BROKEN BY LOVE

MJ MASUCCI

2019©MJ Masucci

This book is a work of fiction. Any resemblance to actual persons, living or dead, or actual events is entirely coincidental. Although every precaution has been taken to verify the accuracy of the information contained herein, the author and publisher assume no responsibility for any errors or omissions. No liability is assumed for damages that may result from the use of information contained within.

All Rights reserved. No part of this publication may be reproduced, distributed, or transmitted in any form or by any means, including photocopying, recording, or other electronic or mechanical methods, without prior written permission of the publisher, except in critical reviews and certain other noncommercial uses permitted by copyright law.

ISBN 978-1-950175-04-8

CHAPTER 1

What am I going to do? I'd already quit my old job at Richards and was meeting with the Vice President of Marketing at my new one, Barker and Perez. I was so excited, I hadn't paid attention to the name of the man who would train me and be my boss, J. Camden Lawson.

It didn't occur to me that it was JC. Yes, *that JC*, the one who had beaten me out for the director's position at my first job. The same one who always topped me in high school and broke off our engagement four months before we were to be married.

I sat in his large office staring at the placard with his name perched on the front of his cherry wood desk. I reached out and ran my fingers over the gold lettering of his name. I was so engrossed in what I was doing, I didn't hear JC enter the room. Behind me, he snorted, and I turned to see his rakish good looks.

He's still gorgeous, with his square jaw, cleft chin, and perpetually stubbled face. I found it hard to keep in mind that this was the man who seemed to win out over me every time. JC was the last person I wanted to be my boss! It was because he still made me moist between my legs. I shifted in my seat and watched him cross the few feet to his desk, as graceful as ever.

JC fixed on me with his steel gray eyes, the intensity of his stare made me shiver and I had to avert my gaze to my lap as I loudly exhaled. He chuckled and opened the folder which had my name, Alexa Stanford, written across the tab on the top.

"I guess I don't have to go over your credentials, Lexi, now do I?" JC said.

"No, you should be well aware of my qualifications, and my name is Alexa."

"It wasn't when we were together."

I sighed. "JC, that was a long time ago."

"It was and it's Camden now."

I started to laugh hard. He had always been JC. Jonathan Camden Lawson, IV. It sounded so pretentious and he knew it. I think that's why he preferred to be called by his initials for as long as I had known him.

JC scowled. "Are you quite finished? I'm not sure we'll be able to work together. You know our history and all."

I gaped at him. "You're going to fire me because YOU broke off our engagement?"

"I broke it off for good reason. Neither of us were ready for that level of commitment." JC's mouth set in a hard line as he narrowed his eyes.

"Most people would remain together to work it out, but you broke it off and broke my heart in the process," I said as I shifted in the black leather chair. It creaked with my movement.

I watched as JC ran his hand through his thick mahogany brown hair. It made me remember how I loved to tug and pull on it while he had his head between my legs. I wondered if it was as soft as I remembered. I loved to run my fingers through the thick strands as he held me in his arms. My chest tightened and a lump formed in my throat. JC knew so much about me, how to boost my confidence with a single look from across the room or a stroke of his pinkie across the back of my hand. I shook the memory away, not wanting to give him any credit for making me feel good.

"It was a long time ago. I've moved on and from what I heard, so have you," JC said.

I knew JC was referring to my recent engagement. He must have spoken to a few of our mutual acquaintances or read the announcement my mother insisted Noah and I have in the *New York Times*. I had moved on, but often when Noah and I made love, JC's face would pop into my mind. The things my former fiancé could do to my body and the mind-blowing orgasms he gave me were hard to forget.

It wasn't because Noah was inattentive in bed, because he wasn't. His brand of making love was very different from JC's. However, Noah Wilton was stable and loving. There was no worry that he would cheat on me the way there was with JC.

"Yes, I have. How is your wife?" I asked.

JC's face tightened. "Brianna is spending plenty of my money in the Bahamas right now. She went on a girl's trip. I'm on my own for a few days. Maybe you could spare some time and we could have lunch."

Once again, I needed to avert my eyes from his gaze because of the dreamy look on his face. Immediately my stomach tightened. "Why?"

JC stared at me, now stone-faced. I could see the muscle in his jaw clenching. "To decide if we can work together without our past interfering."

"JC..."

"Camden!" He said with his eyebrows knitted.

"Camden. I can put aside our past if you can. This is a job, a job that I've long deserved."

I knew I shouldn't antagonize JC, but I couldn't resist.

"You do deserve it and I'll admit, you did deserve the director's job at Carver and Carver, but they gave it to me."

"I'd say that several rounds of golf helped seal the deal."

JC's jaw now bulged with tension. "Let's not dredge up what happened years ago. Please see Darlene in HR. She'll get you set up in your office and you can meet your assistant."

"So, you're not firing me?"

"Don't be ridiculous. I know a good employee when I see one. I have some free time at one. I'll have my assistant make reservations at French's Steakhouse."

My heart jumped. "Why there?" I almost screeched.

"They have great food and I can get a reservation, even on short notice," JC mentioned nonchalantly. There was symbolism in his choice of restaurants. He tried to play it off as if he didn't remember. It was a place I would never forget.

French's was one of the restaurants JC and I frequented when we were together. A friend, Paul Borrego, from our days at NYU, owned it. It had high tan leather booths which offered privacy. The place catered to the business crowd and you couldn't get inside without a jacket. Jeans were not allowed. It was there that JC first got me off in public. My face began to redden at the thought.

"Are you feeling alright? You look flushed," JC asked.

"Fine. Are we done?" *He knew exactly what he is doing.*

"Yes, we're done. I'll speak with you at lunch."

He rose to walk me to the door and stood much too close for my taste. I could feel the heat of his body next to me, his cologne wafting into my nose and my core began to flame. After so many years, it surprised me that just his presence could elicit this type of response.

"Later, Lexi," JC said, almost in a whisper.

I nodded, not bothering to correct my name and hurried out of his office, heading straight for the ladies' room. Fortunately, it was empty. JC was right, my face was bright red. How was I going to work for him when he had this effect on me? I stared into the mirror and smoothed my shoulder length tawny blonde hair. My eyes were bloodshot from lack of sleep the night before.

I freshened up my makeup and smoothed my navy-blue pencil skirt before I headed down to the HR department to find out my office assignment. Darlene, the HR Manager assigned me to an office two doors down from JC. Shit, I wanted to be as far away from him as I could get but as my boss, we would have constant contact anyway.

Darlene gave me the key and I headed down to my office. Upon opening the door, I could see it was tastefully decorated but much too masculine for my liking in rich tones of dark wood, blue walls and brown leather furniture. It wasn't my style, but I could live with it. I hung up my coat on the rack behind my desk and sat down in my black ergonomic chair.

"It suits you."

Startled, I looked up to see JC leaning against the doorjamb with a ridiculous smirk on his face.

"I guess it does, though it is a bit too dark in here for me. I'll have to get some artwork to lighten up the walls."

"The last person to occupy this office was a man. You can request a new paint job, one that would work better for your feminine tastes."

"Thank you, but no. I want to get straight to work. It would disrupt my day."

JC frowned. "For fuck's sake Lexi, they paint at night. Your office would be back together before you came in the morning. I see you still have a touch of perfection."

"I do not, and I asked you to please call me Alexa."

I wanted to smack the smirk off his face. Before I could answer, his cell phone rang. JC fished it out of his shirt pocket.

"Brianna, enjoying yourself?" I heard him say as he headed back to his office.

This was going to be fun. I couldn't wait to get him back when we had lunch. I spent the rest of the morning working on my schedule and organizing my office with my new assistant, Nikki. She was several years younger than me but intelligent and eager to learn. She reminded me of myself at her age of twenty-two. Fresh out of college, pretty, petite and ready to take on the world.

At 12:55, JC showed up at my door.

"Ready to go?"

He nodded at Nikki as she slipped by him when she exited my office. I watched JC as his eyes followed her down the hall. Typical. He still was looking for something on the side even now that he was married. What had I ever seen in him? I knew the answer but ignored it. I grabbed my coat and stepped out of my office to join him.

The elevator ride was awkward and silent, until the tense mood was broken by some other occupants entering from a few floors below ours. JC moved next to me to allow them room. He was pressed right up against me, which I found unnerving. I didn't want the same thing to happen as had earlier.

Fortunately, it was a beautiful spring afternoon with a slight breeze. French's was two short blocks from our building and for that I thanked my lucky stars. I wasn't sure I could handle being trapped next to JC in a cab for any length of time. As we walked to French's, our hands brushed. His touch was electric, and I quickly pulled my hand away as if his were on fire. I could feel my face heating.

"Are you sure you're okay today? Your face is flushed again," JC asked.

"I'm fine. Just hungry."

"Let's get you fed then."

Ever the perfect gentleman, he held the thick smoke glass door for me and ushered me inside. The hostess flashed him a toothy smile and showed him to a booth in the back. We weaved through the round white linen table clothed tables. The restaurant was crowded but there were booths closer to the front. It made me wonder if JC requested this one.

This booth had history for us. It was the one that we had always occupied when we ate here. It was also the one where I first learned how to keep quiet when climaxing. I still remember the look on JC's face when I did and how he sucked on his fingers after, tasting me. Now to think about it made me embarrassed.

"Am I the reason why you're blushing?"

"You're so arrogant. You would think that," I said.

"Well it's just because this is the booth, you know..."

"And did you plan it that way?"

"Not at all. I come here all the time."

"Do you sit in this booth when you do? When you come here with Brianna?"

"No, I don't share this booth with any other women and never have. You were the only one."

I look up at him and see a bit of sadness in his face. I need to change the subject. The noise level in the high-ceilinged restaurant ebbs and flows with conversation of the other patrons, but it's not enough to make me raise my voice.

"What can you tell me about the company?" I asked.

"I trust you did your research on them knowing you."

"I did, but I mean what is the working atmosphere like?"

"It's cozy. Everyone gets along for the most part. There is some competitiveness but it's mostly from the younger, recently graduated set. How do you like Nikki? She started a few months ago and worked for your predecessor."

"She's very competent and bright. I'm lucky because my last assistant was a bit ditzy."

Our conversation ceases as the waiter takes our food and drink orders. I stick to plain seltzer with lime. JC has a beer. I smooth a wrinkle out of the white tablecloth and JC smirks.

"I read about your engagement in the *Times*. Noah is your fiancé's name?" JC asked.

"Yes."

"It said he owns a small security firm. What exactly does he do?"

"He provides security for executives."

"Is there much need for that?"

"There is if you deal with certain countries. Usually his agents travel with the clients."

"Does he do that sort of thing?"

"He used to, but not much anymore. I prefer to have him home."

I began to feel uncomfortable talking about Noah. I felt JC was searching for information about my fiancé. I segue to another topic.

"What about Brianna? What does she do during the day when you're at work?"

"She has hobbies which keep her busy."

"Hobbies?"

"Yes. She has her book club, yoga, spin class, pottery class and a few other things."

I raise my eyebrows. "She doesn't work?"

"Why should she? I make plenty to support us both. She's finding herself. Besides, she isn't much older than Nikki and has plenty of time to start her career."

It doesn't surprise me. JC always could have his head easily turned by a younger woman. At least he did when we were together. I don't know why I was so upset when he broke off our engagement. I should've been relieved.

The awkward silence sets in again and I absentmindedly chew on my bottom lip while I fiddle with my silverware. The next thing I know, JC is dislodging it from between my teeth with his thumb. I want to close my eyes at his touch but instead scowl at him. His fingers are still soft, and I catch a hint of his cologne on them. It raises another memory, one when JC would cup my face and give me the sweetest kisses before we parted for class or said goodnight.

"I'm sorry, I shouldn't have done that. You never did break out of that habit. It always gave you away when you were nervous."

He was right. I was nervous and I didn't know why. We were

just two colleagues having lunch. It wasn't like we were having a midday tryst or anything. I decided to keep the conversation light, asking about what my duties would be and the upcoming projects. I was glad when our meal came because JC seemed to be preoccupied.

Lunch conversation was subdued, and I concentrated on my Quiche Lorraine while he ate his New York strip steak. The end of lunch couldn't come fast enough, and I declined dessert when it was offered.

On the way out of the restaurant, JC firmly planted his hand on my back, gently steering me towards the door. It was an act he had done hundreds of times when we were together. And just that small gesture was making me wet. I felt guilty as we walked back to the office, praying the elevator would have other people in it when we ascended to the tenth floor. I didn't want to be alone with JC. I was fortunate when others entered on the second floor.

We said goodbye at my office door. I watched him gracefully head to his office, ducking into my own before he turned to see me staring. I didn't have even fifteen seconds to compose myself before Nikki breezed in.

"Did you have a good lunch?"

"Uh, yes. It was filling."

She cocked her head at me with a puzzled look and lowered her voice. "How can you deal with being so close to him?"

"Excuse me?"

"I don't mean to sound like a silly schoolgirl, but Mr. Lawson is so handsome. I get flustered when he's around."

You and me both, I thought.

"Nikki, close the door."

Again, the puzzled look but she complied, and I gestured for her to sit in one of the brown leather chairs in front of my desk.

"JC, uh, Mr. Lawson and I have some history."

Her eyes widened.

"We attended high school in New Jersey and college together

9

right here in the city. We dated for three years and right after our graduation, he asked me to marry him."

Nikki's large blue eyes grew wide. "You were engaged to Mr. Lawson?"

"Yes, briefly. We worked at Carver and Carver. He got the marketing position I was up for and shortly after that, he broke off our engagement. I left to work for Richards and that's where I was until now."

"Wow!"

I could see the wheels in her head turning. She probably dreamed about him. If JC wasn't married to Brianna, Nikki was just the type of girl he could go for, all blonde, blue eyed and bubbly with an ass as tight as a drum, totally enamored of him. She had no idea what he was really like.

"It's ancient history. I'm engaged now and he's married."

"I hope I didn't upset you when I said he was handsome."

"Not at all. We should be professional from now on and not talk about his looks."

"I'm sorry."

"It's forgotten. Now let's go over some of the items we need to start working on for the end of the week."

After a full day, I couldn't wait to get home. I was exhausted. I'd taken the rest of my vacation time from Richards and spent the last two weeks home, binging on daytime television and sleeping late. It was a rarity for me since I normally worked twelve-hour days, coming through the door after 8:00 PM to the wonderful smell of whatever Noah had prepared for dinner.

He was a fantastic cook, courtesy of the Wilton's personal chef, Davida, who taught him from an early age. I hoped tonight would be no different. Sometimes Noah worked late, and I didn't see him until well after midnight. However, tonight I was greeted with the aroma of homemade tomato sauce as I opened the door to our loft.

Noah was standing at the six-burner gas stove in a pristine white apron emblazoned with a cursive script that read "Kiss the Cook," which is exactly what I did. He took me in his muscular arms and hugged me, kissing my lips. I buried my face in his chest, inhaling his scent.

"How was your first day?" he asked.

I began to chew on the corner of my lip causing Noah to frown.

"Lexi?"

"It was fine."

"What's wrong?"

"Please don't be angry when I tell you."

Noah switched off the burner and put the pot cover on the sauce.

"Why would I be angry?"

"JC Lawson is my boss."

I watched Noah's face change from worry to amusement.

"Why would I be angry? You were engaged to him and now you're engaged to me. I don't consider JC to be competition. Anyway, isn't he married?"

"Yes, he is. I didn't want you to be upset."

"I'm not upset but you seem to be."

"I was just surprised when I saw his name. I was so stupid not to pay attention to what they told me when I went to fill out the paperwork in the HR department last week."

Noah chuckled, lifting the cover on the pot of water on the back burner. "JC is your past. I'm your present and future. I don't want to talk about your ex-fiancé. I want to have dinner with my fiancée. Go change. Pasta should be ready in twenty minutes."

I breathed a sigh of relief as I headed for the bedroom. A couple of years ago, Noah had purchased the loft and converted it into rooms, two bedrooms, a private office, two bathrooms, a large gourmet kitchen with stainless steel appliances and plenty of windows for natural light.

Noah was everything a woman could ask for, intelligent, hand-some, caring, a great cook and handy with power tools. So why couldn't I get JC out of my head?

CHAPTER 2

After dinner, I cleaned the kitchen since Noah did the cooking. I tried to keep my mind off JC, but it kept drifting there. I was glad Noah retired to his office because my face was red with heat as I scrubbed the dishes in the sink. After, I sat curled up in my favorite wingback chair by the floor to ceiling windows, reading. I must have fallen asleep because I woke up in Noah's arms as he carried me to our bedroom.

"What time is it?" I mumbled, wiping sleep out of my eyes.

"After nine. Your day must have been busy since you rarely fall asleep before midnight."

"I think all that sleeping for the last two weeks got me out of routine. I didn't sleep well last night either. I was nervous about today."

"You should go to bed early tonight. Your next day of sleeping late won't be until Saturday."

Noah sat me down on the king-sized bed and went to the master bath to brush his teeth. I changed into my powder blue nightgown and slipped under the sheets before Noah got back. I think I was asleep when he came to bed because I don't remember him sliding in next to me.

My eyes popped open at 2:23 AM with the ringing of Noah's cell. I heard him talking in hushed tones, but I caught part of his conversation. One of his employees had broken his leg on an excursion with the client. I was crossing my fingers Noah wouldn't have to be the replacement. After he got off the phone, he turned to me.

"Are you awake?"

I opened my light brown eyes to his sapphire blue ones looking at me.

"I am. What was that all about?"

"I have to go to Mexico. Brice Delaney broke his leg riding on a motorcycle."

Before I could answer, Noah rose from the bed to start packing. I turned on my side, tucking the light blue duvet cover around my neck and watched him remove clothing from the dresser, admiring his strong muscular back and shoulders. In fifteen minutes, he was packed, dressed and kissing me goodbye.

"When will you be back?"

"Client is there with his family for another four days. I should be back on Friday night just in time for waffles."

I smiled at the reference to our standing Saturday morning date for breakfast. It was the one meal that was mine to cook. Noah loved my Belgian waffles. I pushed the duvet off and followed him out of the bedroom to the door. He hugged me tightly and I stroked the stubble on his face.

"Call me when you arrive," I said.

"I will. Get some sleep, you have work tomorrow."

"I'm not sure if I'll be able to go back to sleep without you."

"Try. I love you."

One final peck on the cheek and Noah was out the door. I wandered through the loft, stopping to stare out at the lights of the city which dotted the landscape across Central Park. It was now almost 3:00 AM. In another three hours I would have to be up for work. I went to lie in bed but after forty-five minutes of trying to get back to sleep, I gave up. The next few days would be hard on me trying to sleep without Noah.

Instead, I went to take a shower and after, curled up on the wingback chair and picked up my well-worn copy of Jane Austen's *Pride and Prejudice* novel I was previously reading. At five, I got up to get myself a cup of coffee wiping drips from the almond granite island. In about two short hours I would be heading for the office.

I didn't need to be in until nine, but I chose to get in early. It was quiet and I didn't have to brave the heavy crowds on the subway at seven that I would have to an hour later.

I needed to decide what to wear as I stood in the oversized walk in closet. I chose my gray business suit with a white blouse, black heels and curled my pin straight hair. I was ready before seven and headed out into the warm spring sunshine. I loved May. You could say it was my favorite time of year when everything was renewed.

By 7:45, I was sitting at my desk with my travel mug full of coffee, paging through my schedule and checking emails. I heard someone coming down the hall and it turned out to be JC.

"Good Morning, Lexi. You're in early."

I frowned at him since I had asked him several times to call me Alexa. He must have gotten the clue.

JC gave me a lopsided grin. "I'm sorry, I meant Alexa."

"Thank you."

"I'll be in to discuss a few things shortly. We have a full day ahead of us."

He ducked out my door before I could question him. What full day? I thought the projects on my schedule were all that I had to deal with. A minute later JC walked in with his tablet and came around to my desk. He leaned over me and placed the tablet down as he brought up the promotion my predecessor had been working on.

"This is a problem. Our client is very unhappy which is why

the previous person in your position is no longer here. I had to bear his workload until I spoke to Vincent."

I understood he was referring to Vincent Barker, the Barker in Barker and Perez.

I looked up at JC. "What kind of feedback did the client give?"

"First off, the color scheme is completely wrong. It's too harsh. The graphics need to be sharpened and the copy isn't as strong or persuasive as it needs to be."

"I think I can clean this up. When do you need it by?"

"Last week."

I sighed. "JC, I have a full workload."

"Everything will take a backseat for this. We're on the verge of the client dropping us. It needs to be finished as soon as you can. Are you against working late tonight?"

"No. Noah had to go to Mexico. I might as well stay late since I have nothing else to do and I hate going home to an empty apartment."

JC smirked. "Yeah, I remember."

I noticed that he said nothing about me calling him JC. His cell phone rang and he slipped it out of his pocket to answer it. Again, his wife. When he came back, I joked with him.

"Brianna has you on a pretty tight leash. You know checking up on you like that."

Without saying anything to me, he sank into one of the leather chairs in front of my desk, looking weary. It was a look I had seen before, the very same when he sat me down to break our engagement.

"Can I tell you something?"

I nodded. "Of course, anything."

"It's not working out with Brianna. It was a mistake for me to marry her. She's too young, we're never on the same page and she expects so much from me. I'm her fucking husband, not her father."

The revelation about his marriage should've made me happy. Now he knew how it felt but all I felt was empathy.

"I'm sorry. Why *did* you marry her?"

"All the time, my father was trying to get me to date her. I finally gave in and then the pressure started mounting for me to marry her. She's seven years younger than me. I should've said no but all he cares about is his business."

I remember Jonathan Camden Lawson, III. He was an asshole. Always on top of JC to be the best, even in high school. Our senior year, the man grabbed him by the collar after our team lost a debate with a rival school. It was a silly debate and JC was so serious. I felt sorry for him to have a father like that.

"But why, JC? Why would you marry her? Just to please your father?"

An uncertainty crept into his expression. "She was pregnant."

"What?"

I tried to hide my surprise because JC had been so careful when we were together. He didn't want an unplanned pregnancy until we were ready for children.

"I knocked her up. She told me she was on the pill. Brianna is not very good at keeping track of things. She forgot to bring her birth control on a long weekend and that's where it happened. My father was involved in a very important merger at the time with her father. He said he would disown me if I didn't do the right thing."

"How long have you been married?"

"Eleven months."

"What happened? You never mentioned a baby."

"She got her period. Brianna was late, not pregnant. Her pregnancy test gave a false positive."

"That's rare."

"I know, I read up on it, but it was too late. I'd already asked her to marry me and I was stuck. I don't love her."

"You could have broken it off," I said almost sarcastically.

"And bear the wrath of my father while he was going through the merger and risk it? No way. I'd rather be unhappy than have both him and Brianna's father come after me."

I almost felt the urge to wrap my arms around JC and comfort him the way I did when he did poorly on a test or had a tough day at the office, but I resisted. "What are you going to do?"

"Deal with it. I'm married, she's my wife. Maybe in five years I can end it. I never loved her, not the way I loved you."

I feel a deep pang of pain go through me and I start chewing on my lip.

"Stop. I'm sorry," JC said.

"For what?"

"I never should've broken up with you."

I fought back tears. "Then why did you? You hurt me JC. I gave you everything."

"I was stupid. We were young but it would've worked. I wish I could do it all over again."

"You can't. We're in different stages of our lives. You're married, I'm going to be married and hopefully start a family soon."

"Do you love him?"

A look of shock crossed my face. "Noah? Of course, I love him."

"Do you love him like you loved me?"

The truth was that I would never love someone the way I had loved JC, but I would never tell him that.

"Yes, more even. Noah is a good man and he treats me well. I can make a life with him and have made a good life with him."

"But you don't think you could have made a good life with me?"

I slumped in my chair. "JC, you had your issues and you never put me first. It was all about you. In the end, I realized being with you was exhausting. I gave you everything I had, and it wasn't good enough."

"It was. After you left, I felt empty inside."

I didn't know what to say. I knew he was in pain, but I couldn't make it better for him. I loved Noah and we were going to be married in a few short months. JC just sat there with his face in his hands. After a couple of minutes, he scrubbed at his face and got up, leaving my office without saying a word. I didn't have much time to process the exchange we just had because my cell rang.

"So, how is the new job?"

"Mom, it's good. How are you and Dad?"

"Fine. How is your new boss?"

"You know him."

"Really? Who is it?"

"JC."

I waited for it to sink in. There was no love lost between JC and my parents. They had always felt he was all wrong for me. In the end, they were right.

After a short pause, my mother answered. "Oh."

"Before you start to berate him, please don't. This is my job and I deserve it after all my hard work. I can handle him."

"You know best."

I could hear the disapproval in her voice, but I ignored it and quickly cut the conversation off, telling her I had to get to work.

After JC broke it off, I had to move back in with my parents and younger sisters, Megan and Emma. It was the worst time of my life, not only because I was alone after three years but because I had to go back to my parent's house. Fortunately, it was only four months before I got a reprieve. My friend Olivia from college needed a roommate and I jumped at the chance. For three years it was just two single gals on the town until her job transferred her to California.

I was making better money and didn't need another roommate after Olivia left. Then I met Noah. He was charming and sweet. When he got down on bended knee on the bridge in Central Park,

I said yes even though we'd only been dating six months. That was two and a half years ago. The only reason we weren't married yet was because of Noah's schedule. Up until eight months ago, he traveled with clients.

His business had finally picked up enough to hire more qualified employees and now he was mostly at home. I hated when Noah went away. The huge loft we owned was empty and lonely without him. At twenty-nine, almost thirty, I still slept with the lights on when he was not there. I would be doing that for the next few days until he returned. I was lost in my thoughts, thinking about Noah and JC when Nikki came into my office.

"I have your meeting schedule for the week. I wanted to check with you before I set it on the electronic calendar. Mr. Lawson told me to add you into a luncheon they're having in the conference room on Wednesday."

"Luncheon, for what?"

I waited for Nikki to check her tablet.

"The Kingston Group. He said you were working on their copy today. They will be in to discuss the progress. It's a working lunch."

FUCK! I thought. JC never told me I had until noon on Wednesday to get this completed. I wanted to run to his office and wrap my hands around his throat. I wasn't even here two days and he was already piling work on me.

"Fine. Set it and log a reminder for tomorrow at ten."

"Will you be working late tonight?"

"Well, seeing as I have no choice, yes."

Nikki hesitated, looking for words to say and I could figure out what was going on in her mind.

"I don't need you tonight. I can handle this on my own."

I could hear Nikki breathe a sigh of relief.

"It's just that my sister is visiting from Iowa and I wanted to take her out," she said.

"It's not a problem, but I do expect you to work late occasionally. Is that understood?"

"Sure, no problem. Thank you."

Nikki hurried away, leaving me in a cloud of her too strong perfume which was starting to give me a headache. I would have to ask her to take it easy on the spray bottle.

I was fucking annoyed. Just like JC not to give me all the particulars. I decided to confront him while it was still fresh in my mind and I wasn't drowning in rewrites I knew I would need to do. I rose to head to his office, but before I could get around my desk, JC was there in my doorway.

"Could you please shut the door?" I said, my eyebrows knitted as I sat down.

JC eyed me full well knowing my mood because he'd seen the same one many times before.

"Please, Lexi, I seriously can't take any more emotional shit today."

"When were you going to tell me that I needed to have the copy for the Kingston Group done by tomorrow?"

"I was going to tell you now. How did you find out so quickly?"

"Nikki. She came to let me know that my electronic calendar would be updated with the information."

"I'm sorry. I just found out that Mr. Kingston wanted to come tomorrow to see progress. We're overdue and they aren't happy. I need you to wow them."

"I can see this is going to be a long night."

"It will be, and I will be working alongside you so don't worry."

I shuddered inwardly at the thought that I would be here alone with JC at night. I was afraid of my own emotions and what's more, I didn't want to be so close to him.

"Lexi?"

"Good, I think you should work with me on this since it was dumped in my lap last minute."

"We can get sushi. You still like it don't you?"

"Yes, but I don't eat it as often. Noah isn't too keen on it."

"We can do what we used to do years ago. Sit on the floor and eat out of the containers. Remember?"

I did. Our first apartment was tiny and barely had room for a loveseat. Instead, we opted for tons of pillows that we would lay out on the floor. We would order sushi from a restaurant down the street and lay all the containers out on the floor and feed each other. It gave me a warm feeling to think about our fun time.

"Yes, but we need to forget that and discuss the campaign."

I tried to keep my voice even and steady, but it cracked. I didn't want to be reminded of the times we spent together. I didn't want to think about how many times had we made love in that small apartment. That seemed like forever ago.

"I'm sorry if I upset you."

"You didn't upset me. I just want you to stop bringing up the past."

"If it bothers you that much, I'll stop. It wasn't all bad."

"I know it wasn't, but it's long ago."

JC turned to leave my office, saying he was going to get his laptop. I glanced at my watch, not realizing it was close to 4:00 PM. I grabbed my phone and texted Noah. He should have been in Mexico by now and I had not received any messages from him. I waited but nothing came in return. It wasn't like him not to contact me when he was traveling. I began to chew on my lip and when JC came back to my office, he frowned.

"Are you ever going to forgive me for dumping this in your lap?"

"What are you talking about? It's just work."

"You're not even aware that you're chewing on your lip. You always do that when you're nervous or upset."

"It has nothing to do with this," I gestured to the file on my desk.

"Then what?"

"Noah, I haven't heard from him. It's very unlike him not to let me know he landed."

"I'm sure it's nothing. Maybe he has no signal."

I hoped that JC was right. I looked up at him and saw him staring at my lip, almost willing me to stop chewing on it which I did.

"He's fine, you'll see."

As if on command, my phone rang. Noah.

"Hey babe, I'm sorry, connection is shitty here. I tried to text you earlier, but it never went through."

I was just about to reply when static took over and the line disconnected.

"Shit!"

"Was that Noah?"

"Yes, and you were right. No reception."

The corners of JC's eyes crinkled as he grinned. "See, I told you. Stop worrying."

I gave him a weak smile. JC pulled one of the chairs in front of my desk around to sit near me. I found it hard to concentrate with him so close. He smelled wonderful. I think he knew he affected me because he brushed against me more than once. I never said working with JC would be easy, and I was right.

CHAPTER 3

At five, Nikki stopped in to ask if I needed anything. I waved her away, telling her I had the project in hand and told her to go home. I watched JC follow her tight skirted ass out of the office with his eyes and I scowled at him.

"She's a beautiful girl."

"Don't you have enough problems?" I said.

"I can admire her, can't I?"

"As I remember, that was one of your problems when we were together."

"I don't do that anymore, but I can look. And I thought you said no more bringing up the past."

I looked down at my desk. "You're right. I'm sorry."

For the next two hours we worked on the copy and graphics until my neck started to hurt. I excused myself and got up to walk around the office, stretching my arms and rolling my head from side to side.

"You still have that problem with your neck?"

"Yes. It's gotten worse as I've gotten older. I think too many nights bent over my laptop and desk haven't helped."

I sat down again, and JC's strong hand began to massage my

shoulder closest to him. Without realizing it, I closed my eyes at the sensation and remembered how delicious his massages were. I almost moaned. Then I felt a pang of guilt and opened my eyes. What would Noah say?

"Thanks, you can stop now."

I looked into JC's eyes and saw a glimmer of sadness.

"Do you want to order dinner? I'm starving. I only had a salad for lunch."

He didn't answer me but scrolled through his phone. A few seconds later he was ordering everything I loved from the sushi place, Golden Sun, around the corner from the office.

"How hungry do you think I am?" I asked.

"You said you were starving. I can't have you hungry when I need that lovely brain of yours to produce."

I smirked at him and went back to rewriting copy while he worked on improving the graphics on the ad. We could've kept a few of the people from the marketing department, basically my employees, to stay, but I didn't see the point. I had been working copy for years and JC was quite adept at graphics design. It almost felt like we were together again at Carver and Carver.

An hour later, JC was sitting on the small brown leather loveseat and spreading tins full of sushi on the glass coffee table. After he was done, he sat on the floor next to the table and began to eat.

He patted the floor next to him, "Are you going to join me?"

"JC, I'm hardly dressed to sit on the floor."

"Come on, don't be a spoiled sport. It will be like old times."

I decided to sit on the opposite side of the table facing him. I didn't want to be that near to him. Working so closely with him for the past few hours had me aroused. Something I should not be. I loved Noah and he would soon be my husband. The last thing that should be happening was attraction to my former fiancé.

JC finished chewing his piece of tuna and rested his chopsticks on the paper plate. "What do you do for fun? You never told me."

I followed his lead, putting down my chopsticks and looked at him. "I'm involved in volunteer work when I have time."

JC smiled. "You always did have a soft spot for people."

"And animals. I volunteer at the Humane Society."

"Anywhere else?"

"The *Lift Me Up* women's shelter program."

"What do you do there?"

"Organize collections of lightly used business wear. I've also run seminars and mentor to help women get back on their feet."

"Where are these women from?"

"Some were homeless or battered by their significant others. They need a hand to feel self-worth and streamline back into society as productive citizens. We've had several success stories. It makes me feel good to help someone in need."

"You're a good person, Lexi."

"I'd like to think I am. I try. It's a humbling experience. You should join me."

JC nodded and went silent as he continued to eat. When we reached toward the same tin for the last California Roll, I felt electricity as our fingers brushed. I quickly pulled my hand away and JC smiled. I don't think he realized why I had withdrawn so suddenly.

"You can have it. I know it's your favorite."

He picked up the tin and held it out to me. I thanked him and took the last piece of food out of the tin.

"Lexi, do you ever wonder what it would have been like if we had gotten married?"

"I try not to."

The look on his face was full of regret.

"I guess that's my fault. I fucked it all up. I'm sorry it ended so badly."

"You don't have to keep apologizing. I once wanted to be

married to you, but I got over it. It took time but it passed. I'm very happy with Noah."

"I wanted to talk to you about calling me JC. It's fine when we're alone but everyone knows me as Camden. Can you try to call me that when other people are around?"

"If you can call me Alexa when others are around."

"When did you start using Alexa?"

"At Richards. Only my family and Noah call me Lexi."

"How is your family? If I remember, your sister Megan was studying for her masters in biology."

"She received her degree a few years ago and works for Darwin Chemical in Philadelphia."

"That's great. And your other sister, Emma?"

"She's finding herself. First it was acting, now writing. Since she's only twenty-one, my parents let it go. She'll get it together one of these days."

"Your parents, how are they?"

"They still hate you, I'm sorry to say. My mother was not happy to hear I now work with you, well, for you."

JC pursed his lips. "I don't blame her."

"What about your family? Your brother, Hunter?"

"Hunter works for my father's company. He pretends he loves it, but I know different. My father, as you know, can be difficult. It's the very reason why I chose not to work there. I'm the disappointment of the family."

I frowned. "Don't say that. You've accomplished quite a bit on your own."

"Have I? You think I didn't have help getting this position? My father has a lot of pull in this town. The name Lawson opens doors all over."

"I think your merits say it all. You're hardworking and intelligent. I can remember many nights at Carver when you stayed to complete an assignment."

"You did the same. You deserved the job, not me."

"Water under the bridge."

I stood up and started to clear the table of the empty tins. JC helped me clean up and in a couple of minutes we were back in our chairs being professional again. Treading toward personal talk only made me wish it could be like it used to be.

At eleven, I decided it was time to end work for the evening. I was yawning every few seconds and my eyes were getting droopy. I had rewritten the copy that would more than likely satisfy Mr. Kingston.

"I have to go, JC. I'm falling asleep."

"I think we've put in a good amount of work. Tomorrow, I just need to set this up on the video screen and we can work with the copy you rewrote. I think Mr. Kingston will be pleased."

"I hope so."

I shut down my laptop and righted the paperwork in the folder. JC went to his office to get his briefcase and we met in the hallway as I was locking my office door.

"Lexi, I really appreciate you staying. I never would've gotten this done without you."

"That's why you hired me, isn't it?"

"Part of the reason."

"You had other reasons?"

My heart started to pound hoping JC wouldn't say what I thought he would.

"I wanted to be friends again. I missed you."

"I'm not sure if that's a good idea."

"Why? I don't bite."

I started to feel uncomfortable, mainly because I remembered that he most certainly did bite. Many a morning I woke up with small red marks from his teeth while we were making love.

"I know, but our history and all. I'm not sure our spouses would like us to be friends."

"Brianna doesn't know. At least I don't think she does."

"Why wouldn't you tell her you were working with your ex-fiancée?"

"Because she doesn't need to know. It would only create more problems. We argue a lot."

I felt empathetic towards him. Married less than a year and they argued all the time. But nevertheless, a warning voice whispered in her head.

"I'm sorry. Maybe you should seek counseling."

"I think we're well past that. I let her go on the girl's trip because I thought maybe some distance would help."

"Is it?"

"It was until I looked at our credit card statement. Brianna loves to spend. I'm not a multi-millionaire like her father. I can't have frivolous spending."

We walked to the elevator and I wasn't sure what to tell him. As we headed out the door to the building, JC grabbed my hand and pulled me against his chest for a hug. I was taken aback by his actions, but it felt good being in his arms. If I was any other employee, a sexual harassment suit would be in order. But I wasn't any other employee. I was JC's former fiancée.

"Thank you for listening."

He kissed me on my forehead and as he let me go from his embrace, stroked my cheek with his fingers. I resisted the urge to close my eyes and relish his touch.

"I'll see you tomorrow," he said.

"Yes, fine."

As JC headed off in the other direction, I needed to lean against the concrete planters in front of the building. He still made me weak in the knees. After I regained my composure, I headed for the subway. The platform was almost deserted except for a young couple leaning against the dirty tiled wall while they kissed and an old man talking to himself. My phone rang while I waited for the next train and seeing who it was, I immediately felt guilt wash over me.

"Noah."

"Hey babe, sorry to call you so late. Did I wake you?"

I nervously laughed. "No, I'm actually waiting for the train."

"Did you go out?"

"I just got done with work. We have an emergency meeting with a client tomorrow at noon."

"Don't you have employees to work on that stuff?"

"Yes, but they wouldn't be able to give the attention to detail that JC and I could."

The phone went silent for a few seconds. "You were alone in the office with JC?"

"He was working on the project with me. I thought you said you weren't worried about him."

"I'm not but when your former fiancé and you are working late, reminiscing about the old days, things can happen."

Noah could read my mind.

"Don't you trust me? All we did was work, no reminiscing."

"I trust you. I don't trust him. Anyway, I want to let you know I might be out of communication tomorrow. My client and his family want to go to the beach, then to some villa in the hills to have dinner with a relative. Not sure how the comms will be up there."

"I miss you, Noah. I know I won't sleep well until you get back."

I could hear the smile in his voice. "You want me to sing you to sleep?"

It was a running joke we had. When we first got together and were living apart, I called him at 3:00 AM. I couldn't sleep and instead of getting angry that I woke him, he sang to me until I fell asleep. That's when I realized Noah was the one. A month later, he asked me to marry him.

"If I was home, I would say yes."

"You could talk to me until you get home."

I felt a pang of love go through me. It was just like Noah to say that.

"I would love to, but I have a feeling once I get on the train, we'll lose connection."

"Very well. It's an early night tonight. My client is just hanging around in the hotel. If you want to talk, call me when you get home. I love you, Lexi."

"Love you too."

Not realizing, I kept the phone to my ear even after Noah clicked off. I wanted to be closer to him. When the train arrived, I dropped it into my purse. By the time I got home, I was ready to fall into bed. I undressed and slipped under the cool sheets naked.

Sometime around 4:00 AM, my eyes sprang open. It took me some time to realize that Noah was not in bed next to me. It felt lonely not to have him here. I tried to go back to sleep but was getting nowhere and decided to take a shower. I knew I would probably be a wreck by the time the end of the day came with such little sleep.

In the bathroom, I turned on all three shower heads. Noah had designed this bathroom with luxury in mind. The stall was double the size of a regular one with two walls of glass. The three shower heads included one overhead, providing different types of water streams. I took extra time, enjoying the heat as it loosened up my tired muscles.

I always kept the shelves near the tiled shower seat stocked with all kinds of shampoos, body washes and soaps. Today, I felt like using a citrus shampoo and a lemon scented body wash. It woke me up and made me feel refreshed. In no time, I was wide awake.

After I wrapped myself in Noah's thick white terry cloth robe, I made a strong cup of coffee and sipped it while I watched the dawn come over Central Park, illuminating the greenery in fiery reds and yellows. I loved living in Manhattan. There was so much to do and see even in the wee hours of the morning.

My next decision was what to wear. We would be meeting a client today and I wanted to look all business. I searched my side of the walk-in closet for just the right outfit, a grey pantsuit with a white silk blouse. I went to the bathroom and blew dry my hair. I thought about curling it but wasn't in the mood.

A quick addition of some mascara, blush and lipstick made me ready for the day. I grabbed my phone and noticed a text message from JC. I wondered how he got my cell number since I never gave it to him.

Are you ready for today? I hope so. I couldn't sleep at all last night.

I decided against texting him back. I would see him in less than two hours. I took my time filling my travel mug with coffee. This would have to be it for the day. Too much coffee made me jittery and today wasn't the day to be hopping around from foot to foot when we were presenting to clients.

The weather was warm even for this time of the morning. New York was experiencing a blast of hot weather for so early in the year, it was only nearing the end of May. I started to sweat in my suit when walking to the subway and I quickly checked my purse to make sure I had a stick of deodorant. I hoped that they had switched to air conditioning in the building; it certainly was warm enough for it.

JC's office door was open when I strode in at 8:00 AM. It was still early and most of the office staff was not in. I hung up my things and went to his office, stopping at the door to watch him as he worked on his laptop. His thick brown hair was neatly combed to the side and he was wearing his frameless glasses. I called his name.

He looked up and smiled at me. "Come in, sit. You look nice."

"Thanks, so do you."

It had to be said that no matter what JC wore, he looked nice. He would come home sweaty and dirty from games of basketball or baseball in the park and he was sexy. Another memory I tried to purge from my brain.

"Are you ready?" JC asked.

"I think so. I hope Mr. Kingston is happy. Do we need to fine-tune anything?"

"We don't have time. Vincent told me that Kingston pushed the meeting up to nine. He should be here in less than an hour."

I started to panic, but I should be used to it since this happened all the time at my previous two jobs.

"Are you taking the lead?"

"I think you should. You know the copy. I can join in if you need it."

"But I'm not sure I can handle the lead on such short notice," I protested.

JC crossed his arms and smirked. "Still lack confidence in yourself."

"Fuck you," I murmured under my breath.

"Is that an invitation?"

I shook my head as I walked out of JC's office. *Bastard*.

CHAPTER 4

I was fuming as I muddled my way through the meeting with Mr. Kingston. JC had thrown me under the bus, a common occurrence during our past relationship. Luckily, I had enough knowledge about Kingston hand creams to work my way through. He seemed happy enough, especially when I promised to get the new copy to him by Friday. I would have to get the art department involved to draw up some graphics to coincide.

I hadn't seen JC since after the meeting, Vincent wanted to speak with him. I was sitting in my office with the door closed trying to rub away a stress headache. I asked Nikki to hold my calls and I lay down on the couch trying to regain my composure. If I saw JC now, I would lash out and I didn't want to do that since he was my superior.

This was just one more reason why I was glad we were no longer together. JC rarely took accountability for issues that went wrong in our personal and business relationship. He would accuse me of things that were his fault and I was stupid enough to allow it. Love makes you do funny things.

My desk phone rang and I ignored it. *Dammit Nikki, I told you to hold my calls.* A minute later, my cell phone buzzed. The only reason I got up from the couch was because I wondered if it was Noah. He could calm me. I was hoping it was, but my anger flared when I saw a text from JC.

Come to my office. I'm sorry. I fucked up again.

I couldn't resist so I texted him back.

Yes, you did fuck up yet again. You wanted to know why it would never work with us, here's your answer. You never take accountability for anything. You're the vice president of marketing, it was your job to clean up this mess.

My finger lingered over the send button, then I deleted the message, stood up and went to JC's office. His door was partially open, and I walked in, slammed the door a little too hard and stalked toward his desk with my hands clenched.

He smiled with amusement, then as he surveyed my face, the smile disappeared.

"Lexi, I know I…"

I cut him off by holding up my hand.

"JC, you're my superior. You were there to help clean up this mess that my predecessor created. You had a responsibility and took none of it. This is why we aren't together. Your looks and charm can only get you so far."

I was spent and sat down in the black leather chair in front of his desk.

"I know. I just knew you could handle it. You worked on the copy and your skills are impeccable when it comes to that."

"Suppose I didn't have any extra ideas? You would've made me look like a jerk in front of Vincent not to mention the client. You can't do this to me again or I'm quitting."

A look of fear crossed his face and I inwardly smiled. I'd saved his ass and I wondered what Vincent had said to him, so I asked.

"What happened with Vincent?"

"He congratulated me on hiring you."

"Oh, so you get a feather in your cap for me saving your ass?"

"I don't see it like that, but I'll agree because I know you're angry."

"JC, why shouldn't I be?"

"Think of it as trial by fire. You got through your first meeting without faltering."

"No thanks to you," I mumbled.

"I would like to take you to dinner tonight."

"I can't."

"Why, what else do you have to do? Noah is still away and so is Brianna. Don't make me eat alone. I hate it."

I know he did, and I also know he was trying to change the subject. There was no use arguing. It was over and we had been successful.

"If I agree then you're paying."

"I invited you, didn't I?"

"Fine. I have work to do. I not only have to get this copy done for Mr. Kingston by Friday, but I have the Camilla Cosmetics campaign to work on. I need to coordinate with the art department."

"I'll leave you to it. I need to do a few things myself."

I rose from my chair and headed to my office. My head was starting to pound even harder, probably from the limited sleep I had in the last two nights. I couldn't wait for Noah to come home.

I buzzed Nikki and told her to come to my office. I needed help setting up a few things and she could coordinate my schedule with the art department. This was the first time I had a dedicated assistant and I was loving it. When she arrived, we got down to business.

At lunch, I shut my office door, turned out the lights and lay down on my couch. I was exhausted and it was barely 1:00 PM. Right after I shut my eyes, my cell rang. I fumbled for it and swiped the button to answer.

"Lexi, how are you?"

"Noah, I miss you. Come home soon."

"I have some good news. I should be home tomorrow not Friday."

I thanked the heavens. I needed him.

"That's wonderful to hear. Why did the schedule change?"

"My client's wife has a family issue. The earliest flight they could get was tomorrow morning. So I should be back in New York by the afternoon."

"I'm so happy. How is Mexico?"

"Hot, and I got sunburned yesterday. I forgot sunscreen."

"How is work? Are you enjoying being the big boss?"

If he only knew.

"I'm not actually the big boss, that's JC. But I am enjoying the work. I had my presentation this morning."

"And?"

"It went well, a few hiccups."

"Hiccups?"

"I'll tell you tomorrow."

The phone started to crackle and then clicked off. Dammit, must be the poor connection down there. At least tonight would be the last night that I had to sleep alone which I hoped was for a while. I turned on my side and readjusted the pillow under my head. I fell asleep quickly and was woken up by JC. He was kneeling down by the couch and smoothing my hair out of my face. It startled me and I bolted upright.

"What are you doing in here?"

"Vincent and Marco want to see us. I tried calling you, but you didn't answer. Nikki said you were still in your office. I figured you were napping. You really should let someone know when you do that."

"Thanks for the tip," I said, wiping a small bit of drool off the side of my face.

"I'll give you a few minutes to get yourself ready."

He smiled at me as he rose. I sat up and grabbed my purse from the coffee table, taking out my compact mirror. My eyes were puffy with sleep and I freshened up my makeup a little then ran a brush through my hair. I looked tired but there was nothing I could do about it now.

JC met me in the hall, and we headed to the conference room where Vincent and Marco were already. Surprisingly, you could say that they were brothers even though they were not related in any way. Both had dark hair and eyes. They were close to the same height with the only glaring difference being that Marco was heavyset and Vincent was thin. They gestured us to sit down and I started to feel a sense of foreboding.

"We want to congratulate you on today's successful meeting. That being said, we noticed that you two were not in sync."

I wanted to tell them the truth, but let JC take the lead.

"As I said before, this campaign was handled improperly from the get-go. Lexi's predecessor dropped the ball. I didn't think someone of his seasoned experience would require me to hang over his shoulder. I know Mr. Kingston was upset with the progress and that's my fault. I should have checked on the campaign, but I was swamped with other work."

"Camden, I understand but we need you two to be working together. As VP and Director of the same department, you should work hand in hand."

I almost laughed at that because from JC's displays the last few days, he wanted to be more than hand in hand. More like hand down my panties. Instead I bit my tongue to prevent the smile from blooming on my face. JC looked at me and frowned.

"Vincent, we plan on doing that. It's only been a few days but I'm sure by next week we will be on the same page. In fact, I'm taking Lexi out to dinner tonight to discuss just that."

"Wonderful. I hope we won't have any stumbles like this morning, in the future. Keep us informed."

JC hustled me out the door and wrapped his hand around my arm as we walked down the hall. I wanted to shake him loose, but Marco and Vincent were close behind. At my office, he released me, and I gave him a hard look.

"Can we talk?"

"I can't right now. I promised Brianna I would call her. We can talk at dinner."

"Suppose I changed my mind and don't want to have dinner with you?"

"Don't be silly. I'll come get you at five."

He walked away as if dismissing me. I felt my ire building. It would simmer in me all day while I worked on the Camilla project. At five, he ducked his head into my office door. How could he look so fresh after a full day of work and barely any sleep? I, on the other hand, looked exhausted and ready for bed.

"I made reservations at Marino's for 5:30."

Another old haunt of ours. I wished he would stop dredging up the past.

"Why Marino's?"

"Because you love their Chicken Piccata. Do you want me to cancel?"

"No, I'm hungry and I need a glass of good red wine."

"Good, so do I."

"I'll be back in a minute," I brushed past him on my way to the bathroom catching the scent of his cologne.

When I came back, most of the office was empty. The desks in the main area where the assistants sat were dark and the cleaning staff was already emptying garbage cans.

JC had put on his suit jacket and was talking on his cell while sitting on my couch. I tried not to listen, but he was talking loudly to his wife. The gist of the conversation was that she wanted to spend a few more days away with her friends. He wanted her home, probably to prevent her from spending more money. He ended the call by saying her name twice which made me believe that she had hung up on him.

"Everything alright?"

"You don't want to know. Let's go, I need a drink."

In the bright lights of my office I could see that his once fresh look had turned haggard. I guess chasing after a twenty-three-year-old will do that to you.

The cab ride to Marino's was spent in silence. I played with my fingers, not knowing what to say to him. I was curious as to what home life was like for him. Brianna didn't seem like the home-maker type of person. Maybe a few drinks in me would give me the courage to ask, as it turned out, I didn't have to.

As soon as we sat down, a waiter took our drink and food order. JC sighed deeply and started telling me about his marriage.

"I'm sure you've guessed that Brianna is not a typical wife."

"What exactly is a typical wife?"

"Well, one that actually does wifely duties."

I started to laugh because I couldn't believe he used such an antiquated statement. *Wifely duties, really?*

"It's not funny. If I come home to a hot meal once a week, it's amazing. And usually it's something like spaghetti or one of those microwave meals. Brianna is very good at heating things in the microwave."

"Why don't you give her some cooking lessons as a present?"

"Are you kidding? She would just say that I was pushing her to do something she wasn't ready for."

"It's cooking for heaven's sake. You aren't asking her to go to war."

The waiter came back with a bottle of red wine, filled our

glasses and I watched JC down half his glass, then refill it from the bottle left on the table.

"So, tell me about your life? How do you get along with Noah?"

"Noah is wonderful. He cooks, cleans, fixes things. He designed the loft when he wanted to convert it from one big space to several rooms."

"He's an architect, too?"

"No, but he knows what he wants. The bathroom is wonderful. We have a double shower, a large Jacuzzi tub, double sinks and in floor heating."

"Sounds like an expensive project besides Central Park West being an expensive area. I guess the security game is a lucrative career."

"Noah does make good money, but he also invested over the years. His grandparents gave him some stocks and bonds for each birthday and event in his life. The Wilton family made money in real estate."

"That's his last name?"

"Yes, and it will be mine soon."

I watched as JC's expression hardened and he drained his wine glass.

"When are you getting married?"

"In October."

"Why did you pick the fall?"

"It's Noah's favorite time of year."

"I'm happy that you're happy."

I wasn't so sure that was the truth. JC seemed preoccupied with the knowledge of my impending marriage and the possible demise of his.

"Thank you."

I sipped at my wine waiting for something to save us from the awkward silence when I heard my name called. Turning, I saw one of my friends from Richards, Jillian Salazar. She sauntered over with her husband, Damon, in tow.

"Lexi, it's so nice to see you! We miss you at the office. The replacement for you is horrible. Has the personality of a piece of cardboard."

"How's Noah?" I saw her eyeing JC.

"Jillian and Damon, this is my boss, JC Lawson."

Jillian's eyes grew wide as her husband shook JC's hand. She was cold probably because I had told her some horrible stories about him over the years.

"JC, nice to meet you."

We exchanged small talk for a few minutes before our meals arrived and Jillian left with Damon. JC took a bite of his veal scaloppini and looked up at me.

"You told her about me, didn't you?"

"What are you talking about? Told her what?"

"I saw the look she gave me. She was so cold to me that I know you told her something."

"Oh, it just can't be that she didn't drop her panties at the old Lawson charm so I must have said something, right?"

"That's not what I mean…she was pretty rude."

"I might have mentioned you over the years. I don't remember. I did work at Richards for several years."

"I'm sure you said something."

I sipped my wine, ate some of my chicken and avoided making eye contact with him. I didn't feel like getting indigestion, but I could feel the dark cloud hanging over us.

"JC, I'm sorry if you feel I should've just bottled up my feelings. I was hurt in more than one way. I didn't realize before then that someone who said they loved you could ruin a good thing."

His mouth twisted. "I can't keep apologizing for what I did. It was years ago. I think I'm paying for it now, don't you? I gave up someone who would've treated me well, for a business proposition."

"That was your choice. Does Brianna see it as a business dealing?"

"I doubt it. Two of her friends are married and she loves that she's part of the club. Married to an older, good looking successful man as she puts it."

"Does she love you?"

"I don't know. We don't sleep in the same bed. She said I snore and move around too much during the night."

I remember well finding myself at the edge of the bed many a night. JC was a mover in his sleep. We only had room for a full bed in our small apartment, not nearly enough space. At times I would take a blanket and sleep on the many pillows we had in the living room area in lieu of fighting for bed real estate.

"You do move around. I don't remember you snoring, though."

Another awkward pause in conversation allowed me to finish eating most of my piccata. It was the best meal I had in the two days Noah was gone. I was stuffed and leaned back in my chair. JC had also finished his meal and the waiter came over to clear our plates.

"Do you want dessert? They have cheesecake."

"No, I think I've had enough. Sitting at the desk all day is going to make me gain weight if I keep eating this way."

"You have a sexy little figure. I think it's even better than when we were together."

I could feel the blush heating my face.

"JC, you really shouldn't say things like that."

"Why? It's true. You're still sexy, even more so now that you've matured."

"I think it's time to go. I need some sleep. Noah is coming home tomorrow and I'm sure I won't get much."

"Oh, does he often keep you up at night?"

"As a matter of fact, he does. Noah is very giving."

I watched JC's eyebrows raise in surprise and lowered my voice.

"Did you think you were the only one that could give me mind blowing orgasms?"

He smirked and I realized I used the wrong words. "So, I gave you mind blowing orgasms?"

"Maybe, but you're not the only one. Our relationship wasn't only about sex."

"I know that, but the sex was good, wasn't it? At least admit that?"

"Yes, it was when you weren't having it with other women."

He ignored my comment and dug around in his wallet for his credit card. After the bill was paid, we made our way out to the street. The evening was still very warm. Fortunately, I didn't have to walk far to get to the subway station.

"Do you want to split a cab?"

"No. Don't you live in the opposite direction?"

"Yes, but I promised to drop by to see my parents tonight. My mother is getting over a cold. They live close to you."

"I'm taking the subway if you want to join me."

"I prefer a cab."

JC cupped my chin, and for a moment, I thought he would kiss me as he had the night before. I wasn't sure what I would do if he did.

CHAPTER 5

We stared at each other for a moment, and his eyes darted to my full lips. I held my breath, powerless to remove my face from JC's hand. The frustration I felt was a cross between sexual tension and bewilderment. I made my move, heading for the door and pulling out my key. My heart throttled in my chest. I resisted the urge to look back and see if JC was watching as I slipped inside.

Ugh. I questioned why I was having these feelings for JC. Once inside, the throb between my legs drove me to a cold shower as punishment of my betrayal to Noah. If I couldn't resolve my emotions for my former lover, my relationship with my current one would be doomed.

The next morning, I woke up just before the alarm went off at 5:40 AM. I was happy to have slept through the night. My body had wandered over to the middle of the bed and I found myself sleeping on Noah's pillow. The smell of it gave me comfort and I was happy he would be home today.

I quickly showered and again put on Noah's bathrobe. I flipped through the mail I had brought up yesterday and found a plain white envelope, with generous girly script addressed to

Noah. I flipped it over and there was no return address, but the postmark indicated it came within the city.

I was curious as to who sent it but that was Noah's business. I wouldn't invade his privacy by opening the letter. I brought it to his office and laid it on his desk with the other mail. If he wanted to tell me who it was from, he would.

The day went quickly, and I saw little of JC. I think he was embarrassed by his revelation about his marriage. Nikki and I worked on the Camilla project and scheduling with the art department. By five, I still hadn't heard from Noah and I hoped that he'd arrived home safely. I met JC in the elevator when I was leaving for the day. He slipped inside as the doors were closing.

"Hi, I haven't seen you all day," he said.

"I was working with Nikki today. We have the Camilla project. I also finished the final copy for The Kingston Group. I just need you to look it over tomorrow morning and we can send over the proofs for approval."

"Great, I appreciate you taking on the completion. I'll be sure to let Vincent and Marco know you're finished. Let's get together in the morning."

He smiled at me as we stepped out of the elevator and into the noisy lobby. JC walked away from me without looking back and I watched him slip through the glass doors and out into the late spring sunshine.

When I got home, the fragrant smell of roses was in the air and I spied the vase with two dozen red ones on the kitchen table. I kicked off my shoes and placed them in the closet in the entryway, then went to look for Noah. I found him in his office going through the mail I had placed there.

He smiled widely when I entered and stood up to meet me as I came into the room. Embracing me, he buried his nose in my hair then moved his lips to my neck and finally claimed my mouth with his own.

"I missed these lips," he mumbled against them.

I clung to his body and ran my hands up and down his strong back. I felt him twist as my fingers traveled along his ribs and my eyes sprang open.

"Noah, what's wrong?"

"We got into a bit of scuffle at the beach. I took a fist to the back."

"Can I see?"

I lifted his shirt and noticed a large purple bruise in the middle of his back near his spine.

"Do you need ice?"

"No, I'll be alright. One of the locals was harassing our client's fifteen-year-old daughter. When I confronted him, a couple of his buddies jumped on me."

"Where was Victor?"

Victor Talus was the employee Noah was sharing duties.

"He was in the water with the client's son. When he saw what was happening, he came up and assisted me. Those kids had balls."

They sure did since Noah was six five and Victor, six four, both built like brick walls.

"Did you have it checked?"

Noah scowled. "Lexi, relax, it's just a bruise."

"You know I hate when you get hurt."

"I'm fine. I was hoping we could spend some time together tonight."

I grinned. "You read my mind. It's been too long. Do you want me to cook something?"

"I already did. I made turkey chili with corn bread. I figured you were eating out while I was gone."

"I did, but you didn't have to go to any trouble. I know you must be tired."

"I slept most of the flight and my client was kind enough to purchase first class tickets for Victor and me. Our flight was at 4:00 AM."

"I'm so glad you're home."

I hugged him again and headed to our bedroom to change with Noah following close behind me. He scooped me up in his arms on the way and put me down at the entrance to our closet. He sat on the bed and removed his socks, then got undressed. It wasn't a subtle maneuver and I knew what he wanted; I wanted the same.

He stood up naked and pulled me into his arms. His lips pressed hard against mine and I could feel his urgency. There was a tingling in the pit of my stomach, and it moved lower. Noah's rough hands palmed my breasts and rubbed across my nipples, making them hard little pebbles. My skin began to heat under his touch.

Noah's lips continued to explore and left mine to nibble on my earlobe, sucking on it and sending sparks down to my nether region. I could feel my core clench and I fumbled for his erection, grasping it in my hand. He hissed as I ran my hand along his length.

My pulse quickened as his fingers slid between my legs, rubbing my slickness. Noah searched my eyes as he paused at my opening, then he was inside me, sucking at my wetness. I moaned as he held his mouth tight to mine.

"It's been too long," he whispered.

It had been almost a week and that was too long. We often made love several times a week or even in a day. I shivered in anticipation as his fingers plunged in and out, then he removed them. I mewled with displeasure until he picked me up, placing me on the bed and he followed.

He crushed his body against mine and I could feel his hardness against my hip. I wanted him inside me.

"Noah, now," I said almost breathlessly.

He obliged me by positioning himself at my opening and

thrusting inward. His cock felt like steel heat as he entered me, and I heard him grunt as I flexed against him.

Noah was rough with me, thrusting hard and gritting his teeth with each movement. I liked it that way and wrapped my legs around his waist, pulling him tight toward me. His teeth found my nipples and he nipped and sucked at them. I always told him he was raw with sexuality.

He gazed down at me with half lidded eyes, then closed them as he concentrated on our mutual pleasure. I dug my nails into his back, running them up and down his taut flesh. I saw him bite his lip and I withdrew knowing that I'd touched the bruised area near his spine.

"It's alright, it only hurts a little. Touch me."

Instead, I grasped his biceps tightly as he drew me closer to orgasm. Noah could always make me a slave to my lust, and I was that now. I wanted him deeper, harder and faster. He obeyed my request, our flesh slapping together as he sped up his rhythm. And then, I reached the pinnacle of my climax and shattered around his hardness, his name on my lips. A few strokes later, Noah was joining me as he came.

He laid upon me and I uncurled my legs from his waist. His head was buried in my neck, inhaling the scent of my perfume.

"I missed you very much, Lexi. I hate being away from you."

"I love you, Noah."

"Ditto."

He gently pulled out of me and lay on his back. I turned on my side and snuggled against his warmth, my head tucked under his chin.

"Do you want dinner?"

"Nope. I'd rather make up for lost time"

"Then my dear fiancée, that's what we'll do."

Noah pulled the sheet over us and held me close. This is what I loved about him. He always put my needs first. That night we certainly made up for lost time, making love twice more. In the morning, I woke up to the alarm. Our legs were entwined, and Noah gave me a sleepy grin.

"So, today is the end of your first week of work. Would you like to go and celebrate tonight?"

"Sure, what did you have in mind?"

"How about we go to Monster Barbecue?"

"Really? I thought you didn't like eating there."

"It's not that I don't like eating there. I don't like eating there often. I know you enjoy it and it's one of your favorite places, so let's go."

"It's a deal. You make reservations. Are you working from home today?"

"Yes, I have a bunch of paperwork to go through and payroll is due on Tuesday. This upcoming week is going to be busy for me."

"You're not leaving me again, are you?"

"No. I have just enough guys for the weekly scheduling. Brice is out of commission for a while, so I'll get him to help me at the office. We also have a couple of interviews to conduct. Business is getting busier now that it's warming up. I need more employees, or you won't see me all summer."

I bit my lip and frowned. The last thing I wanted was to be away from him all summer. We had several items to take care of for our upcoming nuptials and I didn't want to do them alone.

"Baby don't worry. I'm going to make sure I'm home. I know we have decisions to make for the wedding."

"Thank you. Plus, I hate when you go away. I slept wonderfully last night well except for…you know."

He yawned and smiled seductively, "Would you like to shower together?"

"I love you, Noah, but if we shower together, I'm going to be walking funny all day."

"Is that a bad thing?"

"No, but honestly I'm a little sore."

"We can do other things. I'm in a very giving mood this morning."

"I'd rather you do that in bed tonight."

He slipped out of bed, pouted his lips and crossed his arms. I had to admit how delectable he looked in all his naked glory. I wanted to drop to my knees in front of him and take him in my mouth. The thought turned me on.

"I'm holding you to that."

He planted a kiss on my cheek and then bent down to pick up his discarded clothing from the night before. While I showered, he sat on the vanity and told me about Mexico. I told him about my new job, leaving out parts I knew would cause him concern, like the discussions JC and I had. Noah didn't need to know that JC still held a torch for me even though he was married. When I shut the shower off, he was right there holding a towel for me to walk into. He wrapped it around me and pulled me into a hug.

"I can't wait to spend all weekend with you. I love long weekends."

"Oh my God, I completely forgot that it's Memorial Day on Monday. I was so busy this week and no one mentioned it."

"Well, I get you all to myself this weekend unless you want to go do something? We could go to the South Street Seaport if you like."

"Do you mind if we discuss it when I get home tonight?"

"Not at all. I would prefer just us if you want to know the truth."

"Noah, is that your subtle way of saying you don't want to go to my parent's house?"

"I'm sorry Lexi, but your father acts like I'm a spy. He drives me crazy with his questions. And your mom with the wedding preparations. Does she think that her grown daughter and soon to be son-in-law can't handle them?"

"They mean well. But no, we don't have to go if you don't want to. They haven't even asked me so maybe they aren't having their usual get together."

"Lexi, it's not that I don't like them, because I do. I just want them to let us make our own decisions. It's bad enough your mother was angry at you for a week over the dress you chose. It's your wedding."

"She got over it."

"But it wasn't necessary."

He kisses me on my nose and lets me go, reaching around me to open the glass door to the shower. I finish drying myself while he's washing up and then blow dry my hair. I'm still wrapped in the towel when he comes out, eyeing me lasciviously.

"You look good enough to eat."

"Noah…"

He knows from the look on my face that I don't have time. I have a half hour to dress, apply my makeup and get to the subway, not nearly enough time to do what he has in mind.

"I will expect payment in full when we come home from dinner tonight."

"Oh, do you now, Mr. Wilton."

"I won't tell you what to do but yes."

I swat at his taut ass as I leave the bathroom. Fifteen minutes later, I'm dressed and applying my makeup in the mirror over my dresser. Noah sits on the bed he just made and watches me. Anyone can tell he's in love from the look in his eyes. It warms my heart to have a man so in to me.

"Enjoy your day. I'll be glued to my office chair for most of it."

"What time are you making the reservation for?"

"7:00, I guess. Does that work for you?"

"Yes. That gives me time to get home and change."

He pulls me into an embrace and hungrily kisses me, his tongue gently exploring my mouth. I break the kiss as the butterflies start to flutter.

"You're incorrigible."

"But you'll take me any way you can get me."

"That's true. I'll see you tonight."

It's nearly 7:45 AM and I might just be lucky enough to catch the 7:58 train if I hurry. I do catch it, but I end up standing which I'm used to. The office is still quiet when I enter but I notice that JC's door is open. He peers out when he hears the keys in my hand.

"Lexi, how are you this morning?"

"Fine and you?"

"Okay. Are you ready for this weekend?"

"Yes, a nice present. Just starting and now a three-day weekend."

"You are coming to Vincent's party, aren't you?"

"Uh, what party? I wasn't told."

"At Vincent's home in the Southampton. He has one every Memorial Day weekend and July Fourth."

"I'm not sure that I will be able to make it. I was planning on spending the entire weekend alone with Noah."

"You can bring your fiancé. It's for families though most people leave their children at home. It can get pretty wild at night."

"That's really not my thing."

"You used to hit it pretty hard when we were in college."

"That was years ago. I'm almost thirty."

"You're not past your prime, Lexi. You're a young vibrant woman."

"I'll think about it."

I didn't have much time because Vincent was heading down the hall.

"Alexa. Just the person I want to see. Are you coming to my party tomorrow?"

"Vincent, I'm not sure. My fiancé just got back from a work trip and I think he wants to spend a quiet weekend."

"I won't take no for an answer. I want to see you there. Bring him along. There is plenty to do and I have a private beach."

"Okay, what time?"

"Party starts around 1:00. Bring your bathing suit. Oh, and wear white, it's a theme."

I watched him walk away and my eyes swing to JC who has a wide smile on his face.

"I guess I'll see you tomorrow."

I bet JC did this on purpose. He knew about the party and could've told me on Monday. I wasn't sure Noah would want to drive out to Southampton in holiday traffic. I know he's busy but decide the best time to tell him is now. My fingers drum on the desk as I wait for him to pick up the phone. Noah answers on the third ring.

"Lexi, what's wrong?"

"Something has to be wrong for me to call my handsome fiancé?"

"That's not what I meant. You just left an hour ago."

"I've been requested at Vincent's party tomorrow."

"Oh?"

I can't tell if Noah's annoyed or amused. I drop the other shoe.

"It's in Southampton."

I hear him sigh deeply and I know now that he's annoyed.

"Lexi, I really don't want to drive out to Long Island in holiday traffic."

"I know, I'm sorry but this is a way for me to get to know everyone at the office. I haven't had time. I can go by myself and be back Saturday night."

"I just came back from being away. I don't want to spend another day without you. I'll go, but can we leave early in the morning so we don't have to deal with the traffic? We can have breakfast somewhere until it's time to go."

I inwardly sighed and my heart swelled with love. "Thank you, Noah. I appreciate this."

"You better show me how much appreciation tonight," he growls.

I know he's joking by being demanding but I plan on appreciating him tonight just the same.

"I love you. I'll let you get back to work."

"Love you too, darlin'."

As I hang up the phone, JC shows up at my door, entering my office without an invitation. His stride is graceful, and he sits in one of the chairs in front of my desk.

"Are you coming tomorrow or did your fiancé nix the idea?"

"Why are you so gung-ho to get me over to Vincent's?"

"I'm not gung-ho. I just thought we would have a good time hanging out. I would like to meet Noah."

"Is Brianna coming?"

"Yes. She had a fight with one of her girlfriends and came home last night."

"Well then, I'm looking forward to meeting her," I said sarcastically.

JC looked at me puzzled but said nothing and left my office. Why did I say it like that? I don't care about his wife. He hadn't told me much about her looks, but I was sure she was a petite perfect Barbie Doll with blonde hair. She'll probably stroll around in the tiniest of bikinis.

Except for a quick proofread on the copy for The Kingston Group, my day is pretty easy. I'm ahead of schedule with the Camilla campaign and a new package I'm working on for Kansas City Steaks. I don't see JC for most of the day until it's time to leave. He stops into my office just before I pack up my work for the day.

"Are you staying in Southampton tomorrow night?"

"I doubt it. It's Memorial Day weekend and I'm sure there's nothing available."

"You can stay with us."

"Where are you staying?"

"Brianna's family has a house about a mile from Vincent's house. Why drive home in the dark when you can stay local."

"I would need to see if Noah wants to stay. I know he had some things to do this weekend."

JC frowned. "Lexi, what do you want to do? All I keep hearing about is Noah."

"JC, that's unfair. Noah is very giving, and he would do whatever I want. But I don't want to take him away from his work."

"Then he can go home, and you can stay with us. We can give you a ride back to the city on Sunday or Monday."

"Thank you, but I would rather go home with Noah. I promised we would spend some alone time this weekend."

He knitted his eyebrows together. "Well think about it and text me. You have my number. Don't forget to wear white."

JC walked away from me as I finished up in my office. I didn't think it was a good idea we spend the night at his wife's home; worse was spending the night without Noah.

When I entered the loft, Noah was dressed for dinner and sitting in his office finishing payroll. Soft jazz played on his iPod and he looked up at me as I entered his office.

"So, ready for dinner?" he asked with a smile.

"Yes, I am. Let me get changed. Uh, I have something to ask you about tomorrow."

Noah took off his glasses and gave me his full attention.

"JC and his wife have offered for us to stay in their home tomorrow night. I figured it would be better than driving back to the city in the dark."

He nodded and I thought I saw a hint of a smile. "That makes sense. I'm sure after a full day we'll be pretty tired."

"I'll text JC and let him know that we're going to stay. One other thing, the party theme is white."

"Does that mean we have to wear all white or the decorations are white?"

"Both, I guess. Vincent said to wear white. I have that white bikini; it would be perfect."

Noah frowned. "That thing is very skimpy and doesn't cover all of your ass."

"But it looks fantastic on me."

"I admit that it does, but I prefer the fantastic is only for me."

"Are you jealous?"

"Not one bit. The ring on your finger says that I can touch but others can't"

"Noah, you never have to worry."

I went to the bedroom to change for our dinner at Monster Barbecue. I was starved since I hadn't eaten much for lunch. I texted JC to let him know we would be staying at their home after the party.

We'll be staying overnight if that's alright.

That's great. I'm delighted. I can't wait to see you.

JC's response made me uncomfortable. Our relationship was extending beyond boss to subordinate.

CHAPTER 6

Monster Barbecue was crowded. The air held the aroma of cooking meat and spicy sauce. Because Noah knew the owner, we were escorted to one of the butcher paper clad round tables away from the noisy bar area. After we ordered our drinks, Noah began questioning me about JC as I read through the menu.

"You seem to be pretty chummy with JC. I wouldn't expect it."

"Why?"

"Come on, Lexi. Your relationship ended very ugly and he screwed you over at Carver."

I began to chew on my lip, but Noah didn't seem to notice. "He's my boss, we have history. End of story."

"I just know that if someone treated me that way, I wouldn't be so easy to forgive them."

I raised my voice, but it didn't register much above the din of the restaurant. "Why are you ruining this for me?"

Noah sipped at his water. "I'm not. I'm just trying to understand the dynamic."

"If you're asking if I still have feelings for him, I don't. I deserve this job. I worked hard for years to become director and even though he's my boss, I'm not letting that interfere."

Our drinks came and we placed our food order though my stomach started to feel queasy. I took a big gulp of my martini and stared at Noah.

His face turned passive. "Babe, I didn't mean to upset you. I just want to be sure you're happy."

"Why wouldn't I be? I have the job I want and the man that I love. My life is perfect."

I think Noah realized I was irritated, and he took my hand and kissed it. I smiled at him, but I was angry. This was supposed to be a celebratory dinner and I didn't appreciate the interrogation. For the rest of dinner, we only made small talk. I didn't feel very much like eating and took most of my rib dinner with collard greens and mac and cheese home. Our cab ride was silent as I looked out the window and Noah typed out emails.

As soon as we walked in the door, I placed my food in the refrigerator and headed for the bedroom. I don't know if the day sapped my energy or if it was due to the tension between Noah and me. All I wanted to do was go to bed. Our day would start early tomorrow. I began to undress as Noah came into the bedroom.

"Lexi, please don't be angry at me. I only want what's best for you."

"You could've waited. This was supposed to be a celebration dinner for me, and you ruined it."

"I'm sorry. I should've been more considerate."

I pouted. "Yes, you should've."

"Don't be angry," Noah pleaded.

"I am angry." I continued to get ready for bed, turning my back to him.

"Lexi, please. I'm a jerk. Should I get down on my knees and beg for forgiveness?"

I turned, the thought of him kneeling in front of me begging played in my head. It brought a smile to my face and helped to disarm the situation. Noah took me in his arms and kissed me softly on the lips. He always had a way about him that could make me melt.

"I forgive you. We should go to bed. We need to get up early and pack."

"That sounds like a plan. I want to take a quick shower."

While he was in the shower, I came into brush my teeth and wash my face. I couldn't help admiring Noah's sexy chest and muscular arms as he washed the shampoo from his hair. I was almost asleep when he slipped into bed next to me and I turned on my side so he could curl into my body. He wrapped his arm around me and tucked his hand underneath my left breast. I wondered if Noah could feel my chest thump with a guilty heart.

It's much too early to be awake at this hour of the morning on a Saturday. I reach over to shut off the alarm. I'm vaguely aware of Noah's erection pressing against my ass. We seem to have ended in the same position we went to bed last night. His thumb caresses my nipple.

"Noah, stop it," I said half-heartedly.

"Are you sure?"

"Yes, we have to get out of here or we'll be stuck in beach traffic."

"It's only five. If we're on the road by six, we should be fine."

He kisses my neck and I try to suppress a giggle. He's trying his damndest to get me to give in and it's working as his mouth slips to my earlobe.

"Come on, I'll be quick."

I challenge him, "Oh, so this is all about you?"

"No, it's not. I plan to make you come before I do."

Noah rolls away and pushes me onto my back, then moves between my legs. Tugging at my panties, he pulls them off and puts them to his nose and smiles.

"I wish we had more time."

I know what he means. Noah loves to go down on me but it's never a short process since he enjoys it so much. Usually he makes me come more than once with his tongue before he enters me.

"We don't."

His fingers slip into me and quickly withdraw to be replaced by his cock. I love the feel of him inside me. His thickness fills me and each slow thrust caresses my slick walls. Noah moves to his knees and strokes my throbbing clit as he moves. Slow circular motion with his fingers has me arching my back.

"You're very greedy this morning," he growls.

"We didn't have sex last night."

"No, we didn't but you didn't want it this morning either. Should I stop?"

"Don't you dare."

I'm so close, moaning from the erotic pleasure that he's giving to me. I pull my knees up and Noah smiles. It's a scenario I've repeated many times during our lovemaking. I push hard into his thrusts and then I'm falling apart around him as I climax.

Noah lies upon me and continues to stroke. His tongue caresses my sensitive swollen nipples, first one, then the other. He whispers something that is unintelligible, and I feel him spill into me. He buries his head below my chin, kissing my neck. We're both moist with sweat, breathing heavy as we come down from our orgasms. I kiss the top of his head.

"That was delicious. I wish we could stay here all day."

"We could. Do we really have to go today?"

"I think it would be rude to not show up."

"Maybe we should come home tonight. I'd like to continue what we started here."

"Why don't we play it by ear?"

He lifts his head to look at me with a lazy grin then moves to my side. I glance at the clock and it's now 5:17.

"Noah, we have to get moving or traffic will be a nightmare."

"I'll shower first unless you want to come in with me?"

"No, I'll pack a few things in case we decide to stay."

He jumps over me to head to the shower while I go to the closet to find an appropriate bag to put some clothing in. I find a small suitcase that's perfect for overnight and begin to pack a few things. The dress code is white, and I dig through my closet looking for a pair of white shorts. I don't have any casual white shirts other than t-shirts and I guess that's fine.

Noah comes out of the bathroom wrapped in a towel, his chest still glistening with beads of water. I turn away because I'm still hot from our lovemaking and looking at his practically naked body will just make it worse.

"Finished. You can go in and take this with you."

He yanks off the wet towel from around his waist and tosses it to me. Damn him. He's so fucking sexy that I want to devour him. The perfect V at his hips leading to places I wish I could go right now but we have no time. I scowl at him and take the towel to hang up on the rack.

By the time I'm finished showering, the clock reads 5:45. Noah is dressed in pair of white shorts, white polo shirt and topsiders with no socks, my perfect preppy.

"I packed a pair of swim trunks for you. Do you want to wear them under your shorts instead?" I asked.

"I'm not sure. Do you think we'll actually go swimming?"

"I think so. It's hot out today and at the very least, we can lie on the beach."

"Did you pack your bikini?"

"No, I'm wearing it under my clothes. I'm wearing the white one we talked about."

He scowls. "Oh. The one that I don't want you to wear?"

"Noah, come on. I'm sure there will be women wearing even skimpier bikinis than mine. It covers most of my ass."

"I don't want to argue. Can you at least bring that sarong you wore to Hawaii? The pretty one with all the colors?"

"Deal."

He kisses me and heads to the kitchen to make coffee for our travel mugs. When he comes back, I'm finished packing.

"Let me have the bag. I'll get the car and meet you downstairs. The coffee mugs are on the counter."

After he leaves, I check to make sure I have all our toiletries and my makeup in the small shoulder bag I have. I'm in such a hurry that I almost forget to take my birth control pills with me. Downstairs, Noah is waiting in the SUV. I hand him the travel mugs while I put my seatbelt on and we're off.

It's a few minutes after six and the traffic isn't heavy yet. I'm glad because Noah gets grumpy when he must sit in traffic. The 495 isn't bad by the time we get there and we're making good time. I'm tired and I keep yawning which is causing Noah to yawn. He tells me to stop and I stare out the window so he doesn't see me do it.

When we reach Sunrise Highway, the traffic starts to slow and by the time we hit Hampton Bays, we're crawling. Noah taps his nails against his travel mug and I know he's annoyed.

I wrap my hand around his thigh and knead it, moving up closer to his crotch. Usually he's game but this time he grabs it to stop what I'm doing. I withdraw my hand and put it in my lap. I don't realize it, but I'm biting the corner of my lip.

"Lexi, stop it," he says softly.

"I'm sorry. I should've drove."

"It's no big deal. We have a few miles to go and then we can have some breakfast."

Breakfast, I'm starving and today is waffle day. If we weren't stuck in traffic, I would be home making Noah waffles, our Saturday morning tradition. Finally, the traffic starts to move and we're in Southampton. It took us nearly three hours, but we can have a leisurely meal and relax before the party.

Noah drives around until we find a diner. The parking lot is only half full so I know we can get a good seat. Before we get out, he pulls my arm and leans in to kiss me.

"I didn't mean to snap at you."

"I know. I understand."

He lets me go and I get out of my side of the car. We walk hand in hand into the Seaside Diner and we're seated immediately. The booths are old and the green Formica on the tables could use a makeover, but the place is clean. There's a heavenly smell in the air, probably muffins which is making my mouth water.

After the pink uniform clade waitress serves us coffee and we place our breakfast order, Noah reaches across the table to take my left hand. He starts playing with my engagement ring and I know something is worrying him.

"What's the matter?"

"Nothing, except I might have to go on another business trip."

I try to pull my hand away, but he holds steadfast.

I clench my jaw. "Why? I thought you were hiring a couple of employees?"

"I am. I did but they need to be trained."

"Oh, so this is a training trip?"

"That and a work trip. I want to make sure my employees use the procedures I set in place for our clients. I don't want to be away from you either."

"When is this trip taking place?"

"Next week. The client is making final travel arrangements. Once those are in place, I can set up an itinerary for my staff."

"Is this going to be all summer? We have arrangements to make for the wedding and I prefer not to make them by myself."

"Lexi, it's only for the next couple of weeks."

"Oh, so now it's a couple of weeks? Next you'll tell me it's a couple of months."

I pull my hand out of his grasp and start chewing on my lip again. Noah's face clouds and he reaches over to dislodge my lip from my teeth. I pull my head back because I'm angry with him and don't want to feel his touch. The look on his face says it all, he's hurt, and I begin to feel like an asshole.

"Lexi, please. Just bear with me for a little while."

"I'm trying, but I love you. It's hard when you're away."

Noah smiles, but it's lost on me. I'm upset and I concentrate on pouring sugar into my coffee. I lose count and put too many packets in, making the hot liquid sickeningly sweet. The waitress comes with our food and I ask her for another cup of coffee. Noah digs into his waffles but as hungry as I am, all I do is pick at mine.

I know I'm acting like a brat and he puts up with it because he loves me. I don't want to walk into the party at odds with Noah, so I smile and start eating. The frown he had on his face fades and we're back to us again.

"Have you been to the shelter lately?"

I shake my head, pushing pieces of waffle around some more. "I've been so busy with work. Maggie told me they have two litters of puppies. I love puppies."

Noah smiles at me. "I know you do. Maybe when things stabilize a little, we can think about getting one."

I brighten and put my fork down. "Really? I thought you said no."

Noah grins. "A man can change his mind, can't he?"

My appetite is back, and I take a forkful of syrup laden waffle to my mouth. I've always wanted a puppy, but we've been so busy with everything. I'm glad Noah is warming to the idea.

"Who's going to be at this party?" Noah asks.

"Just work people, I guess. My assistant Nikki is coming with her flavor of the week. Of course, JC and his wife, Brianna, and several other people. I was told Vincent has a huge heated in ground-pool surrounded by a beautiful patio. We can swim there too."

"I'd rather go on the beach."

"Why? I'm sure the water in the ocean is cold."

"I'd just rather."

Noah didn't have to say it, but I knew what he was thinking. He was worried about other men looking at me in my bikini, particularly my ass. Honestly, I didn't know what the fuss was. My body wasn't perfect, and I was sure there would be plenty of other women wearing much less.

"Okay, we can go on the beach."

We finished up breakfast, but it was still early. Then I had a thought, maybe we could drop by JC's home and leave our stuff there before heading to Vincent's. I wasn't sure if he was there yet, but I texted him when Noah used the bathroom and paid the check.

Are you in Southampton?

Since last night. Why?

Can we drop by? We left early so we wouldn't hit traffic and just finished breakfast at The Tin Spoon Diner.

JC texts the address and I let Noah know we can spend a couple of hours there until the party starts. He smiles at me, but I can tell it's strained. It has me wondering why. In the car, I ask.

"Noah, are you okay with us sleeping at JC's house?"

"Yes, why?"

"This morning, you didn't seem happy we would be spending time over there."

"My worry is you. I want to make sure you're okay with spending time with your ex fiancé."

I shook my head. "I told you I'm fine. I can handle JC. It's the past and several years ago. I can't keep dragging this around for the rest of my life. I have a new life and one I love. Stop worrying about me."

Noah reaches over to stroke my cheek with his knuckles, and I lean in against them. I love his thick calloused hands, a product of his intense workouts. I grasp his fingers and press my face into his skin.

"I know you can. You're strong. That's one of the things I love about you."

We pull into a long gravel driveway flanked by two stacked stone pillars. The house is grand with a large porch and beautiful landscaping in the front. As we get out of the car, the front door opens, JC is calling to us as we walk towards it. I sigh, telling myself the next few hours might be hard.

CHAPTER 7

"You must be Noah," JC said as he held his hand out.

I can see him sizing Noah up as if he's a rival. JC is shorter than Noah but not by much and they both had muscular bodies, though JC's is leaner. I see a woman behind him and it's just as I thought, a Barbie Doll. I assume the woman is Brianna. She's blond, petite and gorgeous which makes me feel a little insecure. She pulls me into a hug and my insecurity melts away.

"Camden has told me lots about you, Lexi."

"I hope it's all good," I say with a smile.

"Why wouldn't it be? He told me you're a wonderful addition to the company and making his life easier."

I look at my former fiancé. "I appreciate that, JC."

He shoots me a warning glance and I realize he wasn't kidding; he really didn't tell Brianna about us. I better knock off calling him JC. Apparently, she doesn't notice because she didn't mention it.

I smile because Brianna is wearing a pink string bikini much more revealing than the one I have on under my clothes. Her large breasts are barely covered by the cloth and spill out on the sides. I hope she doesn't plan on playing volleyball because I don't think the strings will hold.

Brianna offers us a mimosa, but I decline. It's barely eleven in the morning and I don't want to get started too early. However, she indulges and fills her champagne flute practically to the rim, then saunters out to the pool area.

"This is quite a place you have here," I said.

"Yeah, fourteen rooms, six of them bedrooms but it's not mine, it's Brianna's parents. They're in Japan right now or they would be here. Hunter is coming with his girlfriend; at least I think it's his girlfriend."

"Anyone else staying?"

"One of Brianna's friends. She's coming later. Let me show you where you'll be sleeping. I hope you don't mind that we share a terrace."

"Why would I mind?"

Noah grabs my hand as we head up the stairs and I feel a bit of tension in how tight he's holding it. I stroke the back of his with my thumb and he opens his grip a little.

The room JC takes us to is enormous. The ceilings are at least fifteen feet high and it's about a third of the size of our loft. It's painted a soothing cream color and a thick area rug the shade of almond is below our feet. He shows us the en suite which makes me happy we don't have to share a bathroom. Then JC opens the double French doors to the terrace which overlooks the rectangular pool. Down below us is Brianna who is sitting on a lounge chair, drinking her mimosa and talking on her cell phone.

"Hey babe, do you want to decide what you're wearing to the party?" JC calls.

Brianna looks up. "This is it. I'm not wearing white. It makes me look washed out."

She flips her blonde hair and continues to talk on the phone. I can see the exasperation in JC's face.

"I'm sorry. She isn't a very good hostess."

"JC, it's fine. Noah and I are very self-sufficient. Besides, we're leaving in a little while anyway, right?"

"Yes, but still."

We hear the doorbell ring and JC excuses himself to answer it, leaving us alone in the bedroom.

"Isn't this some place? I can't believe the size of the bathroom. I thought our bathroom was big." I say.

"He doesn't have it easy with her, does he?"

"Noah, I try to stay out of his business. JC hasn't told me anything about their relationship."

I hate lying to Noah, but the truth would make him uneasy especially with the history between JC and me. We unpack a few things and put our toiletries on the light granite vanity the bathroom before heading back downstairs.

"Shit, Lexi, is that you?"

I turn to see JC's brother smiling at me. "Hunter, so nice to see you."

He scoops me up in a big hug. I always loved Hunter. He's almost the spitting image of his brother, all thick brown hair, and cleft chin minus the stubble. The only difference is that Hunter has brown eyes whereas JC has blue. I kiss his cheek and cling to him. Hunter was always my voice of reason when I had problems with JC. He comforted me when we broke up and we almost landed in bed together.

I introduce him to Noah. "This is my fiancé, Noah Wilton."

They shake hands and begin to chat. Hunter mentions fishing and that's it, Noah is hooked, so to speak. It's one of his favorite activities but he seldom gets to do it. JC gestures me over to the kitchen, leaving them in the living room and probably unaware that we've left.

"Please don't say anything to Brianna about us dating."

"JC, we did more than date. You we're to be my husband."

"Yeah, but it didn't work out so please don't."

"I wish you wouldn't involve me in your baggage. You should've told her when you knew I was working for you."

"She was away. I wasn't telling her over the phone."

"Bullshit. You knew before she left, and you could've told her yesterday when she came home. Suppose Hunter says something? Is he supposed to pretend he doesn't know me?"

"She knows we went to high school together so why wouldn't he know you?"

"I swear JC, I don't want to be dragged into your marital drama."

We stop talking as Brianna comes in for a refill of her mimosa. JC asks her to not drink so much and she narrows her eyes at him. Wow, I almost feel sorry for him, but he deserves it. While he's arguing with her, I join Noah and Hunter. I don't care that their conversation has moved on to investments of which I know nothing about. I just want to escape the awkwardness in the kitchen.

"That's quite a rock you have on your finger, Lexi. When's the wedding?" Hunter asks.

"October. We still have some planning to do."

"Where are you getting married?"

"The Paramount."

"That old theater in Soho?"

"Yes, we wanted something different. The façade is period, but you have to see what they've done to the inside, just beautiful."

"I wish you all the best."

"Thank you."

Noah excuses himself to get a drink of water and Hunter leans in close to me.

"I'll never forgive my brother for leaving you. He's a fool."

"It was a blessing in disguise. We could be like his marriage is now."

"I doubt that. In some ways I think he still loves you."

I smile because I know Hunter's right but I'm in love with

Noah. JC comes in to mention it's 12:30 and we should get ready to leave especially if we want one of the loungers set up on the private beach. Vincent has a huge crowd and a lot of people head out to the sand.

I make sure I have everything I need to take to Vincent's especially my sarong. I don't want Noah upset with me because I forgot it. JC suggests we take one car, but Noah prefers to drive his own. We decide to follow them.

"Lexi, what's up with JC and his wife?"

"I told you, I don't stick my nose into his business. She wants to drink; he doesn't want her to drink. That's what I got from it."

"You're getting defensive. I'm only asking a question."

"I don't want to argue. I want to enjoy this day."

"Fine. I hope you don't mind if I have a beer or two."

"It's okay. I can drive home tonight if I need to."

I know I probably won't have to worry. Noah rarely overindulges in alcohol and normally has a single beer or a glass of wine.

As we near Vincent's address, I'm amazed at the size of the houses. I thought that JC's house was big, but that house could fit in one of these five times or more. Vincent must be doing well because when we pull into the brick paved driveway, we're greeted by a valet who takes the keys from Noah and gives him a ticket.

The house is incredible, and mansion sized. It's stucco with multi paned windows, and two octagon shaped rooms at either end of the home. In the circular driveway stands a fountain with a roman statue. I almost bump into Noah because I'm staring at it. A man in a black butler's uniform holds the door open for us and I feel overwhelmingly underdressed in these opulent surroundings.

We follow JC out to the patio area which is decorated in a beach theme. Beyond the large expanse of green grass and perfectly landscaped property, I see a gate leading to the sand. This is where I want to go but I make my rounds to say hello and meet Vincent's family and relatives. It's during this time that I find out why Marco looks so much like Vincent, they're cousins.

"This is some place," Noah whispers.

I'm happy to see several women dressed in bathing suits including Vincent's daughter, Jennifer. Much like Brianna, her bikini is much more revealing than mine. I decide to do as several women are and remove my t-shirt so that I can walk around in my bikini top.

Noah runs his hand over my back, sending shivers down my spine. But his skin against mine is a turn on. Not the place for it but I can't help it. We circulate for a little while just to be social, but I want to hit the beach. I need to use the bathroom and Noah comes with me.

The one near the huge gourmet kitchen is occupied as is the one in the hall the butler directed me to. I really must go and take a chance by heading up the grand wooden staircase to the second floor. A thick beige wool carpet runs the expanse of the hall that's paneled with wainscoting on the lower half. Beautiful reproductions of famous works adorn the walls, at least I think they're reproductions. I'm not too sure that Vincent could afford a Van Gogh or a Picasso.

"Here's one," Noah says, opening one of the closed doors.

The full bathroom is huge with light granite countertops and white ceramic floors. An oversized garden tub with jets sit in one corner while what looks like a triple sized tiled shower sits on the other. The vanity that the granite countertop sits on is about fourteen feet long with double sinks and plenty of room for toiletries.

Noah turns away while I pee, sweet relief. Then as I'm washing my hands, his arms encircle my waist and he pushes against me. He's hard and I shake my head.

"Are you crazy? This is my boss' house."

"I can't help that I want you."

"We had sex a few hours ago."

"Does that really matter? We often make love more than once a night."

He continues to rub his erection against my ass and my insides are beginning to flame. His hands move to my breasts and his mouth to my neck, kissing where my pulse is. I can feel my heart begin to speed and pound.

"Noah," I caution.

I know I'm past resisting him. He turns me and pulls the strings on my bikini top, freeing my breasts. His mouth suctions my hardened nipples, first one, then the other and I suppress the need to moan by biting my tongue.

With his head buried between my breasts he asks if I still want him to stop. He damn well knows that I'm long gone by now. I can't say no because I want him to much. I let him unbutton my shorts and push them down along with my bikini bottoms. They pool around my ankles and he lifts me onto the vanity. I shiver at the coldness of the granite as it touches my skin.

I hungrily watch him as he drops his shorts, shocked that he isn't wearing any underwear. He pushes my knees against my ass, spreading me wide, then kneels in front of me. I clench my fists because I know what's to come. His tongue slides up my folds and circles my swollen clit several times. I breathlessly whisper his name.

Noah looks up at me and smiles. I know what he wants to do but if he continues, we'll be here for an hour. I shake my head and the smile fades from his shapely lips. He understands and rises, positioning himself between my legs, pressing his swollen head against my opening. In one quick thrust his long cock is in me and I can't stop the moan that's been hanging in my throat.

He shushes me and works into a rhythm while stroking my clit with his thumb. Again, a moan escapes from my lips and he kisses me hard to keep me quiet. I really want to scream because his cock feels so delicious as it slides inside me.

My eyes are closed tight as I suck on his tongue, enjoying the sensation. I can feel my orgasm building and I tighten then climax. Noah pounds into me harder and I begin to slide on the counter. He grabs my hips to steady me then continues his pace. I silently count in my head how many strokes it takes him as I begin to recover from my orgasm, seven, eight, nine…and then I feel his hot release as he softly groans.

He softly kisses my face and then buries his head in my shoulder, murmuring how much he loves me. My voice is hoarse as I echo his sentiments.

"Noah, we need to clean up and get back. We've been away for a while."

"Just let me stay here for a few more minutes. I want you to myself just for a little bit."

I start to feel the guilt rise in me. I should have said we had plans so we could have spent the weekend together alone. I know he was looking forward to it and I threw a wrench in his plans.

When he finally withdraws from me, I'm sticky with his cum. We clean up at the sink with soap and a half a roll of toilet paper. I give a quick check of the counter to make sure we cleaned any evidence of our union; we quickly dress and go back downstairs.

I feel much better. Any residual tension that we had from our little spat is gone. Noah holds my hand and we walk towards the beach. During the time we were missing, the party has gone into full swing. Vincent has a DJ playing music underneath a small open tent and wait staff is circulating with hors d'oeuvres.

"Where did you two go?"

I turn to see JC and Brianna following us to the gate.

"We had to use the bathroom and after waiting at the two downstairs, we went upstairs to find one."

He raises his eyebrow at me, lucky Noah didn't notice. JC knows I'm adventurous with a healthy sex drive. We had sex in plenty of bathrooms at parties when we were together.

The sand is hot, and we hurry over to the few remaining loungers on the beach that aren't occupied. Someone suggests we start a volleyball game. I'm tired and want to lie in the sun but Noah and Brianna join in, leaving me alone with JC. I slip on my sunglasses and ignore him.

"You fucked him, didn't you?"

I'm mortified and pretend I don't hear him.

"Come on Lexi, tell me."

I tear off my sunglass and squint at him.

"If I did or didn't, it's none of your business. He's my fiancé and I don't have to answer to you. I've mentioned the sexual harassment thing before."

"This isn't sexual harassment. I know you so well. You did. You were gone at least fifteen minutes. I don't believe the story that you waited for the bathroom for a while and went upstairs."

"Are you keeping tabs on me?"

"No, I just know you better than you think. How many times did we do that?"

"JC, are you jealous? What bothers you more? That I fucked him, or I didn't fuck you?"

"Why would you think I'm jealous?"

"I have my reasons. Get over me. You're married and soon I'll be married. We have nothing but a working relationship."

I slip my sunglasses on again, stand up and remove my shorts. The look on JC's face is priceless when he sees my ass. I go back to ignoring him and lie down on the lounger stomach first with my head towards him. Even with his sunglasses on I can see he's staring at me. I smile to myself full well knowing what I'm doing to him.

Somehow, I must have fallen asleep because the next thing I know, I feel a towel draped over me. It's Noah and he bends down to whisper to me.

"I thought you were going to wear your sarong."

"I was sunbathing. I thought you only meant when I was walking around."

"Your ass is beautiful but not for everyone else to see."

I turn over and sit up. JC is no longer on the lounger next to me, but I see him in the water with Brianna. I yawn and reach out my arms to hug Noah.

"What am I going to do with you, Lexi?"

"You could marry me."

"That box is already checked. Our wedding day will be here soon enough."

I hear yelling and I look over to see Brianna slogging through the water toward shore. She's complaining about JC splashing her and getting her hair messed up. I watch him follow her out and they join us on the loungers.

"I'm sorry Bri, I didn't know you wanted to keep your hair dry."

"I don't want the saltwater in it. It strips the color."

I smile because it means she's a bottle blond. I wonder what's the real color of her hair. They continue arguing and I try to ignore them. Noah sits on the lounger next to me and asks if I put on sunscreen, I haven't. He finds several complimentary bottles in little buckets next to the loungers and squirts some on his hands, then slathers my legs with it.

I do my arms and chest. He tells me to flip over and I turn my head to the side that JC's on as he does my entire posterior. I can see JC staring, probably wishing it was him touching my body.

"All done. Can you put some on me? My shoulders are getting red."

I do the same to Noah, seductively running my hands over his skin. He leans in and tells me if I don't behave he'll have to take me up to the bathroom again. I can only wish.

When we're done, I stretch out on the lounger for more sun. By this time Brianna has gone up to the outdoor shower to wash the salt out of her hair. JC has parked himself on the lounger next to me and is paging through is phone with his hand cupped over the screen. I'm thirsty and want to get something to drink.

"Noah, can I get you something to drink?"

"A beer would be nice."

"Okay, be right back."

I slip my shorts over my legs. I forgot my sarong in the car, and I don't want to upset Noah by walking around with my ass exposed. I nod at JC as I walk away. Brianna is on her way back with some kind of punch in a big red cup. I'm sure it's alcoholic and that I'll come back to another argument.

Sure enough, when I do return, they're at it again. I pull my sunglasses down a little and roll my eyes at Noah. Seriously, I don't want to listen to their bickering and ask if we can take a walk. He nods and I hand him his beer. There's a slight breeze and it feels good in the hot sun.

"Lexi, I was thinking about the honeymoon."

"Oh? What are your thoughts?"

"We shouldn't go to anything in the Caribbean, it's hurricane time in October."

"Where would you like to go?"

"How about Europe or the UK?"

"Really? I've never been to either one."

"You'll love it. Maybe we can take a tour of the British Isles."

"How about I leave that up to you. Surprise me."

"Are you sure?"

"Tell me the week before we go."

We sit down in the hot sand and I get between Noah's legs with my back against his chest. This is how I love to spend my day with him. I wish we were alone. He massages my shoulders and I close my eyes. We sit there for over an hour, just enjoying the gentle breeze.

"I'm starving. Can we go back to the house to get some food?"

"Of course. I can't have my bride hungry."

What's so crazy is that nothing has changed since we left. JC and Brianna are still quietly arguing. I let them know that we're getting some food and they join us. Maybe that will stop them from arguing. It's close to 4:30 when we come back and there are several trays set up with hot and cold food. The caterer is grilling chicken, burgers and sausage on a large grill, the smell is heavenly.

We start off with salad and work our way up to the heavier stuff. Many tables are set up around the property and we find one in the corner that's unoccupied. JC and Brianna join us. I hear my name called and turn to see Nikki with her boyfriend for the day. She looks adorable in a short white sundress and flip-flops. Her hair is piled high on her head in a bun. JC's leering at her doesn't go unnoticed. The man she's with is cute but not as handsome as Noah or JC.

"How are you, Alexa?"

"Good. You look nice in your sundress."

"Thanks, I wasn't sure if it would be appropriate but judging on all the bikinis here, it's fine."

I introduce her to Noah and JC introduces Brianna. It turns out that Nikki knows Brianna from high school. They were one grade apart. They strike up a conversation. I glance at JC and I can see he's utterly annoyed. Serves him right for marrying a woman seven years younger.

"I have to go to the bathroom, care to join me?" Noah whispers.

"I think once is enough. I promise to make it up to you tomorrow evening."

He frowns but I know he's kidding, and he squeezes my shoulder as he walks away. This gives JC the opportunity to sit next to me.

"Are you enjoying yourself?"

"Yes, I'm glad I came."

"I bet you are."

JC isn't referring to the fact we came to the party but rather that I came when Noah and I had sex in the bathroom.

"That's rude."

"I have no idea what you mean."

I lower my voice so Nikki and Brianna don't hear, "It really is bothering you that I had sex with Noah in the bathroom, isn't it?"

"Why would you think it would bother me."

"Seriously, I think you still have a thing for me. Your actions during the last week have made that clear. Am I going to have to quit?"

"Lexi, I don't want you to quit because of some misunderstanding. I'm just trying to be your friend."

"It seems like your trying to be more. You should work on your marriage."

His face clouds and he moves back over to sit near Brianna. I feel bad to lay the cards on the table, but it needed to be said. I don't feel the way he wants me to. Anyway, what am I supposed to have an illicit affair with my boss? I feel hands on my bare shoulders and see Noah is back.

"Miss me?"

"I always do. Think how it is when you go away?"

"Lexi don't start. I didn't plan it this way. In another few weeks I won't have to worry about it. Brice is handling the interviews and once the training is finished, I can stay home."

"I hope it's quick. I slept horribly while you were gone."

"I know baby. I didn't sleep so well either."

Noah leans over and gives me a hard kiss on the lips. Out of the corner of my eye, I see JC watching our exchange with a look of longing on his face.

CHAPTER 8

Brianna's tipsy, drunk even and in between JC staring at me, he's arguing with her. The sun is starting to set, and several guests have already departed the party.

Noah leans into my ear. "I hope she goes to sleep when we get to the house. I prefer not to be in the middle of their arguing."

"It's none of our business. As long as they don't involve us."

"I'm tired. You think we can go?"

JC must have read our minds, because he breaks himself away from Brianna and heads over to where we're sitting.

"What's up?" I ask.

"Want to go back to my house? The party is winding down."

"Sure. We'll follow you."

We must wait for several minutes before they retrieve our cars and I hear Brianna complaining about how incompetent the valets are. I think she is a spoiled brat. How would she know what it's like to work for a living? She even has the nerve to tell JC not to tip them when they bring their car around. I reach into my purse and fish out a ten-dollar bill which I hand to the valet. I see her from the corner of my eye frowning at me. I hope she takes the hint.

"Lexi, I wish we could be alone tonight."

"I know Noah, I'm sorry. If I had the energy to drive home, I would."

"As long as we can leave early tomorrow."

"I'll let JC know that we are."

The drive to JC's is quick and the driveway is filled with cars when we arrive. Hunter must have brought over a whole crew. We hear yelling and splashing when we enter the house. Sure enough, there are about ten people there. Brianna grabs Nikki's hand and they head out to the pool. I look from Noah to JC and shake my head.

"I'm tired but we're not going to be able to sleep with this noise."

"I can tell them to leave if you want," JC says.

"JC, that would be rude and I'm sure that Brianna would give you a hard time."

He looks out the window and his wife already has a beer in her hand. I have no idea where she is putting all the alcohol and why she isn't majorly drunk.

"It looks like the guys are going into the pool house," JC said.

"Why? What's in there?"

"They play poker. Do you want to join in? You were quite the card shark if I remember."

"I haven't played for a while. Noah do you want to play?"

I can see he was looking at me expectantly, so I nod and he heads over to the pool house leaving me alone with JC.

"Are you going to play?"

"No, I would rather hang out with you if you don't mind. I think we have some issues to discuss."

"I seriously don't want to discuss them now."

"This is our best chance. We can't at work and you're busy after work. Please Lexi?"

I know it's a conversation we need to have. I'm still wearing only my bikini top and shorts. I tell him to let me go upstairs to change. The air conditioning is making me feel cold and I want to put on a sweatshirt. He tells me he'll wait for me in the living room and I head upstairs to change. I pull some clothing out of my bag and realize that I took Noah's gray sweatshirt instead of mine. It's pretty big on me but it allows me to forgo a bra which is fine with me. No one will be able to tell.

JC is waiting for me and he made me a cup of tea, Earl Grey with lemon in it. He remembered and I'm flattered.

"Thank you. You remembered."

"I would never forget something like that, Lexi," he says softly.

I pick up the delicate china cup and take a sip. He even put in some honey. It makes me wonder if he purchased the Earl Grey just for me or it was here in the house. JC was always doing little sweet gestures for me when we were together. Too bad he couldn't keep his dick in his pants.

"Okay, so where do we start."

He sighs, "I think we have a bit of tension between us."

"We really don't until you make references to my sex life. That bothers me a lot. Why do you do that?"

"I'm sorry. We have so much history together. I feel so foolish for letting you go. I never dreamed my life would be this way. I married someone I should have said no to. I let my father talk me into it and then I got stuck."

"JC, are you still in love with me?"

I stare into his blue eyes hoping he's going to be truthful with me.

"Sometimes I think I am. I don't think there was a time I wasn't"

This is a huge revelation to me. In high school he made me miserable. I would work so hard and he would best me on almost everything academic. It was one of the most frustrating times in my life. I was surprised when he approached me in college and asked me out. I only did it to see what he was really up to.

"I don't understand. You disliked me in high school."

"I pretended to dislike you in high school. I really did like you."

"Then why did it take you a whole year to ask me out in college?"

"Because you were dating that guy, what was his name, Randy?"

"Yes, Randy Gates. He was nice enough, but he was more into his car than he was into me. Who drives in the city?"

"But you dated him for a year."

"And you were dating a lot too. I used to see you on campus with one blonde or another. I was amazed when you asked me out since I wasn't your typical."

"I liked women, not just blondes."

"Yeah, I know. Even when you had me you liked women. I forgave you time and time again because I loved you. You hurt me so much."

I can feel tears stinging my eyes and I flutter my eyelids to push them back.

"I was so stupid. But after I asked you to marry me, I didn't do it again."

"No, you did something worse. You stole my job and broke off our engagement months before our wedding."

"If I could take it all back I would. Do you love Noah like you love me?"

"JC, I loved you. I love Noah. He's never given me any reason to do otherwise. He would never cheat on me or hurt me."

Brianna comes into the house with Nikki and interrupts our conversation.

"Tea? You're drinking tea? It's hot out."

"Brianna, stop being rude."

"Fuck you, Camden."

It's obvious she's drunk and she gets up in a huff to go back outside.

"I can't believe you take that from her," I whispered.

"I told you, our relationship is beyond repair. I've mentioned a separation, but she said that's out of the question. She doesn't care about our marriage, only the appearance. Her friends are jealous she has an older, successful husband."

"JC, you have a choice. You don't have to stay with her if you're unhappy."

"And risk having my balls cut off by my father and hers? It's more than I can stand."

"You don't work for your father. So why are you so afraid?"

"My salary pays for certain things and then some things are supplemented by my father and hers."

"Like this house?"

"Yes, like this house. If I want to forgo the good life, then I can leave her but there will be consequences."

"I'm sorry it's so complicated for you. I want to be your friend; I really do but you have to stop making rude comments."

"I promise I will. I missed you the past few years."

We continue to talk about things and hours go by until I notice on the clock above the fireplace that it's nearing one in the morning. Noah is still playing cards in the pool house and with a three-hour drive back to the city, we better go to bed if we want to get up early. I rise to head to the pool house.

"Where are you going?" JC asks.

"To get Noah. I forgot to tell you that we want to get back to the city early tomorrow."

I see his face fill with disappointment and my heart hurts for him.

"I thought you would stay until Monday."

"I can't. We were supposed to spend the weekend together alone and I promised Noah we would at least have a full day or two together."

"I'll go with you. Hunter and his buddies can get pretty boisterous."

When we walk in, the place smells like a bar. Seven men sitting at the table and all of them are smoking cigars. Noah is doing well and has a big stack of chips in front of him. I'm upset to learn that besides the three beers he had at Vincent's, he's consumed several more and is drunk. I tap his shoulder.

"Hey baby, I'm beating the pants off these guys."

"I'm sorry to spoil your fun but if you want to leave early tomorrow, we need to go to bed."

"I decided we should stay for the rest of the weekend. Everyone is."

This is news to me since he wanted to get home. I wonder what changed his mind.

"Fine. I'm tired and I'm going to bed."

"You're mad, aren't you?"

The guys around the table let out a big "Ohhh" in unison. I'm embarrassed. JC tells them to shut up and to make sure they clean before they come up to bed. He ushers me out and grabs my hand to take me upstairs. Brianna is asleep with Nikki on the couch. I can feel my face burning with embarrassment.

"Come on. We can sit on the terrace."

We go through the French doors in my bedroom and sit on the cool tile floor. I can feel tears threatening to spill over my cheeks. Noah has never disrespected me like that before.

"Don't cry Lexi, he's drunk."

"I'm so embarrassed. Noah isn't like that and I don't know what's gotten into him."

JC rubs my back and before I know it, his hands are under my sweatshirt and stroking the soft skin of my back, tickling my spine. When we were together, he would lie behind me stretched out on the couch and do this very thing. It would always soothe me especially if I had a rough day.

"I always loved how smooth your skin is."

The only reason I let him continue is because I'm so angry at Noah. I know it's wrong and what makes it worse is that JC is still in love with me. I'm leading him on and after the display in the pool house; he might think he has a chance.

"You need to stop."

"I know you don't want me to."

"I do. Please."

He removes his hand and pulls me onto his lap. Another mistake that I allow to happen, but I'm upset. I cling to him and bury my head against his neck. He smells like the ocean and fresh air. I feel his arms embrace me and he begins to rock. Then the kisses come. First on the top of my head and then my cheek and finally my lips. I respond, then push him away and scramble from his lap.

"I'm so stupid. I'm sorry JC, I can't do this."

"It's alright, I shouldn't have done that, but you feel so good in my arms again."

I rise from the terrace floor just in time to see Noah helped into the bedroom by Hunter and another guy from his group. He stumbles to the bed and lies on his back. Within seconds, he's snoring loudly.

"Sorry, Lexi. He just kept asking for beers," Hunter says.

I thank him and realize that JC is no longer on the terrace. This is very unlike Noah and I wonder what's eating at him. Perhaps I nagged him to much about going away and he just wanted to let off some steam.

When I'm left alone with Noah, I pull off his sneakers and get ready for bed. I don't know how I'm going to sleep with the racket from his snoring, but I somehow manage to fall asleep.

During the night, Noah rolls over and hogs the bed. I try to push him over but he's all dead weight and my efforts are futile. I end up taking a blanket I find in the closet and sleeping on the small sofa in the sitting area of the bedroom. It's not as comfortable as the bed, but I'll make do.

I keep tossing and turning most of the night. My brain won't shut off about Noah's behavior and more troubling, JC's. I need to set both of them straight. At dawn, I hear movement and see Noah trying to figure out where the bathroom is. He finally turns on the light and without looking in my direction, goes toward the door.

This is my chance to get back into bed and I do. I snuggle under the sheet and pretend I'm sleeping. I feel the bed depress with the weight of Noah and then he turns out the light. He strokes my hair and I suddenly feel depressed, then the tears come, silent at first but turn into sobs.

"No, Lexi, don't cry. I was an ass."

"Noah, how could you talk to me that way," I whisper through my sobs.

He pulls me against his chest, and I inhale the scent of his skin.

"I was drunk and stupid. I have some things going on that I can't tell you about now. I need to work them out and then we'll sit down and talk."

I'm tired and satisfied with his explanation. He cuddles me against him in his strong arms and I fade to sleep. When I wake up, the sunlight flooding the room, Noah's no longer in bed. I check my watch and it's nearly 11:30 AM. I haven't slept this late since I was with JC in college.

My normal routine for Sundays is to get up early, make coffee and read the paper. Then I work on bills and finally a few hours of housework. Ever since Noah and I moved in together, he handles all the bills related to the loft and I handle any bills related to me. I protested that I wanted to contribute but he wouldn't hear of it. So, my bills are minimal except for my college loan which is almost paid off anyway.

I stretch and just as I'm about to get out of bed, Noah comes into the room with a tray. It has pancakes, bacon and orange juice on it. He's got a smile from ear to ear and so do I. It's been ages since he made me breakfast in bed, but I guess he really feels horrible with how he treated me.

"I might just forgive you if the pancakes are good."

"JC made them, and the juice is fresh squeezed."

He puts the tray on the bed next to me and I pick up the glass of juice. It tastes wonderful and Noah put in ice cubes. I love my juice cold and always put a few cubes of ice. I taste the pancakes and they're wonderful, chocolate chip with slices of banana on the side. The bacon is crispy, greasy and salty. Just the perfect mix to counteract the sweetness of the chocolate.

I'd like to give credit to Noah for this, but I know it's all JC. These were always the types of breakfasts he made for me when I was angry at him for staying out to late with his buddies. After all these years, he still remembers.

"This is delicious."

My hunger is voracious, and I shovel food in my mouth not worrying about what a pig I must look like. I've been lucky my whole life not to gain weight with the way I eat. But I'm going to be thirty in a couple of months, and I need to start being more careful.

Noah sits on the bed next to me and takes a napkin to wipe at a dab of syrup on my chin. I can see how apologetic his eyes are. He is trying to make up for the horrible way he treated me.

"Lexi, can you forgive me for the way I acted?"

"Noah, it's forgotten but you promised to tell me what's been going on with you."

"Give me some time and I will. I need to get everything together."

I really start to wonder what the problem is. I hope he's not sick or having money issues. If it is money, I make a good salary and can help. If he's sick, I hope he tells me soon.

"How long do I have to wait?"

"Not long, you have my word."

I finish breakfast and he took the tray away which gives me some time to freshen up in the bathroom. I take a long shower. The shower heads have different settings and I get involved playing with them until Noah comes in to see what's taking me so long. I show him and he smiles.

"You're acting like a little kid."

"We should get one of these."

"That shower head costs about eight hundred dollars."

"Eight hundred dollars? For one shower head?"

"Yes, I priced it when we were renovating the master bath."

"I think we can survive with the one we have."

"Good. Now do you mind getting out of there so we can go downstairs?"

I stick my tongue out at him and he raises his eyebrows.

"Remember what I said about sticking your tongue out?"

I do. The deal is that if I stick my tongue out, I need to use it on him. I'm game but we already crossed the line by having sex on the vanity in my boss' house. I think the next time we do; it should be at our apartment.

"I remember."

"Then stop doing it."

Again, I feel the urge to stick my tongue out but roll my eyes instead and turn off the shower. In fifteen minutes, we're sitting on lounge chairs in front of the large in ground swimming pool. I only brought one bathing suit so I'm wearing my white bikini. Brianna is wearing a hot pink number and Nikki a bright orange one.

Frankly, I'd like to cover up. I feel self-conscious being near women with perfect bodies. Noah gets up and dives in the pool leaving the chair next to me open which JC sits in.

"What's the matter."

"Nothing. I'm a little chilly."

"It's eighty-four degrees."

I put a towel over my stomach area and thighs. I notice from the corner of my eye that JC is laughing.

"What's so funny?"

"You're embarrassed aren't you," he whispers.

"Not even close."

"Lexi, those girls can't hold a candle to you. Your body is beautiful."

"JC, you're talking about your wife."

I glance over at Brianna. She's on the far side of the pool with Nikki, Hunter and Noah along with a few other guys, their playing water basketball.

"Brianna is not exactly natural."

"She's not?"

"No. She's had breast enhancement, liposuction and a chin implant."

I'm flabbergasted. She's very pretty and her body is perfect.

"She looks great."

"Sure, the finest money can buy. I prefer your body to hers any day."

"JC, you can't talk like that," I whisper.

"Why not? It's true. I love your tight, little body."

"Because you just can't."

I can feel a blush starting to creep up my neck. I'm desperate to change the subject.

"Thank you for the pancakes and the fresh squeezed orange juice."

"What about the bacon? Just the way you like it. See, I do remember."

"That wasn't the problem with our relationship."

"What was? I want to know so I don't repeat the same thing."

"Number one, you fucked other women," I growled in a low voice.

"I don't do that now."

"You shouldn't since you're married, but I have my doubts."

JC frowns. "Why the fuck would you say that?"

"Because you've been making overtures toward me since I started working for you. You need to understand, I'm marrying Noah. I won't cheat on him."

"I won't cheat on Brianna either. I'll leave her first but there's only one woman I would leave her for."

"Then I guess you're staying married."

"You should reconsider."

"JC, you already said her father and yours would cut your balls off."

"So, you would reconsider if I left Brianna?"

"Don't twist my words. I'm marrying Noah, period."

His eyes shoot up. "JC, honey, can you make us some drinks? Maybe a pitcher of Mimosas?" Brianna calls from the pool.

"Isn't it a little early to start drinking? It's only 11:30."

"By the time you make them and get glasses, it will be closer to twelve, please?"

"Sure."

JC gets up to go make the drinks and I follow him into the house, leaving my towel on the chair.

His eyes sweep up and down my body. "You see how sexy you are. Your stomach is flat as a board and your legs are nice and shapely."

"Please don't start. I just came in for a bottle of water."

"Stay while I make the drinks?"

His pretty blue eyes plead with me and I climb onto one of the stools in front of the wide expanse of gray granite. JC moves around the kitchen getting a tall glass pitcher and the ingredients he'll need to make the mimosas.

"So, what do we have coming up at work?"

"You really want to discuss work? It's a holiday."

"Then what do you want to talk about?"

"Us, being friends."

"JC, I can be friends with you, but you can't make comments regarding the past. Let's leave our past in the past."

"I want to know, was it really that bad? When you look back on our relationship, was it as terrible as you make it seem?"

"No. We had some good times but then we also had some very bad times. And it ended on a horrible note."

"I know. I also know that I was the reason for a lot of those bad times. I'm sorry for the things I did to you. You deserved better."

"Why couldn't you give me better when we were together?"

"Because I didn't know what I wanted back then. I thought I had it all sewn up. Go to college, find a wife, get married, have a successful career, maybe some kids."

"But you have almost all of that now, well except for the kids."

"Brianna doesn't want kids and I'm not with the person I want to share all of that with."

"I wish things were different but they're not."

"I guess it could be worse. I could be Hunter, pretending to love my job and really hating it. I know he's miserable, but he loves the money too much to start out from scratch with another company."

"But he has experience. He wouldn't be starting out from the bottom."

"He thinks that he'll be looked upon as getting his position because he knew the boss. Hunter is too proud to deal with that assumption. He would rather stay where he is."

"Why didn't you ever work for your father?"

"You're kidding, right? You saw how he treated me in high school. That stupid debate contest we lost. He went crazy like I was going to be put in front of a firing squad. It was embarrassing and I told myself I would never work for him, ever."

"It was years ago. Is he really still like that?"

"He's worse if you ask me. I'm not quite sure how my mother deals with him. Probably because he's away so much. She is free to do whatever she wants."

"I always liked your mother."

"She loved you. I don't think she's forgiven me for breaking up with you."

"She doesn't like Brianna?"

"Not a bit. She thinks Brianna is a spoiled brat, which isn't far from the truth. Her father gave her whatever she wanted. I can't afford the lifestyle she wants. Noah seems like he's pretty well off."

"How would you know that from looking at him?"

"Hunter was discussing investments with him and told me. Noah has quite an extensive portfolio including real estate holdings."

"His grandfather got his start in real estate. He bought several rundown buildings around the city many years ago. The Wilton family still owns and manages buildings including the one we live in."

"Oh? So, you get the family discount?"

"I'm not sure. Noah insisted when I moved in that he would take care of all the bills involved with our general living expenses. I wanted to contribute but he wouldn't hear of it."

"That's pretty generous of him."

"That's the way Noah is. He's always been kind and generous to me."

"Where did you meet him?"

"Richards was doing a marketing campaign for his company. I handled it and by the end, he asked me out."

"He waited until the end?"

"Not really. He asked me out before, but I told him when our business is concluded, I'll decide."

"A bit arrogant of you, wasn't it?"

"Not at all. I didn't want to mix business with pleasure. A protocol I want to continue to follow."

JC smirks at me as he turns to take plastic cups from the cabinet.

"Can you try this and make sure it's tastes okay?"

I nod and he hands me a cup with a small amount of the Mimosa mixture. It's sweet and tasty.

"It's very good."

"Let me take this out to Brianna before she complains I'm taking too long."

"I'll come. It's a bit chilly in here with the air conditioning."

He prepares a tray, but I notice he's staring at my breasts. Sure enough, my hard nipples are straining against the fabric of my bikini top. I feel my face heat and stand up to go outside. JC is behind me and his fingers stroke my spine as he balances the tray in one hand. My stomach twists as I walk faster, away from his touch. I know what this is about, and it can't happen.

CHAPTER 9

When we get outside, the warm air is a welcome and my nipples return to normal. Noah waves to me. He's hugging the wall by the deep end and his wet hair is slicked back. He swims over to the side that I'm on.

"Can I have a swig of your water?"

"I can get you a bottle if you want?"

"I just need a mouthful."

I hand him my half empty bottle and he drinks most of what's left, then hoists himself out of the pool. I admire his glistening muscles. I look up to see Brianna giving JC a hard time about the amount of alcohol in the mimosas and Hunter laughing at him. Again, I feel sorry for JC.

Noah leans in and kisses me then pulls me against his wet body, his hand snaking around and squeezing one of my partially exposed ass cheeks.

"I hate this bikini in public but for me, I love it," he whispers.

The move is not lost on JC and out of the corner of my eye I see him intently watching us as Noah presses a kiss to my lips.

"Do you want to take a shower together?" Noah asks.

"I already took a shower, remember?"

"This one won't be to get clean."

"I don't feel comfortable doing that here. We could go home."

"I like it here and I won a hundred thirty-eight bucks at poker last night. Hunter's friends are coming over for some more tonight."

"They are?"

I give him an icy stare and he knows why.

"I'm not getting drink."

"Noah, it had nothing to do with your drinking. It had to do with the things you said."

"Lexi, I was just blowing off steam. I needed a break. I already apologized."

He was right, he did but that didn't take the sting out of the words he spoke.

"I'm sorry but your behavior upset me. This is the last I'll say about it."

"Thank you. I'm going to shower."

After Noah goes inside, I settle back down on the lounge chair and tip my head up toward the sun with closed lids. I hear someone sitting next to me but don't open my eyes.

"Trouble in paradise?"

"Mind your own business, JC. Everything is fine."

"Good, glad to hear it."

He doesn't say anything further to me, but I can feel the tension between us. I open one eye and see him reading a magazine. The others are whooping and hollering in the pool while they splash each other and swim.

By mid-afternoon, the temperature has pushed near ninety and JC is still giving me the silent treatment. I'm not in the mood to swim so I head upstairs to change into shorts and a tank top. Noah hasn't come back down, and I find him asleep on our bed in his towel, I leave him to slumber while I dress. To wake him, I run my fingers over the ridges of his stomach and his eyes flutter open.

He yawns loudly. "Hey baby, what time is it?"

"Nearly three. You've been up here for a couple of hours. I was wondering what happened to you."

"I was pretty tired."

"Your towel is wet. You should get up and dress."

"In a minute."

Noah yawns again and smiles wickedly at me, then starts to untuck the towel at his waist. He throws it open and he's lying before me in all his naked glory.

"Are you trying to entice me?" I ask.

"Maybe. Is it working?"

"It might be, but there are people in the house."

Noah begins to stroke himself. His cock is semi-rigid by the time I decide to lock the door and get undressed. I can already feel my core start to flood as I pull off my tank top, shorts and panties. As I reach back to take off my bra, he tells me to keep it on and holds his hand out.

I approach the bed and he pulls me on top of him. His cock is rock hard and sandwiched between us. He wraps one muscular arm around me and the other gently pushes my head toward his lips, holding it firmly in place. His kisses send my stomach into a wild swirl. I'm lost, forgetting any residual anger.

I run my hands through his thick hair and wiggle my hips over his erection. A low rumble erupts from his throat. Noah reaches back and unclasps my bra, then pushes me up while he holds the straps. My breasts are free, and his hands explore my naked flesh, rolling my nipples between his thumb and finger. I moan as he continues to play.

"Lexi, you're so beautiful."

I push back until his length is between my slick lips and I slide back and forth lubricating it with my own juices. Noah's breathing is heavy, and I notice his jaw is tight with tension. It means he's holding back. Pushing off his belly, I get on my haunches and center myself, then grasp his cock and guide it into me as I sink to his base.

"Fuck, you feel so good," Noah groans as I begin to move.

His hands grip my hips tightly, his nails digging into my tender flesh. I use his stomach for balance but after a minute, he sits up and pulls my legs around his waist, burying his head between my breasts. I feel his arms embrace me and we begin to rock, back and forth.

I don't know for how long we are in this position, but I don't care. I love the intimacy of it especially when Noah's mouth finds my breasts and he begins sucking and kissing them. It's then that I realize I'm whimpering; low little mewls with each movement. My orgasm has been building and climax is not far off, but I don't want to come, it feels too good.

"Noah, stop moving."

He looks up from what he's doing to my breasts with a puzzled expression.

"Are you alright?"

"I just want to savor this. I don't want to come yet."

"I'm not sure I can stop," he pants.

He again buries his head in my breasts. I grip his shoulders and we rock together until I feel the tight clench of my womb, then divine ecstasy as I come. Noah follows close behind, filling me as he releases. I go limp in his arms and we continue to rock until I feel him slip of me.

He moves me off his lap and onto the bed, curling his sweat laden body around mine. His warm breath caresses my shoulder as he holds me. I can feel his heart thumping against my back.

"I love you so much, never forget that."

"I feel the same, Noah."

He fades into a light sleep and I hear shuffling outside our door, then a pause. I hope whoever it is doesn't try the door because they will know what we've just done since it's locked. I hold my breath and then I hear shuffling again as they move away.

I fall asleep cuddled in Noah's arms and when I wake, we're still in the same position. The sun has sunk lower in the sky and I estimate its near dinner hour. I'm hungry since I haven't eaten since this morning.

"Noah, wake up."

I feel him snuggle deeper into my back and he mumbles something unintelligible.

"I'm hungry."

"Can't we just stay here for the rest of the night?"

"We can if you don't mind missing your poker game."

That gets him moving. He lets me go and sits up to look at the time on his phone that he placed on the bedside table.

"It's early yet."

"What time?"

"A little after seven."

"What? I haven't eaten for hours. I need food."

"Then food you shall get."

He rises from the bed and drags me up. I see his eyes travel over my naked form and I smile. If I wanted to, I could get him to stay in bed all night with me.

"Don't give me that smug look, Lexi."

"I have no idea what you're talking about."

Noah slaps at my bare ass and I yelp in surprise.

"Let's take a shower and I'll show you."

I back away from him but he catches my arm and pulls me to him, then lifts me over his shoulder. We spend more than a half hour in the shower. It starts off innocently enough, soaping each other but the stimulation is arousing, and we end up having sex again. Sometimes, I can't get enough of Noah.

We hurriedly get dressed and when I open the door, I can smell something cooking. Downstairs someone has been busy on the grill. Everyone is sitting around the granite counter in the kitchen eating steak, burgers and hot dogs along with several salads.

JC looks up at me as he shovels half a burger in his mouth. It's a look of longing as if he knows what Noah and I have been up to. I look away and grab a paper plate from a stack at the end of the counter. Noah does the same and we load up food on our plates and sit at the dining room table where Hunter and one of his friends were.

"Where were you all day?" Hunter asks.

"Why did you miss us?"

"No, we thought you went home. We need a chance to win our money back from this card shark," he gestures to Noah.

"Kid, I'm going to take more of your money tonight."

They argue back and forth while I concentrate on eating. I end up having two burgers, a big mound of potato salad and coleslaw. Brianna comments on how much I can eat, and JC mentions that I always ate a lot. She looks at him funny and he realizes the mistake he made. He ends up correcting himself by saying because we have lunch together. I guess it's a good enough explanation because she goes back to drinking her wine.

I'm surprise that Nikki hasn't said anything, but I guess that JC asked her not to discuss work situations with Brianna. In my opinion he should have told her about us already but it's not my place.

After dinner, JC turns on the gas-powered fire pit and we roast marshmallows around it. At nine, Hunter's buddies come over and all the men except JC head to the pool house to play cards. Brianna and Nikki follow leaving JC and I to clean the kitchen.

I'm not thrilled that there's a mound of dishes to clean but I don't complain. We are staying in this wonderful house for free. JC dries while I wash and though I think it's a bad idea, we reminisce about this very activity in our first apartment. You could barely move in the tiny space, but we were in love and didn't care.

"We had some fun times in that apartment, didn't we?"

"Yes, we did. It was cozy and it was ours."

He pours me a glass of white wine and we sit on the patio in front of the fire pit. Strangely, I'm more comfortable with him than I've been in the last week. We joke and laugh. He doesn't bring up anything about Noah and I being up in our room all afternoon.

"So, have you decided what you're doing for your birthday?"

"Not really. I think Noah has plans but he won't tell me. I just hope that he doesn't have to travel around that time."

"That would suck. I'll make you a deal, if he's away, I'll take you out."

"JC, that's not necessary. I'm sure my family will want to see me."

"You'd rather spend your thirtieth birthday with your family then me? I'm insulted."

I stare at the serious look on his face and he bursts out laughing.

"You're a jerk."

"Yeah, but you love me anyway."

"I wouldn't go that far."

"Admit you at least like me."

"Fine, I like you in the least."

"Clever, Lexi."

We spend the next hour talking about the old times.

The door to the pool house is open and I can hear them yelling and having a good time. I don't want to seem like a mother hen and check to see if Noah is drinking. I just have to trust that he isn't as he promised.

I decide to sit by the pool and dangle my feet in the cool water. It's still very warm out and the water feels good on my bare legs. JC sits near me and jokes around, trying to push me in the pool. I finally get pissed at him, stand up, lose my balance and end up in the pool with a huge splash.

He's laughing so hard he doubles over, and I see my chance to get him back by tugging on his arm, pulling him in. He doesn't look happy but then he doesn't seem to mind and takes off his shirt revealing his lean muscular torso. I pull off my shirt and swim in my bra and shorts.

Climbing onto the diving board, I notice he can't take his eyes off me. What is he staring at? I dive off and swim for a few more minutes before I start to feel cold. I tell JC that I'm going to change and when I get into the bathroom, I realize why he was staring at me. My plain white cotton bra is see-through! I can see my nipples perfectly through the wet fabric.

My face turns crimson when I think of the eyeful, I gave him. As much as I'm trying not to entice him, it's happening inadvertently. I feel violated but it's not his fault.

CHAPTER 10

The second part of the weekend goes a little better. Noah and I don't have another argument and he won another two hundred dollars, not that he needs the money. On Monday, mid-afternoon, we prepare to leave. I want to get home before all the traffic backs up. I seriously am not in the mood for a grumpy Noah.

We quickly pack out stuff and say goodbye. I tell JC and Nikki that I'll see them bright and early the next morning. Noah makes plans to hang out with Hunter sometime. They're like best buddies now. Who would have thought that my current fiancé would become friends with my ex-fiancé's brother?

On the way home, Noah can't stop talking about what a great time he had. It's funny because he doesn't have many friends except for Brice, his brother Lucian and Pavel, his accountant. I'm waiting for him to ask what I talked to JC about, but he never does. I'm a little annoyed that he doesn't show the slightest bit of jealousy now when he did before.

The sounds and sights of the city are welcomed and very different from our weekend. Horns blare, taxis barrel down the avenues and pedestrians are walking the streets enjoying the wonderful weather.

At our building, he drops me off and leaves to park the car. I get the mail and there's another one of those letters with the girly script and no return address. This time the postmark is from Massachusetts. I wonder if this is what Noah has to discuss with me.

I don't want to invade Noah's privacy but when I get upstairs, I hold the envelope up to the light hoping I could get a clue as to who it's from. I can't see anything, and I get startled when Noah enters, dropping the mail on the floor.

He scoops it up and pages through it, handing the envelopes addressed to me, then heads to his office. I want to ask about the letter, but he'll tell me when he's ready. I hear him on the phone a few minutes later. When I come to his office door, he hangs up quickly. This is very unlike him, to be secretive.

"I have to leave town on Wednesday morning."

"What? So soon."

"Yes, Brice scheduled a client and I need to train Tom Devoe, one of the new guys. It's only until Saturday. Once he and the other guy are trained, you can have me all to yourself."

"I guess I better find something to do when my bout of insomnia hits."

"Why can't you sleep when I'm not here? This place is secure."

"I just can't. I'm used to you being with me. Besides, I never had a place all to myself. I either lived with a roommate, JC or you even in college."

"But you had your own room at your parents."

"But there were four other people in the house."

"It's only a few days and then maybe another trip to train the other candidate."

"Why can't one of your senior guys train?"

"Lexi don't start. It's my company and I want them trained correctly. I can only do that if I do the training."

"I'm sorry, I just miss you."

"I have a few things to do. Why don't relax and I'll meet you on the terrace in a little while."

Noah is hard to read and I'm not sure if he's being considerate or condescending. I decide to unpack, do laundry and prepare my outfit for tomorrow. I hunt around the refrigerator for something to make for dinner. I'm not much in the mood to cook so I put together a salad with some leftover chicken.

After I'm done, I shower and put on my new robe. I'm wondering if Noah will find it enticing. It's been sitting in my closet for the last month. It's short, barely covering my ass cheeks. I love the feel of the soft, slippery pink satin on my naked body. I'm in peering into the refrigerator when I get my answer. Noah's behind me with his hands on my ass, then my breasts.

"When did you get this? I've never seen it before," he growls.

"About a month ago."

My breath hitches as he unties the belt and his hands are touching my flesh, fingers pinching my sensitive nipples.

"Are you wearing this for a reason?"

"Not particularly."

"I think you're lying."

I giggle because he knows me so well. He presses against my back and I can feel his hardness through the thin fabric of my robe.

"Do you want something from me?"

"You know I do."

He moves me over to the counter, pushing me forward and spreading my legs. His fingers move to my sex and I'm already aroused before they find my swollen clit. Noah pushes my hair to the side and plants feathery kisses on the back of my neck. I push back, letting him know what I want.

He withdraws his fingers and I hear the zipper to his shorts. He groans as the head of his cock pushes through my moist folds.

"Is this what you want?"

"You know it is," I gasp as he slips his head into me.

"Maybe I should make you wait."

I feel him withdraw, his head poised at my opening. I push back because I want him inside me, and he holds my hips firm so I gain no leverage.

"So greedy tonight, Lexi."

I start to whimper, and he thrusts into me hard, making me gasp at the full feeling of him as he stretches me. His fingers once again find my clit, rubbing it in small circles, applying delicious pressure. In the distance, I hear his cell ring and his movements slow almost to a stop.

"No, Noah. Please."

He picks up his movement, but his fingers fall away from my clit and both hands clench my bare hips. Three more strokes and I feel his hot release fill me. He pulls out, kisses me, apologizes for coming first and walks away. I'm bewildered because I have no idea what just happened.

His behavior is unacceptable especially since, one, I feel disrespected and two, I haven't come. I follow and find him in his office with his now semi-erect cock hanging out of his shorts, still glistening with our juices. He's on the phone checking the voicemail of whoever called. Noah looks up in surprise.

"When you're ready to tell me what your problem is, I'm here to listen."

I stalk off to take another quick shower. When I get out, he's still in his office but the door is closed. I feel sick and in no mood to eat. I find the rattiest pair of pajamas I have, unappealing yellow flannels with a rubber ducky motif and a hole under one of the arms. It's a little too warm for them but I have nothing else even close to being this ratty.

I slip into bed. It's before nine but I'm exasperated, annoyed and upset with Noah. I want to be asleep when he comes into the bedroom. Sometime during the night, I feel his arms reach for me and I shrug them away. They withdraw and when I wake up the next morning, he's on his side of the bed, practically at the edge.

I'm still upset but I have to go to work, and I can't let our relationship issues get in the way. I head to the shower and when I come out, Noah is not in bed. I'm not about to hunt for him. I quickly slip on a plain white cotton panty and bra set, not feeling sexy enough to be more daring.

By the time he comes back into the bedroom, I'm fully dressed in a black business suit and I brush past him without so much as a word. He wraps his hand around my arm and holds me fast to my spot.

"Let me go Noah. I'm not ready to have a conversation with you."

"Can't you forgive me?"

"For what? What do I need to forgive you for?"

"For my behavior last night."

"You think that's the only thing?"

"I don't understand."

"You've been very out of sorts lately. Then you tell me that you're working on some issues and to be patient. My patience is running thin."

"As soon as I get back from this latest trip, I promise to tell you."

"Noah, are you sick?"

"No, why would you think that?"

"Because you're being very secretive. We've been together for two years and I've never seen you act like this."

"It has nothing to do with my health. It's a delicate situation and I should know where I stand after this week."

"Fine. I'll be patient but I expect an explanation as soon as you come back."

"You'll have it. Now can we just make up for the time being?"

I let him lean in and accept the kiss he plants on my cheek. I'm not in a forgiving enough mood to allow him to kiss my lips. He realizes this and doesn't try anything further, instead, going to the closet to get clothes for the day. I head to the kitchen to fill my travel mug with coffee only to discover that we're out of pods for the Keurig.

I don't know why but it's the last straw and I feel hot tears prick my eyes. It's only coffee, what the hell am I getting so bent out of shape for? But it's enough to push me over the edge that I've been teetering on since last week. I grab a tissue from the box on the counter and leave before Noah sees me. A few days ago, I would have wanted his comfort but today, I don't.

The walk to the subway station makes me feel better. It's warm in the early June sunshine and I turn my face towards the sky, almost tripping over the sidewalk. I feel my face start to heat with embarrassment, but no one was paying attention to me anyway.

I get into the office before JC. Nikki is not in yet, so I check my electronic schedule to see what's on the agenda for the day. I see that my afternoon has been rearranged. I was supposed to have lunch with Vincent, Marco and JC but now I only see JC's name next to mine.

Seriously, I'm not in the right state of mind to have lunch with him alone. I don't like his advances, no matter how small, though he did promise not to act this way in the office. I check my emails and find two from clients that I have upcoming projects with. I need to schedule appointments with them. I guess I can have Nikki handle that.

I'm lost in thought when JC comes in. He leans his head in to say hello and gives me a wide smile. I always loved his teeth, so straight and perfect. I nod causing him to frown.

"Lex, is everything okay?"

"Yes, I'm alright," but as much as I try, my voice is wavering.

He comes into my office and shuts the door, then sits in one of the chairs in front of my desk.

"You don't seem alright. Are you still upset with Noah about this past weekend?"

"JC, his behavior is very irregular, even when we got home last night."

I'm not about to give fuel to JC's fire by telling him about what Noah did when we were having sex.

"How so?"

"He's hiding something from me. He told me to be patient and he'll tell me when he gets back from his trip on Saturday."

"He's going away again?"

"He has to train an employee. I hate being alone in the loft."

"You still don't like that after all these years? I bet you still sleep with the lights on when you're alone."

I smile sheepishly because he does know. He took a few business trips when we were together, and I couldn't sleep while he was gone.

"So, what of it?"

"Don't get defensive, I'm simply stating a fact."

"I hate sleeping alone."

He smiles wickedly, "I can join you if you need a stand in."

"JC, stop joking."

"I'm not. I can help you out. Brianna is once again going away. Her parents rented a house in Cape Cod for the month of June."

"Are you taking a vacation?"

"I can't. Too much to do even though it's supposed to be slower in the summer. I might go for a weekend or two. So, we can have dinner if you want or just hang out after work."

"When is she leaving?"

"She's already gone. Left this morning with two of her friends."

"She does have the life, doesn't she?"

"Yes, that's my spoiled little princess."

I see his face cloud as he says sit and his forehead wrinkles.

"You know you can do something about it. You don't have to be miserable."

"I'm resigned to the fact that I'm stuck for a while."

"That makes no sense to me."

"It should since you know my father."

My heart hurts for him because I do know. Even with everything he did to me when we were together, I still feel bad. Though I know I shouldn't, I ask a question that is highly personal.

"JC, how often do you have sex with her?"

He raises his eyebrows in surprise.

"Why do you ask?"

"You're newlyweds. Most newly married people have sex quite often but from what you're telling me, I'd be surprised if you did."

"And you'd be right. We haven't had sex in a few weeks, but she has been away."

"But you were together this weekend."

"We had guests in the house. Not a very opportune time to have sex."

I don't want to mention that Noah and I had sex in JC's house.

"What about when she's actually home?"

"I'm not sure if Brianna likes sex or just doesn't like sex with me. I've tried everything. I wouldn't be surprised if on her little excursions, she fucked other guys. I mean she's twenty-three, what woman that age doesn't want sex? Maybe I'm wrong."

And maybe you're comparing your wife to me when I was twenty-three. We had a lot of sex when we were together, sometimes rushing through the door from work, tearing off each other's clothes and falling into bed.

"JC, you shouldn't speculate especially about something so serious."

"What am I to think? It's almost like she's repulsed by me. But we're getting off task. We were talking about Noah."

"There's nothing to talk about. He's going away, I'll be alone and wondering what secret he has until he gets back."

"Do you think it's bad?"

"I don't know. It could be anything. I don't stick my nose into Noah's business. He hasn't given me any reason to."

I check my watch and notice we've been talking about our shitty private lives for almost a half hour. I have work to do and I let JC know that I need to get to work. As soon as he leaves the office, Nikki comes in to discuss our schedule for the week.

"Shit! Camden was just here. I need to ask why Vincent and Marco aren't joining us for lunch."

"Mr. Lawson requested I make that change. He didn't say why."

"Where did he ask you to make the reservation?"

"French's. He said you are familiar with their food."

Yeah, I'm familiar with more than their food. I'm familiar with JC's habit of getting me off in our booth when we were together. No doubt he will request our seating in the back of the restaurant.

"I am but I'm not in the mood. Can you change it to Marino's?"

"Sure, I'll call and cancel the reservation."

We discuss a few detail items before she leaves. I go to JC's office. His door is closed, and I can hear him loudly talking, the hostility in his voice is apparent. Instead of waiting, I go back to my office and wait before I buzz his phone.

"Yes?"

He definitely is perturbed. I wish I hadn't asked Nikki to change the reservation.

"JC, why French's and why aren't we having lunch with Vincent and Marco?"

"You know why French's. Neither partner can make the lunch. They have a client meeting downtown."

"Excuse me if I don't want to be reminded of the past."

"You love French's. Are you embarrassed?"

"Of what?"

"The things we did in that restaurant."

"Sex doesn't bother me. The fact that we're no longer together and you need to constantly remind me of what we did there, does."

"Fine. You can change the restaurant then."

"I already did. Marino's."

"I'm busy. I'll come to your office at lunchtime."

"Later then."

I hang up and begin work. I spend part of the next two hours at a meeting with the art department. I have two projects I need to get graphics for. By the time I come back to my office, it's close to the time to leave for the restaurant. I take my compact out of my purse and touch up my makeup.

"You don't need to do that."

I look up to see JC standing at my door.

"That's your opinion."

"You're beautiful. I'm sure others will agree."

"Thanks for the compliment but can we keep this strictly business?"

"If that's what you want."

I grab my purse and I follow him down the hall to the elevator. It's annoying to me that I have to keep telling him to stop making comments. Surprisingly, it's just us two in the elevator and I'm waiting for him to say something. This is another place we've had sex. Not this building, the one when we used to live together.

Late one night we had come home from a party. We were both a little tipsy and very horny. He slipped his hand up my dress and it was on from there. Lucky there were not cameras in the car because security would have got an eyeful. I blush at the thought and look over to see JC staring at me.

He nods and I know he has figured out what I was thinking of. This makes my face heat even more and he smiles. I avoid his eyes until the doors open on the main floor.

"I know what you were thinking."

"Do you?"

"Would you ever be able to ride in an elevator without thinking of it?"

"Contrary to what you believe, I can ride an elevator without my mind drifting to dirty thoughts."

"I'm glad you can because I find it incredibly hard especially when the woman I did it with is right next to me."

"JC, I thought you weren't going to do this anymore. I can't stress enough that it's not going to happen between us. I love Noah."

"Are you sure? You seem to have some doubts."

"I'm sure. Nothing he tells me is going to end our relationship."

My cell rings as he hails a cab. It's Noah and I know that JC is trying hard not to listen but it's impossible in such a combined space. My face turns grim as Noah tells me that he has to leave this afternoon. I start chewing on the corner of my lip as I hang up. There's JC's thumb again to dislodge it.

"Noah has to leave early?"

"He said the client changed reservations. I won't see him until Saturday evening. I guess I'm in for a few days of little sleep."

"My offer still stands."

"I'm sure it does."

We make small talk about the office during the trip. I'm trying to avoid any personal talk. Maybe I'm overreacting but my emotions are all jumbled. I'm hurt Noah is leaving. I thought we could discuss what happened the night before.

"Give him a chance, Lexi. I'm sure it's nothing."

As time goes by, I'm not sure that's true. Noah's never acted this way. Conversation is kept light between us. I think JC finally realizes I'm never going to be available to him again. I wish it was different but we're both involved with other people.

I don't eat much and take my food, shrimp scampi, back to the office. At least I won't have to cook tonight. JC comments and I tell him I had a big breakfast even though I had no breakfast or dinner the night before. He knows me to well to know that if I don't eat, something is really bothering me.

We part ways at my office, and I shove the container of food in the small refrigerator in the corner. I spend the rest of the afternoon immersed in working on copy. It helps take my mind off things until it's time to leave for the night. I don't relish spending time in our empty loft and I silently curse Noah as I walk to the subway.

CHAPTER 11

At the loft that night and after dinner, I'm bored. My mind starts to drift to the letters that Noah has been receiving. Who could the letters be from? Though I know it's wrong, I go to his office. He rarely locks his desk as I found out the last time I went looking for some tape. However, this time, all the drawers are locked.

There's a tin box on the desk where Noah keeps his stamps and I take a chance that the key would be in there, it is. My hands shake as I unlock the top middle drawer. In it, I find the envelopes with the letters. I hate doing this, but my curiosity and fear get the best of me. The paper used is pink and lined. I unfold the first one and begin reading.

Noah,

It was so nice to finally meet you. I was never told much about you and I've often wondered what you're like. Having dinner with you was much appreciated, and your offer to finance my studies is too. I don't need the funds since I was left an inheritance by my grandfather. Do you remember him? I heard he didn't like you very much. It was yet another reason why I was hesitant to contact you. Now that he passed, I think I have a right to know things that were kept from me. I'm coming to New

York to take a tour of NYU in a few weeks. Please let me know if we can get together.

Rory

Who is Rory? I had never heard Noah mention anyone by that name. From the sounds of it, this is a lost relative. I slip the letter back in the envelope and pick up the other one. My hands are still shaking, and I need to put the letter on the desk so I don't make myself dizzy reading it.

Noah,

My mother wants to see you again. I didn't think she would, but her eyes lit up when I told her I'd been in contact with you. She asked me all kinds of questions. I think we can start emailing, texting and calling without worry. You mentioned you can visit Boston in early June, is that still a possibility? If it is, please let me know when you'll be here. I'm so excited to see you again.

Rory

My stomach started to turn. It was early June now. Noah never told me where he was going for the trip with his client. Could it be that he lied to me? Now the letter I first read makes sense. I think Rory is Noah's daughter. I shove the letter back into the envelope, put it in the drawer and lock it.

I don't know how to feel about what I just read. It bothers me greatly that Noah didn't think he should tell me about this as soon as he found out. If this is his daughter, then she was born when he was barely out of his teens. Noah just turned thirty-five so that means he was about eighteen or nineteen. Why hadn't he mentioned this before?

I realized that I haven't heard from him since this morning. He usually texts me to let me know when he arrived, and if he's alright. I run off a quick text and I'm surprised when he gets back to me immediately.

I'm fine. Tonight was busy with my clients. I should be settling into bed soon and I'll text you then.

I want to ask for more information, like where he is and who he's with, but I resist. I need to allow him time to explain and I'm hoping that I don't have to pry to get straight answer.

I end up doing something I rarely do, turn on the television. Flipping through the channels keeps my mind occupied and not thinking of the answers I want to hear from Noah. The ringing of my phone wakes me up, I must have dozed off. I shake the sleep out of my head, glad to see that he's calling me instead of texting.

"Noah?"

"Yes baby. I'm sorry I didn't let you know I was okay when we landed. It's been crazy today. The client's wife left her carry-on behind and I had to send Tom to get it at the airport. Then she said some jewelry was missing. So after all the filing of reports and I'm beat."

"You never told me where you were going."

"I thought I did. We're in Vancouver."

"Washington?"

"No, Canada."

"Oh, so it must be dinner hour there."

"It is, but Tom is handling it. It's the first test I'm giving him. I'll head down after I'm done talking to you. I needed a break. The client has four children all under the age of ten. Not easy to keep them in line."

We chat about a few other trivial things and questions abound are at the tip of my tongue but it's not the time for them. We can talk when Noah gets home. I end the call with him by telling him I love him, but he doesn't return the sentiment. I hang up feeling a sense of foreboding.

The next day my mind is not on my work. Nikki has come in to go over some directives and has had to keep pulling me out of my thoughts.

"What's with you today, Alexa?"

"I'm just a bit tired. I didn't sleep very well."

"Did Noah's snoring keep you awake?"

"No, he isn't home. He had a business trip."

"That's the best time to sleep. You get the whole bed to yourself."

"Nikki, I wish I had your enthusiasm, but I don't sleep well alone."

"I have my own apartment and I love it after sharing a dorm suite with three other women."

"I haven't lived alone in quite a while."

She lowers her voice to ask, "Did you live with Mr. Lawson?"

"I did. We had a small apartment together after college."

"And after that?"

"I went back to live with my parents, then moved to an apartment with a roommate. After she moved to California, I lived by myself for several months until I moved in with Noah. I hated sleeping alone on the nights before I met Noah."

"He seems nice. When are you getting married?"

"October if we can ever get all the arrangements finished."

A knock on my door ceases the conversation and Nikki opens the door to reveal JC.

"Camden, what can I do for you?"

"Mr. Kingston. He is unsure of the completed copy you provided."

"But he approved it. He said it was a go."

"He wants an afterhours meeting tonight to discuss some changes. Can you clear your schedule?"

"I have nothing going on tonight. It won't be a problem."

It's nearly three now and I wonder why this wasn't brought to my attention earlier in the day. Not that I have anything to do after work. At least I won't have to wander around the loft alone all night. I'm fortunate because Megan has an interview in the city with a company in midtown on Thursday. She'll be staying with me both Thursday and Friday nights.

"Great. Meet me in the conference room at five."

He walks out, closing the door behind him.

"I know this might sound inappropriate, but he really is gorgeous."

"Nikki, don't get caught up in Camden's looks."

"I'm sorry. I shouldn't have said that."

"No problem. I think we're done here. See that the graphics for the Camilla ad get finished by tomorrow afternoon. I want them on my desk by the end of the day."

Nikki nods and gets up to leave. When she's gone, I suddenly feel exhausted. Lack of sleep and the stress of worrying about Noah are starting to take their toll. I yawn and take a sip of my cold coffee.

"Ugh."

I spit it back into the cup. I get up to get a fresh cup and almost run into JC as I'm leaving my office. He has his travel mug in hand, and he laughs when he sees mine in my own.

"We had the same thought. You look tired. Are you not sleeping?"

I yawn again, "Noah's gone for the week so what do you think?"

"I guess so. I sleep great when I have the bed to myself. Brianna hogs it most of the time, stretching out. I end up at the end of the bed and sometimes go sleep on the couch in my office."

"You have an interesting relationship. Why don't you just get a new bed, a king sized one."

"That's what we have already. It's still not big enough."

Of course, when we get to the break room, the empty coffee pot is sitting on the counter. We look at each other and I take it to the sink while JC prepares a fresh filter for brewing. There's an awkward silence between us as the coffee brews and I busy myself by washing out our mugs. His hand stroking my hair startles me.

"JC, don't," I whisper.

"I couldn't resist. I always loved your thick hair. Remember when you would put your head in my lap, and I would stroke it? It always soothed you when you had a hard day."

I give him a stern look as I hand his clean mug back to him. I can feel the heat on my face and I'm sure my cheeks are the color of crimson. Damn him, why does he keep doing this to me? I keep my head down, not wanting to look at him. As the coffee pot finishes brewing, I add a splash of milk and a packet of sugar before I get ready to fill my mug.

I turn and JC is holding the pot for me to put my mug under. I still don't look at him as he fills it, then his own. I take a sip and relish the heat of the liquid as it slides down my throat. I hope it gives me the boost that I need. He looks at his watch.

"Another hour and I'll meet you in the conference room. Don't be late because I'm sure Kingston will be here early."

"Sure, no problem."

We walk back to our offices together, not speaking. I'm glad because I don't want to make small talk. He shouldn't have touched me, it's too familiar. I spend the next hour going over the Kingston file wondering what we will have to change. The copy was good, and he liked it, now he doesn't. At 4:50, I gather everything together and head to the glass walled conference room. Sure enough, Mr. Kingston is there with his son. I can see JC talking with them.

They welcome me in and all stand when I enter the room. I thank them and we all sit down at the large conference table. JC takes a seat next to me and his knee rubs mine as I discuss with Mr. Kingston the changes in the copy. I keep a smile pasted on my face the entire time even though I'm on the edge of frustration.

The changes that are requested are much like the previous copy from my predecessor. I quietly explain that the copy I wrote up is more persuasive along with the new graphics, but Mr. Kingston is adamant. His son sits glaring at me as if I said something offensive. He looks like he isn't older than twenty-two. Nepotism at its finest.

JC takes over after I present, and smooths out the bumps so that everyone is happy, everyone but me. I'm busy and thought we had put this account to bed. Now I need to rewrite the copy and ask the art department to draw up new graphics. After the Kingston's leave, I just sit in the chair trying to figure out what just happened.

"Lexi?"

"Yeah?"

"Look at me."

I look up at JC and he can see I'm upset. I have no room or time to do rewrites.

"We can work this together. Knock it out of the park tonight. Do you mind staying?"

"I might as well. I can't do it tomorrow because Megan is staying with me. I haven't seen her for a few months, and I'd like to spend time with her."

"How is she?"

"Fine as far as I know. She just went through a pretty rough breakup. I think it's part of the reason why she wants to move away from Jersey. She has an interview tomorrow here in the city with Nolan Pharma."

"That's great. Wish her luck for me."

I laugh and smile at him.

JC grins back. "Yeah I know; she still hates me for breaking your heart. I wish she'd get over it since it's been several years."

"I think she took our breakup harder than I did. Though I did take it pretty hard."

JC's face clouds and his eyes darken.

"Don't remind me that I made the worst mistake of my life."

I don't know how to reply to that statement. As I head to my office, I hear my cell chiming behind my door and hurry to get it before it goes to voicemail. It might be Noah. I get to it just in time.

"Hey babe, how are you?"

"I'm fine, still at work. I have to work a little late."

"With who?"

"JC. A client that I thought I was done with asked for a rewrite. I need to get this out of my hair because I have tons more to do."

"Is anyone else working late?"

Do I detect a note of jealousy in his voice?

"Nikki," I lie.

"Okay. How was your day?"

"Good, busy. Megan is coming tomorrow to sleep at the loft."

"I completely forgot about that. Will she be staying all weekend?"

"No, back to Jersey on Saturday. She'll be gone before you get home I think."

"I'm sorry to miss her."

No, you aren't. Noah doesn't like Megan very much. He says she's like my father and sticks her nose into everyone's business. I see it as she is protecting me. I wonder what she'll say when I tell her what I found out or should I even tell her?

"I'll let her know you said hello."

"I have to go. We're heading out on to do some fishing."

"Be careful and I love you."

"Love you, too."

Finally, I get some sentiment. He hangs up and I sit at my desk deciding what to do first. JC knocks at my door to ask if I want to order Chinese. I was hoping I would be able to eat at home tonight.

"I guess so. If I don't, I'll be starving by the time I get home."

"Should I order your favorite?"

"You remember my favorite?"

"With the amount of times you ate it, I should."

He smirks and I nod my head while he orders. It's amazing he remembers my favorite is coconut shrimp and spring rolls. It has been almost seven years since we broke up.

When the food comes, I'm famished. JC won't let me pay for

any of it and that annoys me. We aren't dating and I can more than afford a meal. I wish he was this way when we were together. Back then he was always short of money and constantly borrowing from me. That is until he got the director's job.

"Lexi? Are you alright?"

I'm deep in thought and didn't hear a word he said.

"I'm sorry. I was thinking about something."

"What? When we used to eat dinner on that small coffee table we had. Remember?"

"I do. We did have some fun times."

We had fun times, but we also had horrible times. JC could always seem to bring the worst out of me especially when he wandered in drunk reeking of some woman's perfume. Then the arguments would start, and he would pass out in our bed, snoring so loud that I ended up sleeping on the pillows in the living room.

I kept telling myself he would change. In the morning, he would sweet talk my panties off and we would have phenomenal sex. I think I was addicted to the sex and that's why I forgave him all the time.

"Lexi, I'm sorry I couldn't give you what you needed back then. I'm sorry I hurt you. I was careless with your heart."

"It was a long time ago," I mumble into my container of coconut shrimp.

JC doesn't reply, concentrating on his food. We finish our meal. In the last two weeks I've eaten more meals with JC than I have with Noah.

It takes us over four hours to finish the rewrites and the new graphics which JC is a whiz at. He made the art department's job easy. I'm yawning every twenty seconds and realize it's time to go. Maybe I'll sleep tonight. If not, then Megan is not going to be happy with me falling asleep early.

"Want to share a cab?"

"I guess so. I'm not in the mood to walk to and from the subway tonight."

We pack everything up and get ready to leave. JC is the perfect gentleman, holding the elevator for me to step in and out first, holding the door to the building and the cab. I'm so tired that I put my head on JC's shoulder as the cab heads for the loft.

He begins to stroke my hair and I feel his arm snake around my shoulders. I must have fallen asleep because the next thing I know, he's gently shaking me awake. My nose is full of his scent and I find myself feeling turned on. The one thing that makes me totally awake is my brain screaming, NOAH.

I pick my head up so quickly that I hurt my neck but feeling the way I do. I can't get away from JC fast enough. I slide out of the cab and thank him, then practically slam the door in his face and run to the elevator. I don't realize I forgot my purse and once I get in my apartment, I text JC but get no answer until I hear a soft knock at the door. JC is standing there with my purse dangling from his fingers, a smirk on his face.

"You ran out of the cab so fast that you forgot this. I usually don't have that effect on women."

I snatch my purse out of his hands and then wonder what I should do. Do I invite him in? Do I tell him I'm tired and I'm going to bed? I'm sure the cab we were in is gone and he'll have to hail another. I also know he has nowhere else to be. Brianna is in Cape Cod.

He leans in and whistles at the soaring ceilings and the wall of windows opposite the entry door. I don't invite him in, he does that all himself and I inwardly sigh. The way I feel, I just want to take a hot shower and to snuggle under the sheets, but here JC is, begging for my attention. I worry where that might lead.

CHAPTER 12

"This is some beautiful place. Give me a tour."

I'm not in the mood, but I don't want to be rude. I take JC around to all the rooms and he comments on the décor, the paintings and the view. He spies the desk in Noah's office, and I can see the wheels turning in his head. JC fucked me several times over the desk in his father's office. If the man knew, he would be livid. His parents were out for the week and we had to feed and walk the family dog, a precocious beagle named Chauncey.

We ended up sleeping over there for a few nights. It was nice to have some space to move, not like our apartment. If his parents knew we defiled several surfaces in their home, we would never be invited back. But that's what JC did to me back then. All he had to do was give me one of his smoldering looks and I was done.

"You don't mind if I change, do you? I would like to get into something a bit more comfortable," I said.

"Sure, knock yourself out. I'll wait."

I head into my room not sure of what would be appropriate to wear. I can't very well wear my ratty flannels or my slinky nightgown. Instead, I opt for a pair of jogging pants and a polo shirt.

"You do look comfortable and gorgeous," JC says as I approach after changing.

Before I can say anything, he's pulling my long hair out of my collar. His fingers brush against my neck and it feels electric. After all these years and he still has the power to do this to me. I back away before he can touch anything else.

"Do you want something to drink?" I ask.

"Sure, what do you have? A beer would be good."

Beer I have, and by the time I'm done removing it from the refrigerator and opening the bottle, he's got his tie off and his shirt partially unbuttoned. I can't stop staring at the tan muscled flesh he's just revealed. I used to love to run my tongue between his two pecs right up to the hollow at his throat when we were making love. I take a beer out for myself and open it.

"JC, why do you say those things?"

"I'm telling you what I think."

"But you shouldn't."

"Shouldn't what? Say what I think and feel."

"I loved you once, but I love someone else. I can't return how you feel."

He frowns. "Are you sure you can't?"

"What do you mean?"

"I see the way you look at me sometimes. It's not any different than when we were together."

"It is," I insist.

"You used to give me those same looks just before we ended up in a sweaty heap in bed together."

"That was years before when I was young and naïve."

"Seriously, I don't think you were ever naïve. You loved me and I treated you poorly. I should've cherished you and now it's too late."

I sip my beer. "Yes, you should've. But now I'm marrying Noah in a few months. I'm happy. Can't you just be for me?"

"I can, but that doesn't mean I have to like it."

JC takes a long pull on his beer and rubs at the stubble on his chin.

"I decided to ask Brianna for a divorce."

This is news to me because a few short days ago he said he was stuck.

"When did you make that decision?"

"This afternoon when I got this picture."

I watch as he scrolls through his phone, then hands it to me. The picture I'm looking at is a bikini clad Brianna kissing a dark-haired young man. I feign shock because frankly, I'm not. I saw the way they interacted at the beach house. It was like a woman and her servant, not her husband.

"Who sent you that?"

"Brad McConnell, remember him?"

My mind recollects the name but I'm having trouble placing him.

"No. Name sounds familiar but I don't remember his face."

"Worked with us at Carver? Tall guy, used to shave his head and when he let the hair grow back, he was partially bald."

Now I remember. He was an obnoxious ass kisser especially after JC got the director's job. I hated that asshole.

"He sent you the picture?"

"Yes. He's on vacation with his girlfriend. He came to our wedding and knew Brianna. I doubt she remembered him. It's not the worst of it either. He sent me three more pictures of this guy fondling Brianna's breasts and her slipping her hand down his shorts. That's my fucking wife. How do I know this is the first guy?"

"I'm so sorry. How do you plan on telling her?"

"I feel like driving there this weekend and shoving the pictures in her face. She can't get away with a story now. I've suspected. God knows what she did when she was away last week. Probably fucked some cabana boy."

I want to say to him, *how does it feel?* JC cheated on me and it hurt. It hurt that he didn't love and respect me enough to be monogamous. He was always waiting for something better to come along. That's not what he said when he broke up with me, but it's what I felt. I refuse to chastise him and offer support.

"Just do what you think is best. You have an out now. If your father wants to argue, you can show him the pictures."

"He probably will still give me shit. Always trying to explain things away. I really wonder why my mother stayed with him all these years. I never told you, but I caught him cheating on her when I was in high school."

My mouth drops open. "Are you serious?"

"Do you remember the debate against Hillside that we lost? He went crazy on me. It wasn't that we lost, it was because I saw him, and he knew. It happened the day before the debate. I was sick about it."

I think back to the day. JC was normally clear and concise in debates, but I noticed he was scattered. He hesitated several times almost as if he lost his train of thought. After it was over, I thought he just didn't care. We were graduating in a few weeks. Now it all made sense.

"I knew something was wrong that day. You weren't yourself."

"I'm sorry I was such a jerk to you in high school. I don't think I ever told you that when we were together."

"Frankly, I was shocked when you asked me out in college. I thought you hated me."

JC takes a long pull from his beer, "Quite the opposite. We didn't run in the same circles back then and I didn't have the courage to break out of that mold."

"What do you mean by that? I wasn't good enough for you?"

"Not at all. You were just different than the girls I dated. I was a jock, you were more, academic."

"You mean a nerd?"

"No, don't twist my words. You didn't care about sports; I did but I also did well in academics. Did you forget?"

How could I, JC always bested me, and it annoyed me to no end. I didn't date much in high school though there were plenty of guys who asked.

"Not at all."

"You didn't date much in high school. Why?"

Strangely, this conversation we're having never took place in the years we dated. Maybe it was because JC just didn't care back then.

"I just didn't. I wasn't interested I guess."

"Did you lose your virginity before you got out of high school? I know I wasn't your first."

Yes, another question he never asked me when we were together. He probably assumed I had my share because we always had phenomenal sex. That usually comes with experience.

"Why are you asking me these things now? You never cared when we were together. As I recollect, you never even asked me how many men I slept with before you."

"I don't remember you ever asking me that question either."

"It didn't matter to me and guessed you slept with quite a few."

"So, getting back to my original question, were you a virgin when you graduated?"

"No, I wasn't."

His eyebrows lift because I think he's surprised. He expected me to say yes.

"Who was it? And when?"

"You wouldn't know him. He didn't go to our school. In fact, he was in college."

"Really? A college guy? When?"

"I was a senior and he was my mother's college roommate's son, a junior at Dartmouth. I knew him throughout my life. I hadn't seen him for a few years but when I did, it was instant attraction. He filled out in those intervening years. One thing led to another and before I knew it, I was naked, and we were having sex."

"In your parent's house?"

"In the basement, you know, in the family room. It started off innocently enough. We were watching a movie with the whole family. Everyone but us went to bed. He would be sleeping down there on the sofa and told me that he was tired. I started to leave, and he said I could go upstairs or join him."

"Just like that, you joined him?"

"It was time already. He was hot and we were alone."

"He seduced you?"

"I wasn't naïve. I knew what he wanted, and I wanted it too. He didn't take advantage of me. I was almost eighteen."

"But he was what? Twenty, twenty-one? He knew what he was doing."

It sounds like JC is jealous and I inwardly smile knowing he's annoyed he wasn't my first.

"He was almost twenty-one. We slept together and just before dawn I went upstairs to my bedroom."

"Did you sleep with him again?"

"A few more times. He wanted to date, but with him at Dartmouth and me at NYU, I didn't want a long-distance relationship."

"Do you still see him?"

"Of course not."

"I didn't mean that way. I meant do you see him at functions."

"Well, yes. My mother is good friends with his mother. So parties, graduations, you know, stuff like that."

I glance at the clock on the wall and realize it's getting late. JC needs to go because I'm beginning to fall asleep.

"I'm exhausted. I think I'm going to call it a night."

"Are you sure?"

"Yes, I am. Between the long workday and this beer, I'm ready for bed."

JC drains the last of what's left in his bottle and hands it to me.

I put it in the sink to wash it out for recycling and I feel his arms embrace me from behind. For a few seconds I close my eyes, remembering what it's like to be in that place. Then I push him away.

"I'm sorry. I just feel so lost right now. I'm not sure what my next move is with Brianna."

"JC, I'm always here to talk. I want to be friends."

He gives me a weak smile and pecks me on the cheek. I walk him to the door and see him out. After I close the door, I realize that my heart is pounding in my chest and I'm breathing heavy. It's a reaction that shocks me. After all, it's only JC. He's part of my past, Noah is my future.

Speaking of Noah, I haven't heard from him since about five. Usually he calls me before he goes to bed but it's nearing eleven and I haven't heard a word. I check my phone to see if I missed a text and there's nothing. I'm annoyed but in no mood to deal with him. I want to go to bed.

Fifteen minutes after I brush my teeth and put on my t-shirt, my phone rings. It's 11:15 and if it's Noah, he should know better since I'm usually asleep by now on a work night. I glance at my phone and I'm surprised to see it's JC since he just left here a little while ago.

"What's wrong? You just left me?"

"I didn't want to, you made me go."

I deeply sigh. "So, what is it?"

"I'm home and it's too quiet in this place. Remember we used to lie on the pillows in the living room with the lights out and the windows open, listening to the sounds of the city?"

"JC is there a reason you're calling me so late?"

"I can't sleep. I know you won't so I thought we would talk until one of us does."

Is he serious? This isn't high school and I'm long past the cheerleader sleepover stage, not that I was one.

"Fine. I'm exhausted so I'm sure I'll go first."

He switches the phone to speaker, and I hear the water running. He must be in the bathroom brushing his teeth. A couple of minutes go by before I hear him speak.

"You still there?"

"I'm not asleep yet if that's what you're asking."

"Are you in bed yet? I bet I can guess what you're wearing."

"I thought we were going to talk?"

"We are talking. Can I guess?"

"If you must."

"I bet you're in a t-shirt and panties. One of those short t-shirts that show your stomach. Am I right?"

Dammit, he is. Why did I tell him to guess because now he has that image in his head? It was a gimme anyway because I always wore t-shirts and panties to bed when we were together. That's if I wasn't naked after sex with him which was almost nightly.

"Too easy. I always wear that to bed."

"I bet you're wearing a sexy little pair of panties or is it a thong?"

"Does it matter?"

"Yes, because you have an incredible ass and a thong would be such a turn on."

"JC!" I caution.

"Okay, I'm sorry but it's true. Do you want to guess what I'm wearing?"

"Boxers?"

"Guess again."

"Pajama pants, no shirt?"

"Still wrong. One last guess."

"I don't know. What else is there?"

"Give up?"

"Yes, what are you wearing?"

"Nothing, I'm completely naked."

I'm startled by his admission and my mind starts wandering.

"Lexi? Did you fall asleep on me?"

"No, I was just thinking about something. Why are you naked?"

"Because Brianna isn't home and I can do whatever I want when she's not home. I prefer to be naked, but she accuses me of trying to push her into sex. It's been over two months since we had sex, God forbid she throws me a mercy fuck once in a while."

I almost laugh at poor sex starved JC. "Think of it this way, at least you don't have to worry if she picked up a disease from one of her side dishes."

I feel horrible the minute the words come out of my mouth, but I can't take it back.

"You're right, I should be thankful. At least if she ends up pregnant, she can't blame me."

"JC, are you sure about ending your marriage?"

"Absolutely. I made my decision. Neither of us are happy. As far as I'm concerned, this is a marriage of convenience."

"What do you mean by that?"

"Well, it's convenient that she married a guy who can take care of her. She doesn't feel the same way though. I'm the one shelling out all the money for her trips and hobbies, yet I get nothing in return. She can't even make a grilled cheese sandwich for me when I work late."

"I'm sorry it didn't work out for you."

"I made a mistake when I let you go. I wish I could take it all back."

We're back to that again and I seriously don't want to discuss it especially since I'm upset with Noah.

"JC, I'm falling asleep here so before I do, I want to say goodbye."

"Are you sure?"

"Yes. It's late and I don't think there's enough coffee to keep me awake if I don't get at least four hours of sleep."

"Okay, I'll talk to you tomorrow."

JC hangs up and I put my phone on silent, placing it down on my nightstand. My mind is going in a million directions. Soon he'll be free when he divorces. Will he press me even more about getting together again once that happens?

CHAPTER 13

Three hours later, I'm awake. It's 2:40 in the morning and I'm not happy, mainly because of the disturbing dream I experienced. Having visions of your fiancé cheating on you with a mystery woman aren't comforting. I need someone to talk to and I start wondering if JC is awake. Should I text him? I do.

Are you awake or did you finally go to bed?

I'm awake. I went to sleep for about two hours and now I'm wide awake. If I come over, will you make me breakfast? I haven't had one of your home cooked meal in ages.

Is he nuts? He wants to come over so I can cook him breakfast. I seriously think about whether I should say yes. I know I'm not going to sleep, and I hate being in this big apartment by myself, especially when it's dark out.

I'll tell you what. If you get me an extra-large cup of Seattle blend from Beansy, then I'll make you pancakes.

Beansy is a cool little coffee shop a couple of blocks away. They're open twenty-four hours a day so I know JC can get me my favorite at this hour.

It's a deal. Do you have any maple syrup?

Yes. I also have strawberries.

You know a way to this man's heart. I'll be over in about twenty minutes.

I start heading to the kitchen and realize that I'm in my panties and t-shirt. I go back to the bedroom to put on the sweatpants I wore earlier. I probably should put a bra on, but I'm in no mood. My breasts are firm enough, maybe not as firm as Brianna's but not bad for an almost thirty-year-old.

I prepare things while waiting for JC to get here. My hair is hanging in my face and I find a hair band in the kitchen junk drawer to make a ponytail. By the time JC knocks on the door, I have the batter ready and the pan waiting. The aroma of coffee hits me as I open the door.

I'm surprised to see him carrying a garment bag and a smaller bag with him. I wonder why he brought them.

"What's with the bags?"

"After you feed me, I'm sure I won't feel like heading the several blocks to my apartment to get ready for work. I figured I would just do it here if you don't mind."

The fact was that I did mind. I felt weird having JC dress in the home that I shared with Noah when he wasn't here. I decided not to make a big deal out of it, so I just shrugged and busied myself with the pancake batter. I sipped at the coffee, relishing the rich taste as it passed over my tongue, then I started to make pancakes.

We chit chatted about mundane things, anything to keep JC from talking about my ass or whatever other body part he fixated on. As it turned out, that fixation was my breasts. I was a bit chilly in the air conditioning and my nipples were straining against the cloth of my t-shirt. I ignored him hoping food would avert his gaze. I placed a plate of stacked pancakes in front of him, but he kept looking at me and making me uncomfortable.

"Try them and tell me if I still make good pancakes."

"I'm sure you do. They look delicious."

I handed him the maple syrup and our fingers touch. He

brushes the back of my hand with his thumb before taking the bottle in his hand.

"Are you joining me?"

"Yes, I'll just have one."

"You can eat more. You look thinner than when we were together."

"I'm fine with one. I told you, I'm almost thirty and I need to watch my weight."

"Says who, Noah?"

JC sounds almost annoyed.

"No, Noah would never say that to me. He isn't like that."

"Some men are."

"Well he isn't. It's my decision."

I watch as JC shovels a big forkful of pancake dripping with syrup in his mouth and he closes his eyes.

"These are so good. You remember when you used to make them with bacon crumbled in the batter? So good."

"Yes, I remember. I haven't had that in a long time."

"We should go for burgers on Friday. Noah's not going to be home yet is he?"

"No, but Megan will be here. She's staying with me until Saturday morning."

"We can all go out together."

"JC, she's still pissed at you."

"It's been years and she hasn't gotten over it yet?"

"I can't force her."

"Why is she still upset? You got over it."

"It took me a long time and I was a mess for a while. She saw how miserable I was during most of it."

I didn't want to reveal so much to him but if JC didn't know, he should. I want him to feel guilty about what he did even though it was years ago. I watch him closely and he seems to be deep in thought, his fork full of pancake in midair, dripping syrup onto his plate. JC puts his fork down and gives me a sad look.

"Can I tell you something?"

"Since we're being so candid with each other these days, why not?"

"I knew I made a mistake as soon as I broke up with you."

"Then why didn't you tell me that? I lost you and quit my job all at once."

"You didn't have to quit."

"Oh, and work for my former fiancé who just broke up with me?"

"You could've moved to a different department."

"You were the director of marketing. I would have seen you and had to answer to you no matter what department I was in. It was best to end it."

"You could've had a career at Carver."

"I have a career and I finally have what I want."

JC starts eating again, avoiding my gaze while I finish making my pancake. By the time I start eating, he's finished and is carrying his plate to the sink to wash. He reaches over and takes the pan and spatula, washing them. I'm actually astonished because when we were together, he would stack dishes in the sink and leave them for me.

"You've become domestic since we were last together."

"I've become a lot of things since we were together. I've changed, matured. I hope you can see that."

"I do and I just want to have a good working relationship with you."

"Is that all you want?"

"What else is there?"

"Friends. If I can't have you for myself then I at least want to be friends."

"JC, I'm not sure that's a good idea. I don't know how Noah would feel about it especially if you get divorced. You're no threat now that you're married."

"Is he worried?"

"I doubt it. He didn't seem worried when I told him you're my boss."

"Then why wouldn't it be a good idea if he doesn't care?"

"I just don't."

I realize he hasn't touched the plate of strawberries I left on the counter. I push the plate over to him and he selects one.

"I'd love to feed these to you."

"Definitely not."

"Why not?"

"It's too, too intimate."

My face begins to warm because we spent a good amount of time feeding each other when we lived together.

"You're blushing."

"Because it's embarrassing."

I see the wheels turning in his head and I wait.

"Why because it was so sensual when we did it before?"

"JC, do you want to fuck me?" I blurt out.

I watch his jaw drop as he ponders what I've just asked him. He doesn't have to say yes because it's written all over his face. He does.

"I'm almost shocked that you asked that but if you want to know, yes."

"You do know that isn't going to happen. We've been there done that."

"So, if we were both single you wouldn't consider it?"

"But we're not. You're married and I'm going to be married."

"Maybe there will be a time you're not married. I'm considering myself already divorced."

"Thanks for the vote of confidence. I love Noah and I hope we stay married until death do us part."

"You believe in the fairytale. I believe in reality. Things happen to drive people apart."

"I think we have a good shot to make it."

As I spoke those words, something niggled at my brain. Noah

was acting strangely and maybe what he had to tell me when he got home would drive us apart. But it was something that would make JC work even harder to get me into bed with him. He would put doubts in my mind.

"It's after four. Do you want to watch TV for a little while?"

"Actually, I was wondering if I could take a nap on the couch? I think all this starch and sugar is making me sleepy."

"If you want to, be my guest. I probably should do that same. I could wake you at six."

"That's perfect."

He heads to the couch and kicks off his sneakers. I go to my bedroom and stretch out on the bed but forget to set the alarm for six. I don't know what time it is when I smell something wonderful and feel a hand on my shoulder.

I open my eyes to see JC touching me, freshly showered. I'm wide awake and feeling defensive. I bolt up in bed and he takes his hand away.

"I'm sorry. It's almost 6:15, you didn't wake me at 6:00."

"Why is your hair wet?"

He looks at me sheepishly, "I hope you don't mind. I needed a shower."

"I have to go in myself."

I just want to get away from this awkward situation especially since he's in my bedroom. The bedroom where I make love to Noah. I get out of bed and go around him, practically slamming the door to the bathroom. I take a quick shower and when I come out, he's no longer there but the lingering smell of his cologne is.

Within ten minutes I dressed in my gray business suit. I put my hair in a ponytail and take another five minutes to work on my makeup. When I come out of the bedroom, he's sitting on the stool at the breakfast bar eating strawberries I left on the counter.

"These are really good; you should try one."

"I already brushed my teeth."

"You're missing out."

"I'll survive," I say a bit annoyed.

"I'm taking the car service this morning. Do you want to come?"

Are you fucking kidding! You're having them pick you up in front of my building?

"Since you're going the same way, might as well."

"Lexi, what's wrong? Did I do something?"

"No, I'm just tired."

"So, is that a no for burgers tomorrow?"

"I told you that Megan is coming to stay."

"I can bear her wrath."

"Can we discuss this later?"

One uncomfortable and silent car ride to the office later, I'm settled at my desk, coffee in hand. Fortunately, JC is not in the building long. He has two client meetings and has to go. I breathe a sigh of relief.

Several hours pass and I'm pissed off. I haven't heard from Noah in almost twenty-four hours. This is becoming a habit with him. Before when he went away, he would always call me whenever he got a free chance. Now I feel like I have to chase him.

By the time five rolls around, I still have not heard from him and JC is nowhere to be found. Megan didn't call me either and I'm wondering if she's going to be sleeping at the loft tonight. I guess I'm on my own.

On the subway, my phone rings. Of course, cell service is intermittent, and I lose the call before I can even answer. Once I'm out on the street I see three missed calls from an unknown number and two voicemails. I listen and sure enough, it's Megan. Scatterbrain must have gotten a new phone. She should be at my apartment on Friday. She met some friends for drinks, and they invited her to stay over. So much for missing your big sister.

As I'm walking in the door, I almost trip over a bag, Noah's bag. He's home and didn't even tell me. I call to him and get no answer but when I go in the bedroom, he's in the shower. I'm glad he's home even though I'm annoyed by his lack of communication.

I strip my clothes off quickly and walk into the bathroom naked, softly saying his name as I step into the shower enclosure. He wheels around and grabs me against him. His mouth is all over mine, tongue pushing deep in my mouth and curling around my own. I'm surprised by his behavior.

"I missed you so much," he says after releasing my mouth.

"Why didn't you call me? I was worried."

"I'm sorry. The client's son got into some trouble and I was involved trying to straighten it out. Stupid kid got arrested for public urination."

"Is that why you're home early?"

"Yes. They decided to cut their vacation short though we got paid the full amount. Tom got some training but not as much as I would've liked him to have. I probably have to go on another trip to feel comfortable with him going alone."

I groan. "I hate when you're gone."

"I know but I'm here now," he growls.

His cock is hard and pressing against his stomach. My core clenches and immediately starts to flood. I want him ever since JC started his seduction earlier this morning. The fact that he was here with me alone will not be revealed or Noah might have a fit.

"I'm glad you are."

His mouth latches on to my nipple and he sucks, hollowing his cheeks. I don't want or need foreplay; I just want him to fuck me. I've been craving him for the past two days. I think if he wasn't here now, masturbation would have been on the table tonight. But he saved me from a lonely orgasm.

I push him off my nipple and pull his face up to mine. I want to kiss him, and I do, hard. I wrap my hand around his girth and slowly stroke him. A low-pitched rumble comes from his throat and he begins to finger my clit. It's not what I want, I want him inside me.

"Fuck me," I mumble.

He breaks the kiss and pushes me, face first against the glass, spreading my legs a little with his hand. I feel his cock pressing against my opening from the back and with one thrust, I gasp as he pushes inside me. His hand splays against my belly as he pumps into me. He moves his hand so that his thumb is working my clit. I want to scream because it feels so good.

"Yes," I moan.

This one word seems to spur his ardor and he really starts to move, his hips slamming against my ass as his cock pistons in and out of me. I feel a quick orgasm coming on and I grit my teeth as it takes hold. He moves both hands to my hips and continues to pump until I feel him spilling into me with a loud grunt. I want more but I know this is probably only the beginning of our night. Noah is still inside me and his head is pressed into my wet hair.

"I love you Lexi."

We're locked together for another minute and then he pulls out and turns me around to face him. He embraces me and moves me under the rain shower head as he reaches for the shampoo. Noah loves to wash my hair and I like when he massages my scalp.

I close my eyes and feel his hands work the shampoo into a lather. It feels wonderful because he's using just the tips of his fingers. When he finishes, he pushes my hair back and pulls me towards him. His cock is hard again and pressing against my belly, it hasn't even been five minutes since the last time he came.

I reach up to wipe the water out of my eyes as he takes my hand and pulls me over to the shower seat in the corner of the stall. He sits and I stand above him wondering what he wants. I decide he wants me to suck him and drop to my knees in front of him. Even before I take him in my mouth, his eyes are closed, and I hear a small moan from him as he anticipates.

Even in the shower, I can see a bead of dew pooling on his head and I lick it with the tip of my tongue.

"Fuck, yes, I love when you do that."

I do it again as another bead replaces the one, I just licked. He moans as I swirl my tongue around his head and then take him in my mouth. He's gentle but I can feel his hand on the back of my head. Noah wants me to take him deep and when I do, he exhales loudly. His hand is no longer on the back of my head but clenching the edge of the shower seat.

I work his cock in and out of my mouth which elicits a series of loud moans from Noah. When I cup and fondle his balls, he bucks, gyrating his hips. It throws off my rhythm, but he doesn't seem to mind. His eyes are closed, and his top teeth are pressed over his bottom lip as if in deep thought.

I hollow my cheeks as I take him deep, sucking hard. This causes Noah to moan loudly.

"Don't stop, I'm going to come."

I take him almost to his base and can feel his release hit the back of my throat. He gently bucks and I feel several more spurts. When he finishes, he slumps against the wall, stroking my wet hair from my face as I clean him with my tongue.

"You're incredible, you know that?"

I smile but I can feel my face start to blush. Two years of having sex with this man and it still embarrasses me when he gives me compliments about my prowess in bed.

I rise to my feet and he reaches over for a washcloth so he can wash my body. What I just did has made me hot and bothered. I want him inside me, but I know it's too soon. I hope that he will use his tongue when we get to the bedroom.

After we shower, he wipes me dry and blow dries my hair. I love when he pampers me. When we're done, he takes me by the hand and leads me to our bed, then goes in the closet. He comes out wearing a t-shirt and boxers. I'm a little disappointed because I thought we were going to have more sex.

"Lexi, what's the matter?"

"Nothing. I'm just tired."

"I know that face. What's wrong."

Should I tell him or wait until he goes to sleep and masturbate? I decide to tell him.

"I missed you and I thought we were going to make love."

"We did make love. Do you want more?"

"I do, but if you're tired."

"That's not what I asked."

"Then yes, I want to make love."

"Seriously, I'm not sure I have anything left. I didn't sleep well last night. The hotel we were staying in was full of kids on a trip and they made noise a good part of the night."

I'm not in the mood to argue but again, this is peculiar behavior for Noah. He could go all night even with two hours of sleep. Now that he's home, I want to ask him about what he had to tell me. He promised he would. It's late and I decide to acquiesce.

"Can I expect you'll make it up to me tomorrow night?"

"You know I will."

He pecks me on the cheek and climbs into bed next to me. Within minutes, he's softly snoring next to me. I just realize that I'm still sitting on the bed naked. The hell with it, I think. I slip under the sheets that way, but sleep doesn't come as readily as it did with Noah. I toss and turn for a while. A few things are bothering me relating to the closest men in my life, Noah and JC.

I'm horny and it might be the only thing that's going to help me to fall asleep. What I do next is horrible and something I haven't done for years; I fantasize to JC as I masturbate. I think about the feel of his tongue on my clit. That does it, and within two minutes, I come, silently mouthing his name. After I'm done, I feel the guilt bubble up in me. I did this with my fiancé sleeping right next to me.

CHAPTER 14

The next morning, I wake before the alarm. I have a headache and Noah is still sleeping. He's on the other side of the bed. Usually he's right on top of me with his body curled around mine. I might be overreacting, but I'm hurt. He was away from me for a few days and I would think that he would be more affectionate.

I reach out and poke him. He stirs, grumbles, then starts to snore. Screw it then. I get up and quickly shower. By the time he wakes, I'm dressed for work and sitting at the breakfast bar finishing the last of the strawberries.

"Hey babe, why didn't you wake me?"

"I tried but you just grumbled and went back to sleep."

"I'm sorry about last night. If you have some time this morning…"

I'm more than satisfied, thank you very much.

"I need to get to the office. Rain check until tonight?"

His blue eyes darken, and he comes over to me to kiss my neck and suck on my earlobe. I know what he's trying to do but I'm not in the mood for a quickie.

"Enough Noah," I say in a stern tone.

"Wow, excuse me."

"I'm sorry. I didn't mean it that way. Are you home this weekend?"

"Yes. Nothing on the schedule that needs me out in the field."

"Are you we going to talk?"

"Talk?"

"You said you wanted to talk to me something. I'm curious."

His face tightens. "Uh, yeah. I guess."

"Noah, I could call in sick if it's serious."

"It's not. I'm just not sure how you'll take it."

"That only worries me more."

"Lexi, it's not what you think but it is important you know before we get married."

I'm silent for a minute because it must be serious if he wants me to know before we become man and wife. It's getting late and I have much to do at the office, so I need to get going.

"Can we talk tonight?"

"I want to. I think it's best we do it as soon as possible."

"You could have told me before you left."

"No. This is something I don't want to just drop and go. You might have follow-up questions and it's best they are asked while I'm here."

"Fine. I'll see you tonight."

I kiss his cheek and he pulls me into a full embrace, cupping my ass while his tongue invades my mouth. I shrink away quickly because if he keeps that up, I'm going to be late.

"Behave."

"It's not easy with you smelling so good. You're hot, Lexi."

"Thank you, Noah, so are you."

I smile at him as I walk out the door.

Thirty minutes later I'm sitting at my desk when JC pokes his head in my door. I can feel a heated flush on my face when I think back to what I did in bed and the shower even though it's none of his business.

"How are you this morning?"

"I'm good. How are you?"

He comes in and closes the door, sitting in one of the chairs in front of my desk.

"I told Brianna last night."

"You drove to Cape Cod?"

"Fuck, no. I called her. I wasn't driving five hours to ask for a divorce."

"You told her over the phone?"

"You sound upset. She cheated on me."

"What was her response?"

"She started to cry and begged my forgiveness. I asked her how many more there were. She admitted to three more. I think it's higher than that."

I fixed my eyes on his. "JC, did you ever cheat on her?"

"Why would you ask me that?"

"You know why."

"No. I thought about it, but I didn't. I'm not that person anymore."

"So, what is your game plan?"

"I told her I would pack her things and she can come get them whenever she gets back. The apartment is in my name only. She can go back to live with her parents. Their apartment is much nicer than mine, I'm sure she'll love moving back there."

"How do you feel about everything?"

"I feel free. I woke up this morning and was whistling. I can get used to sleeping alone again. I want it. Are we on for burgers tonight?"

"I can't. Noah got home yesterday, and Megan is coming over this afternoon. Should be fun since they don't really get along."

"Oh. He doesn't like Megan?"

"He says she's too much like my father, always questioning him. He hates when people invade his privacy."

Fuck, I forgot to remind Noah that Megan is coming over this afternoon. It also means that we won't be able to have the discussion until she goes home tomorrow.

"Oh, one of those."

"What is that supposed to mean?"

"I question when someone is so private. Does he have something to hide?"

"Not at all. Noah runs a business where he needs to maintain confidentiality. He can't talk about his clients or they would never hire him again."

"I just find it strange when someone is so closed off."

"He's not closed off."

"Not when he has alcohol in him."

"I don't like where this conversation is going. Do you have something to say about him?"

"Yes, I do. I don't like how he treated you on Memorial Day weekend. He embarrassed you."

I begin to laugh, and JC gives me an annoyed look.

"YOU, don't like how he embarrassed me? You used to do it to me all the time."

JC grips the chair arms. "I was an immature dick. Is that what you want me to say? I would never do it to you now if you were mine."

"But I'm not. Now you can have whoever you want. You're free to fuck as many women as you like."

He rose from his chair to leave but not before he left me a parting word.

"The woman I want is unavailable and I will regret that for the rest of my life."

After he leaves, I think about what we had. Why do I keep bring this up in my head? Is it because I have doubts about Noah? I really don't until recently. His behavior has been different from any other time I can remember. I hope that once he tells me what he has to tell me, he'll go back to the old Noah.

I get busy with work and spend a good two hours going over some things with Nikki. It's time I give her more responsibility since she is my assistant. I'm finding that I have my hand in too many things and I need to farm some out. I give her the task of speaking with the graphic artists for one of the projects we're working on. She can handle it.

By the time I'm finished going over everything with her, it's close to lunchtime. I know I have something to do but I can't remember what it is until I get a text from Noah.

Was there something you forgot to tell me?

FUCK! I once again forgot to let him know Megan was coming. She must be there early.

You mean Megan?

Yes, I mean Megan. She just showed up and is asking me where she's going to sleep. You should have told me because I need to clean my files out of the guest room.

Just push them aside. She's not going to look at them.

Please don't tell me what to do. Those files are confidential. I just can't leave them there for her to look at.

. . .

I don't like the tone of his text and I decide to ignore him and go back to work. Probably not the best idea because five minutes later he's calling me.

"What the fuck, Lexi. You ignore me?"

"Don't speak to me like that. I don't appreciate it."

"You don't huh? I don't appreciate when you don't tell me things."

"Really? Look who's talking. How dare you Noah."

He starts ranting and I put the receiver down and lean back in my chair, rubbing my temples. This is a Noah that I haven't had to deal with in a very long time. Not since he was under a lot of stress when he was expanding his business about a year ago.

I pick the phone up after I hear silence. "Are you done?"

"Yeah, I'm done. We'll discuss this later."

He hangs up and I'm left staring at the phone. I seriously hope that what he has to tell me is not catastrophic. He said it wasn't, but with his behavior, drinking and lack of consideration, I'm beginning to wonder.

I skip lunch because I begin to feel nauseous from our conversation. JC passes by and asks me if I want to go across the street to the deli, but I tell him no. I don't think I can keep anything down. A half hour later he's back and brings me something in a large plastic cup.

"I told you I wasn't hungry."

"Lexi, you have to eat something. You'll like this."

I pop the cover and inside's a raspberry vanilla shake, one of my all-time favorite flavors. But the place I usually get them from is way uptown. How did he get this?

"Where did you get this?"

"I bribed the kid behind the counter at the deli. They have vanilla shakes, so I just asked him to add a dash of vanilla and some fresh raspberries."

I'm overwhelmed that he would do this for me. I'm nothing to him but an ex and he's giving me more consideration that my freaking fiancé. I'm emotional and I blink my eyes quickly to push back the tears I feel ready to fall.

"Thank you, JC. That was very thoughtful of you."

"Lex, what's wrong? You seem out of sorts."

"It's nothing, I'm okay."

"No, you're not okay. You seem upset. Is it what I said this morning? I'm trying to make it up to you with the shake. I didn't mean to say anything bad about Noah. I just want to make sure he's treating you well. I care about you."

"Thank you but I'm fine. We just had a little bit of a spat. I forgot to remind him about Megan coming tonight. He's upset because he has some confidential files in the guest room that he has to move out. Plus, she just got there and well, they just don't get along. Actually, she gets along okay with him, but he tolerates her."

"I'm sorry. That must be tough since you want your family to get along with your fiancé. We never had that problem."

"No, they loved you until you broke my heart."

"And I feel like shit about it. Does your dad still golf? Maybe we can drive up to the Rye Golf Club, I know he loved it there when we used to go."

"He would love that, but Noah would probably freak out that my ex was having a golf outing with my father."

"Then ask Noah to come."

"Noah hates golf. He says it's the most frustrating game he ever tried to play. He has no patience for it."

JC grins. "So, something I'm better at than him."

I shake my head. "It's not a contest and I'm not the prize."

"I didn't mean to imply that you were."

I dismiss him. "Thank you for the shake but I have work to do."

"I'll talk to you later. Think about the golf."

Ha, I could just see my father telling my mother that he's going to play golf with JC. She would yell at him and ask him how he could spend the day with someone who broke his little girl's heart.

I sip at the shake that JC got me, it's wonderful and I'm grateful because the more I drink the more I realize that I was so hungry. I finish it and go back to work, but I can't concentrate. I keep thinking what's waiting for me when I get home. I know that Noah will be in a foul mood, probably more than the one he was in when we last spoke.

I trudge on and at 4:45, Nikki comes in to show me graphics on her tablet. She tells me she emailed them to me, but I didn't answer. I check my email and she's right, she sent them for approval a half hour ago. They're good and I knew I could count on her. I give my approval.

"Do you mind if I leave for the day?" Nikki asks.

"I think it would be okay. I'm leaving in a few minutes."

"Thank you."

The train ride home is not pleasant. The car is packed with people who smell like they just ran a marathon. The man next to me is wearing jogging attire and he's soaked with sweat. To top it off, with each lurch of the train, he rubs his sweaty body against me. Tonight, first thing is a shower.

It's hot out and the sidewalks are teeming with pedestrians. I'm envious of the ones dressed in shorts and t-shirts, like they don't have a care in the world. By the time I get in the door of our building, I'm the one sweating and smelling like I ran a marathon. Of course, the minute I get in the apartment, Noah stalks out of his office with an angry look on his face.

"Where's Megan?"

"She went to have dinner with one of her friends. She said she would be back by seven. That gives us enough time to have a talk. Come to my office."

It's a demand, not a request. I'm not one of his fucking employees.

I clear my throat. "I'd like to change first. Maybe take a quick shower."

He clenches his fists at his sides and the knuckles turn white. "And I don't want to wait to say this."

"Noah, I'm hot and tired. I worked all day and I want to be comfortable. If you want to talk, then come into the bathroom with me while I shower."

He just stares at me and crosses his arms but I'm not giving in. I need to freshen up and if he doesn't want to wait, too bad. I head to the bedroom with him right behind me. He stands there while I undress and grab my robe then follows me into the bathroom, not saying a word while I step into the shower.

Noah is still there leaning against the vanity when I get out and he looks hungrily at my body but keeps his arms crossed while he does it. He hasn't said a word and as soon as I'm dressed, he takes me by the hand and leads me to his office.

"Sit. I want to get this out before Megan comes home."

Now it's my turn to cross my arms and stare at him. I don't hide my annoyance.

"I would've appreciated a heads up with Megan. Do you know what she did to me after she got here? She began questioning me about our relationship. What the fuck did you tell her?" he growls.

"Noah, I haven't spoken to Megan at length in a few weeks. We've been playing phone tag. I can't help it if she feels there's something wrong with us."

"You think that?"

"I didn't until Memorial Day weekend. You've been acting like an asshole to me."

"Me? What about you with this little stunt today?"

"You've been hiding things from me, you got drunk, you fucked me and took off when your phone rang. You haven't been the Noah I know and love. I forgot to remind you Megan was visiting. I hardly think that constitutes me being so terrible."

I watch him work his jaw and rub the back of his neck. I know he is thinking about what I just told him, I can almost see the wheels turning in his head.

"You're right. I've been detached lately. I want to talk to you about why but I'm not sure it's a good idea with Megan here overnight."

"For fuck's sake, I'm not waiting anymore. Just tell me already."

He reaches into his desk and removes the letters I previously read. I bristle with the knowledge that I invaded his privacy.

"These two letters are from someone I thought I would never have contact with again."

My eyebrows go up in surprise. "Who are they from and what do they say?"

He hands them to me, and I open them up as if it's my first time. I know what they say but I can't tell him that. I look at the girly script and pretend to read through them.

"Who's Rory?"

"Rory, or Aurora, is my daughter."

My jaw drops as I try to process the information, he just told me. How can he have a daughter and not have told me?

"What? A daughter? How, how old is she and why haven't you told me this before?"

"Vivian, Rory's mother, was together with me when we were in our late teens. We were high school sweethearts. We had a passionate love affair into the summer after our senior year. I was heading off to Stanford and she was attending USC. I got her pregnant."

He stops talking so he can let that sink in. My straight arrow Noah got someone pregnant.

He continues. "I wanted to marry her. I would've transferred to USC to be with her and we could've lived together. We would have worked it out. But her parents were livid and said she would take a year off college to have Rory and then go. Our marrying was out of the question."

"They forbid you to marry?"

"Yes, and worse, my father cut me off. He said if I wanted to go to Stanford, I would have to pay for it. So, I enlisted in the Marines just to spite him. The Barton's, Vivian's parents, worked on her that first year. Telling her how horrible I was to leave her. By the time I came home for Rory's birth, Vivian hated me and said if I truly loved her, to let her and Rory go. I wanted the best for my daughter and I agreed to cut off contact."

I place my hand over my mouth. "You gave your child up?"

"Not parentally. I'm still her father."

"Of course," I mutter.

"Lucian was able to get pictures of Rory every so often to send to me. He maintained a friendship with Vivian, then she left Boston and I had no idea where she was. For years I thought about Rory. Of course, I finished my military tour, went to Boston College four years later and got my degree."

"So how did you find Rory again?"

"I didn't. She found me. Vivian was back in Boston living with her family. Her father died and Rory found information for Lucian. She contacted him and he led her to me. Rory has been accepted to NYU and will be starting in the fall. She graduated high school early. I want a relationship with her."

"Noah, you could've told me this from the beginning, I would have understood. Why didn't you tell me you had a child out there?"

"I didn't know if she would ever be a factor in our lives. I met her; she looks just like her mother but with my eyes."

I could just picture a young woman with Noah's gorgeous sapphire blue eyes.

"Do you have pictures of her?"

"Yes, she sent me these while I was away this past week."

He hands me his phone. On it is a picture of a beautiful young woman with sandy colored shoulder length hair and his very eyes. I scroll to the next picture and it's of her on the beach with another gorgeous woman but this one is older; both have curvy figures. I can only guess that this is Vivian. I feel a pang of jealousy as I gaze at the screen. Vivian fills out a bikini better than I do. A few more pictures and I hand the phone back to Noah.

"She's lovely."

"You'll like her. I hope you can be friends since you'll be her stepmother."

I think about that. At twenty-nine, I didn't expect to be a step-mother to someone only twelve years younger than me. But then again, Noah is almost seven years older.

"When do I get to meet her?"

"She wants to come down next week. I was thinking of having her visit a couple of weeks before school starts to stay with us. She's going to be staying in a small apartment with one of her friends from Boston who's also attending NYU."

"So, she won't be staying with us full time?"

"No, she doesn't need me hanging over her shoulder. She deserves to experience college life away from her parents."

I agree with that. I couldn't wait to get away from mine when I went to college. It was only across the river, but it gave me a sense of freedom and got me away from Megan and Emma's drama.

"She can join us for dinner every so often."

"I'm sure she would like that. Thank you for being so under-standing."

He kisses me on the cheek and when he does, I'm indifferent to it. Why? I never felt that way about his kisses. Usually I crave his touch but not tonight. I guess it's because I'm tired, or maybe it's something I can't put my finger on.

CHAPTER 15

I'm in the kitchen eating a small container of vanilla yogurt when Megan walks through the door. I haven't seen my middle sister in months. She's gorgeous and her hair looks lighter than its usual strawberry blonde and a lot longer, down to her lower back. I look at her green eyes with envy since I have light brown. She seems to have matured since I last saw her.

"You've lost weight."

"Yep, twenty-two pounds. No more eating ice cream at night with Jeremy."

"Megan, I'm sorry about your break-up."

"He was an asshole. He didn't deserve me and I'm glad I found out now before it had gotten serious."

Gotten serious? They had been dating for over two years. Jeremy was kind of geeky, but he had a great sense of humor. I know he loved having my beautiful sister on his arm when they went to company functions. Jeremy was an executive for a hedge fund. I wonder how it went all wrong, but I don't want to open up her healing wound by asking.

"So, what are your plans?"

"I'm moving to Manhattan. Nolan extended an offer to me this afternoon."

"That's wonderful. Congratulations. Big changes for you. Did you tell Mom and Dad?"

"Not yet. You know how they get. All weepy that I'll be leaving the nest. I haven't lived in the nest for three years."

She flips her blonde locks out of her face and starts chewing on her thumbnail.

"When do you start at Nolan?"

"Two weeks. I'm giving a week's notice at Darwin and taking a week to move and enjoy the city. We can hang out more now that I'm going to live in Manhattan."

"I'd like that. We haven't spent a lot of time together in months."

"Tell me about your new job. Mom said you're working for JC?"

"He goes by Camden now, but I don't call him that any more than he calls me Alexa."

She lowers her voice, so Noah doesn't hear through his open office door.

"Is he still so fucking hot?"

"Megan! I don't pay attention to that. One, I'm with Noah and two, he's my boss."

"So, he was beautiful. I would love to run my tongue over his abs."

"You're hopeless. He's married anyway."

"Really? Hunter didn't say anything to me."

"You talk to Hunter?"

"I did more than just talk to Hunter."

"Please tell me you didn't."

"A few times but not in a while. What can I say? He's awesome in bed."

"Was this before or after Jeremy?"

She starts biting her thumbnail harder and looks at the floor.

"During?"

"It was towards the end of our relationship. I met Hunter on Fire Island before Memorial Day and well, one thing led to another. He's so hot, too."

"And now?"

"Now we're just friends. We talk all the time."

Great, so my sister is best friends with my ex's brother. Just perfect.

"How's Lucian?"

"He's good. He should be coming to New York in July."

"You have all the luck being surrounded by beautiful men. You always had handsome boyfriends."

"Megan, I barely dated in high school."

"Yeah but after, you always had a hot guy. I was jealous sometimes."

"You were homecoming queen while I spent my time in the library and debate team."

"You could have dated if you wanted to. All my male friends were in love with you."

"That's nice to know since they were all three and a half years younger than me."

"I'm sure plenty of guys your age wanted to go out with you."

"JC did."

"Really, he did? Why didn't he ask you?"

"He was too busy fucking around. He didn't date, he fucked."

"I miss him."

"I thought you hated him."

"I got over it. I wish you were with him still."

Before I can answer, Noah comes out of his office.

"So, what are you girls talking about?"

"Girl stuff. Unless you have an opinion about mascara, I doubt you'd be interested."

"I like when you wear it. You have mile long eyelashes."

He takes me into his arms and dips me, then plants a kiss on my nose. I know it's for show because Megan's here. Our relationship is on the icy side tonight. But I play along. I don't want my sister telling my parents that another engagement of mine is in trouble.

Noah goes to the living room and turns on the television to watch something sports, probably a baseball game, I can hear the announcer. Megan and I talk about all the things we missed in each other's lives. I'm glad she's here because I miss girl time. My best friend, Olivia, is moving back to Manhattan soon and that will give me someone else to commiserate with.

Later than night, I'm lying in bed and Noah slips in behind me. He pulls me close and begins to knead my breasts.

"No. I'm so not in the mood."

"Did I do something wrong? I thought we resolved everything."

"You resolved everything. I need time to absorb what you told me. You can't make everything alright with sex."

I feel him shrink away from me and move to his side of the bed. I'm still pissed off about his behavior over the past couple of weeks.

"Lucian called me today. He's coming to visit at the end of next week."

"I thought he was coming in July?"

"My father has a big development deal he's working on. He has to go to Japan in July, so Lucian is going to have to cover the other ongoing projects while he's gone. He doesn't trust anyone else."

Figures, the great Richard Wilton. I still can't believe he cut Noah off with paying for college. It must have been painful to have your parent take away their support when you needed it most. I'm surprised that Caroline, his mother, didn't have something to say but then again, she's had problems with alcohol over the years. It might have been one of the times she was drying out in some Palm Springs Rehab Center.

"Is he staying with us?"

"More than likely."

I like Lucian. He's different from Noah, less high strung. They look nothing alike except they share the same sapphire blue eyes and sandy colored hair. He's shorter but nonetheless handsome, just in a different way.

"Maybe Megan can join us."

"Whatever."

I frown. "Noah, that's a child's response. You need to get along with Megan; she's going to be your sister in law."

"Don't remind me," he mumbles.

The word "dick" is at the tip of my tongue because that's what he's being. I don't give him the satisfaction of a reply and turn over on my stomach to go to sleep.

In the middle of the night I feel Noah snuggle up against me and pull me onto my side. I wake partially but once I'm in his arms, I quickly fade back to sleep. I don't want to fight, I love him, but lately, our relationship is strained. I'm awake and rising from bed for a much-needed cup of coffee when Noah stirs, leaning on his elbow.

"I hope you're prepared because, I'm going to fuck you hard tonight."

Any bad feelings I had from the night before has dissipated with sleep and I feel my belly clench at the mention of him fucking me. I want it now, but we can't. Instead, I get back in bed and snuggle against him making Noah growl in my ear not to tease him. I'm so comfortable, I don't want to get up. I have time since it's only 5:30.

Noah is not about to behave, and he slips his hand in my panties, I'm wet and he nips my ear as his fingertip touches my clit. I protest but that fades as he stimulates me with his fingers. I'm panting when there's a knock on the door. Noah withdraws his hand and I bite my lip.

"Megan, what's up?" I call.

"I'm leaving. I need to get back early," she says through the door.

I try to get up, but Noah is holding me down as he sucks my earlobe.

"Let me up or else after she leaves, I lock myself in the bathroom."

"You wouldn't!"

He lets me go and I go to the door to kiss my sister goodbye and walk her to the front door. We briefly talk about getting together for lunch and I let her out, locking the door behind her. Apparently, she needs to get some things from Jeremy's apartment and wants to get a head start.

When I come back, Noah is standing near the bed and stroking himself. I feel my belly clench a few more times at the erotic sight of him, his thick cock sticking straight out. I want it inside me.

"Okay, I'm heading for a shower."

"Oh no, you're not!"

Noah grabs me and in one quick move, pulls my nightgown over my head, then hooks his fingers in my panties and tugs. I'm naked and he slaps my ass, pushing me toward the bed. I get on all fours and he comes up behind me, rubbing his fat head against my soaked folds.

Noah teases me by pressing against my opening, then pulling back. I whimper, anticipating how he's going to fill me and with one hard thrust, he does. I can feel myself stretching and conforming to the size of him. He grabs my hips and moves in a slow rhythm. *What happened to fucking me hard?*

"Harder."

He pays no attention to me but instead, I feel his fingers on my clit, rubbing which sends shockwaves through me. I want him to make me come and I start begging for it. His fingers move faster, and he pumps harder. The feeling is so sensual especially when he leans over and runs his tongue up my spine.

I'm moaning and ready to break apart which I do, exploding around him. When my orgasm finishes, he stands up, grasps my hips and starts pounding me. He murmurs my name with each movement until he releases with one mind numbing thrust, holding himself deep inside me until he's finished.

This is just what I needed. I need to know Noah is in sync with me. I feel any disagreement we had has just been repaired over the last fifteen minutes. He pulls out and I lie on my back with him next to me.

"You're hot, never forget that. You're always going to be my number one girl."

I know what he means by that. He's trying to allay any fears I might have that when his daughter comes, I'll take a back seat to her. Actually, I expect it. I would never want to get in the way of his relationship with his child.

It's almost six when I start to get up, but Noah pulls me back, "Just a few more minutes. You have plenty of time."

I snuggle against his chest and kiss the smooth skin near his nipple then touch it with the tip of my tongue. His eyes are closed but I hear a low rumble in his throat as I continue.

"Lexi, keep it up and you're calling in sick today."

Oh? Sex all day? We haven't done that for a long time, but I can't stay home. Since it's Friday, I need to complete some copy and hand it off to JC for approval making next week a light week for me. I'm looking forward to it since the Kingston Group has been a thorn in my side since I started two weeks ago.

I lie in Noah's arms for another fifteen minutes then get up. He's right behind me, pulling on a pair of sweatpants and a t-shirt. He's going to work out in our small home gym. It's stocked with a top of the line elliptical, treadmill with incline and video, weights, a heavy bag and other assorted gear. He's been after me to work out too, but I don't have the motivation like he does.

Noah has training in martial arts and holds a second-degree

black belt in Karate. He hasn't had to use it much but I'm sure that his clients feel more secure knowing this. I know I do.

When I come out of the bedroom a half hour later, dressed in my burgundy shift dress, Noah's still in the gym. I can hear him grunting and I peek my head in to see what he's doing. He's running full speed on the treadmill and his white shirt is soaked and clinging to his muscular frame. He smiles at me and continues to look at the video screen.

He bought this treadmill that connects to trainers from all over the world. You can run up mountains, through valleys or city streets. It should come with a valet for the price, but it keeps him in great shape, and I appreciate it.

I head to the kitchen to see if I can scrounge up something to eat. The refrigerator is getting pretty bare and I think it's time we go food shopping. I could probably stop after work and pick up some groceries. Noah didn't mention what he has on his schedule today so maybe he can shop.

I decide on a bowl of raisin bran with the last of the milk. As I'm eating, Noah emerges from the workout room wiping his face with a small towel. He's all sweaty and leans in to kiss me on the cheek. Even though he just worked out, his scent is masculine and sexy.

"We're almost out of food. Do you want to pick up some groceries today?"

"Shit, Lex, I have so much on my plate today. Can you do it?"

I sigh. "I'll pick up some after work. I hope I can be home by seven."

"Thanks babe. I'm up to my eyeballs in paperwork."

I watch as he walks toward the bedroom. I'm tired but if we want to eat, I better find the energy to pick up food tonight. I wash my bowl and put it on the drain board then fill up my travel mug with much needed coffee.

The subway is more crowded than usual, and I stand holding onto the strap with one hand while balancing my briefcase and coffee in the other. The office is a flurry of activity when I get in and I wonder if I missed a meeting. Normally when I get in at eight, it's quieter than it is today.

Before I can even sit down, JC is in my office asking about the two campaigns I need to finish. I tell him that I'm almost done, and I should have the copy to him in an hour or two.

"What's going on? Did I miss something?"

"Neil Barker is coming in today."

"Who's Neil Barker?"

"He's the majority silent partner. He put in a good chunk of the funds to get this place rolling."

"I wasn't aware they had a silent partner. I thought Vincent and Marco were the owners."

"They are, but Neil does have a stake in the company. He's a good guy but usually comes occasionally to assess operations."

"Should I be concerned?"

"You? No. I'm sure he'll be impressed with you. Just finish the copy please. I have a meeting in the conference room at 9:30."

He walks out and I sit in my chair to finish my work. Nikki comes by and I farm a few minor details out to her so I can concentrate on completing my items. I get up and close my door so I can work in silence. At 10:45, I get a knock at my door.

"Come in."

In walk JC, Vincent, Marco and one other man who I can guess is Neil. He's dark like Vincent but taller and thinner with long brown hair tied back in a ponytail.

"This is Alexa Stanford, our new marketing director," JC says.

Neil holds out his hand as he comes towards me. I start to rise but he waves me to sit back down which I do.

"Alexa, very nice to meet you. I heard you did a wonderful job with the Kingston Group. I received a personal call from Kingston himself. Anyone that can satisfy that man is worth their weight in salt."

"Thank you. It was a challenge, but JC was very helpful with his assistance."

"Ah, you're one of those who can't take a compliment without thanking the little people."

I wonder if he's joking and the smile on his face tells me he is. I smile back and he chuckles. We make small talk and then everyone but JC leaves my office.

"Do you have that copy for me?"

"I told you I would. Check the server. You can proof from there."

"Neil likes you but what's not to like."

"Thanks, but I hope you're referring to my work and not something else."

"He isn't like that."

"I wasn't talking about him."

He scowls at me and rises to leave. I feel a pang of guilt for making that snide comment but he's out the door before I can apologize. Oh well, I don't have time to chase after him.

I don't see him for the rest of the day and when it's time to leave, his door is closed with no light illuminating from under the door. He might have left but I didn't even see him pass by my door which has been open since this afternoon. I've been glued to my seat and forgot to eat lunch or pee for that matter.

I go to the bathroom before I leave and decide how nice a hot bath would be followed by a glass of wine on the terrace. Then I realize that I need to go grocery shopping. Fuck, I'm in no mood.

On the train, I make a list of items in my head as shoulders of other riders bump into me with the movement of the train. I want to get in, grab the essentials and get out of there quickly. The sooner I get home to start my weekend, the better. I'm looking forward to spending some alone time with Noah. I want to discuss his daughter a little more extensively.

The grocery store is three blocks from my apartment. I'm standing in front of the apple display deciding which ones to get when someone whispers in my ear.

"Your ass looks divine in that dress."

I turn to see JC behind me with a huge grin on his face. I want to slap it off.

"Stop looking at my ass."

"It's hard not to when it's so enticing."

"Try. What are you doing here?"

"Same as you, shopping. Since you won't go out to burgers with me, I need to get some food for my apartment."

I check out the small shopping cart he's wheeling around. Cheetos, rolls, cold cuts, beer, red licorice, bananas, hummus, onion dip and a stick of salami. How the fuck does he maintain that beautiful body when he eats all this stuff?

"Is this the bachelor basket? I still see you haven't lost your penchant for licorice."

"It's my favorite and I am considering myself a bachelor. I spoke to my lawyer this morning and he's drawing up divorce papers."

"How do you feel about it?"

"It's so freeing. I can breathe again. I'm waiting for the fallout though. I'm sure old Jonathan the third will be calling to bitch me out. Tell me I'm making a huge mistake. For him it's a mistake but the merger is finished so I'm not quite sure what his problem will be. I'm through making myself unhappy to make him happy."

I nod. "I told you that. You can't live your life for him. You have a good job and you don't rely on him to take care of you so why worry about him?"

"Seriously, I still care what he thinks. Can you believe that? I can't shake that shit from when I was a kid looking for his approval."

"It's time you let it go."

He reaches up and strokes my jawline with his thumb. I resist the urge to close my eyes as a memory of him doing this emerges from the past.

"You always have my back."

Anxious to escape what I feel is becoming an awkward moment; I tell him I have to finish shopping. Never mind the fact that his touch has caused my stomach to have butterflies. He can still excite me. JC tells me goodbye and I'm not shocked that his hand brushes my ass as he walks by.

CHAPTER 16

I complete the shopping in less than a half hour, weaving around dawdling shoppers. The cashier line is another story. All the check-outs are busy, and I page through a tabloid as I wait. By the time I reach the gum snapping blue haired girl at the counter, I'm exhausted. I just want to go home already.

As if waiting for me, JC meets me in the front of the store. He's just checked out too and he has a couple of cloth bags in his hand. I forgot to take mine and the plastic on the four bags is making my hands sweat. Juggling them with my briefcase is no easy feat, they're heavy.

"Give them here."

I look up and JC is holding out his hand. He's switched the cloth bags to his right hand is offering his left. I'm grateful and hand him two of the four bags.

"Give them all to me. You look exhausted."

"No," I protest but he puts his hand on the remaining two bag's handles and I give them over to him. We live a few blocks apart and he can drop me off then head to his apartment building.

"I didn't mean to offend you this morning," I blurt out.

"Lexi, it's to be expected. When will you realize some of the things I say I do for shock value?"

"That's not very professional of you and bordering on sexual harassment. If you were any other man..."

JC smirks. "I thought we were friends?"

"We are but at work, you're still my boss and it's inappropriate."

"I promise to try to control myself. It's not easy when I'm around you."

I guess that's the best he can do but I'll take it. I feel like he wants to test me to see how strong my resolve is.

"Megan asked about you yesterday," I say.

"I thought she hated me."

"She's gotten over our breakup. She said she misses you."

He lowers his voice. "You know she hooked up with Hunter before."

"You knew?"

"You didn't?"

"No, she just told me last night. I can't believe it."

"They always had chemistry. Didn't you notice how they flirted with each other when we were together?"

"Yeah, but they were teenagers."

"I caught them making out once. Hunter had his hand up her shirt."

I scowl. "Why is it that I'm just finding out about this now?"

"I knew you'd be upset so I didn't say anything. Plus, I promised Hunter that I wouldn't say anything."

"Oh, that old bros before hos?"

"Lexi, you're hardly a ho."

"I know, I'm just saying."

We weave our way around people walking dogs, a pair of skateboarding teens and kids texting before we arrive at my building. JC hands the bags in his hand over to me. I kiss his cheek.

"Thank you for your help."

"Enjoy your weekend."

"Without Brianna, that won't be hard. Call me if you want to hang out."

I nod and head into my building. In the reflection of the glass door, I see him watching me as I go inside. When I get upstairs and unlock the door, I can hear conversation going on, Noah's voice and a woman's I don't recognize. I bring the groceries to the kitchen and start unpacking them. I don't want to bother him if he's with a client, so I keep quiet.

"Lexi?" he calls.

"Yes, Noah."

"Can you come to my office."

"Give me a minute."

I put the last of the groceries away and go to his office where I see two women with blonde hair sitting in front of his desk facing him. They turn as I enter.

"This is Vivian and my daughter Rory."

I smooth my dress and walk over to shake their hands. The picture I saw of Vivian didn't do her justice. She's stunningly beautiful and well groomed, with soft gray eyes, high cheekbones and perfectly straight white teeth. Rory is the image of her except she has Noah's blue eyes. They make quite a pair and I'm sure could turn heads when they walk down the street.

I immediately feel inadequate next to Vivian with my tawny blonde hair and light brown eyes. Nothing stands out on me compared to her.

"Noah's told me a lot about you," Vivian says.

"I hope it's all good."

I glance at him and he's got a strained smile across his face.

"Vivian and Rory came to the city to make final arrangements for her apartment. I thought we could have dinner with them if you're up to it."

I'm not. I just want to take a bath and relax but now I need to entertain his daughter and, I guess Vivian is his ex-girlfriend or baby mama.

"Sure, where would you like to go?"

"How about French's? You're always talking about what great food they have."

Seriously Noah! Why don't we just pick the table in the back where JC got me off several times in the middle of dinner crowd. But Noah has no idea the things we did in that booth. I wouldn't dare tell him.

"Do you really want to go to mid-town on a Friday? French's is probably going to be crowded."

"I thought you could call Paul and see if he could get you in. After all, you do have an in since he's the owner and you're friends."

I sigh. "Let me call him."

I go to the bedroom and dial Paul's cell, sincerely hoping that he can't accommodate us. I'm in no mood to change and travel for dinner. Unfortunately, Paul promises to give me a table for 7:30, which gives us a little under an hour to get there. I let everyone know and head to the bedroom to change. Noah joins me a few minutes later.

"Lexi, are you upset with me?"

"A little advanced notice would have been nice."

"I'm sorry. I was busy all day and they showed up a couple of hours ago."

So, you couldn't text me and give me a heads up?

I stand in the closet in my bra and panties deciding what I should wear. I'm not in the mood to dress up and I can go casual, but I don't want to look like an old rag next to the stylish beauty queens. I select a pair of beige linen slacks with a black lace trimmed silk camisole top. I realize I'm going to have to change my bra to strapless.

When I'm dressed, Noah saunters into the bedroom as I'm applying a fresh coat of makeup. He kisses my shoulders and runs his hand down my arm. I'm feeling heated but that slowly disappears when I think about how annoyed I am with him.

"Ready to go?" he asks.

"Yes, let's get this over with."

"You say it like you're going to your execution."

"I'm sorry. I'm tired."

"You can stay home if you're not up to it?"

Hell no. And look like a bitch in front of your daughter and ex? No way. I need to assert my possessiveness over Noah from the start. I want this woman to realize that he's my soon to be husband, not just the father of her daughter.

I take his hand and we walk out of the bedroom together. Rory and Vivian are sitting on the couch and smile when we come out.

"You make such a lovely couple," Vivian says.

"Thank you. Shall we head out?"

Dinner goes better than expected. The restaurant is crowded but Paul has come through and given us a great table in the back, the one and the same table JC and I did inappropriate things. I'm embarrassed and my cheeks burn even though Noah is not aware of why.

"Babe, are you okay? Your cheeks are flushed. I hope you're not getting sick."

He launches into how proud he is of me for getting the director's position at Barker and Lopez which further embarrasses me. Vivian and Rory are gracious and offer their congratulations. I let them carry the conversation through the meal while I dig into my steak. I haven't eaten since breakfast and I'm starved.

Paul comes by to chat and mentions I need to tell JC to stop by because he hasn't seen him since we had lunch together. Noah scowls at me and I realize I forgot to mention that we went out to lunch on my first day. I didn't think it was a big deal since it was just to get acquainted in our working relationship.

I'm positive that after Vivian and Rory part ways with us, Noah will give me the third degree. I'm not looking forward to tonight. In the cab home, he doesn't say anything, nor does he touch me. It's a sure sign he's pissed off about my lack of revelation.

When the cab pulls up to our building, I get out and go inside while he pays the driver. He places his hand firmly on my back when the elevator comes and steers me into the elevator. We can't talk because there are other occupants but as soon as we get into the loft, it's on.

"Did you forget to tell me something?" he growls.

"Noah, it was a business lunch."

"With your ex."

"With my boss. It wasn't like I was going to fuck him."

"He wants you and you encourage him."

"Where the fuck is this coming from?"

"I saw you on Memorial Day weekend. You spent a lot of time with him."

"Yeah I did, while you were playing cards and getting drunk."

I stalk off to the bedroom to change. Noah seems itching to continue the argument and follows me to the closet.

"You're not going to let me forget that, will you?"

"It was so unlike you."

"First off, let's not get off subject. Why didn't you tell me you had lunch with JC if it wasn't such a big deal? Where did you go after?"

I turn with a shocked look on my face. Is he accusing me of cheating on him?

"Back to work. Do you think we went to a hotel room? I don't understand why this is an issue now. It happened two weeks ago; can we move on?"

"Where else have you been with him?"

"Well if you want to know, he helped me carry the groceries home today."

"Why was he shopping with you?"

"He wasn't. JC just happened to be there."

"Don't you think it's coincidental? What else haven't you told me?"

I think to when JC came over for pancakes. If I tell Noah, he'll lose it. He also doesn't know t JC is getting a divorce. This would all be fuel for the fire, and I don't want to add to it, so I keep quiet.

"You know everything. Why are you jealous all of a sudden?"

"It's not all of a sudden."

"So, you tell me you're okay with me working for JC but now you have doubts?"

"It's not the working for him I have a problem with."

"Noah, why don't you just come out and say it? You're afraid I'm going to end up fucking him, aren't you? Tell me the scenario because I'm really curious."

He glares at me; I can see his jaw clenching and the vein on the side of his forehead is becoming pronounces.

"I know guys like him, that's all. You said he cheated on you so why wouldn't he cheat on his wife?"

"You're not saying that. You're saying you don't trust me, not him. I don't understand how you can say that. Have I done anything to make you feel that way?"

I can feel my eyes start to burn as the tears threaten to come. I try to force them back, but I lose, and they spill over my lids. I face my clothes and sniffle then start to sob. Noah reaches for me and I push his hands away, rush past him to the bathroom and lock the door.

He knocks and calls my name several times, but I ignore him. Is this what he's been thinking about me? That I'm going to cheat on him? We've been together for over two years and I've never seen this behavior from him. Plenty of men have paid attention to me during that time but he just shrugged it off. Now it's an issue?

I think that there are only two factors that have recently occurred to drive his reaction. One, that I now work for my ex and two, that he now has contact with his ex. He mentioned Vivian a few times and, in that time, he always seemed to become dewy eyed. Maybe it's him who wants to cheat. Maybe he's still in love with her since their relationship ended so abruptly.

I don't know, but whatever the problem, we better fix it soon. Our wedding is only four months away. I wipe away my tears and decide to draw a bath. I can use it after the busy week I've had. I pour in bath beads as the water is running. It fills the air with the rich scent of vanilla.

I spend almost an hour in the tub, refilling it when hot water when it starts to cool. I don't hear from Noah during that time and it's fine with me. I'm so angry at him I'm not sure if I want to share the same bed with him tonight. I'd rather sleep alone in the guest room.

My skin is pruny by the time I come out, dry myself and put on my robe. Noah is not in the bedroom and it's well past eleven. I find him in the living room watching a baseball game that went into extra innings. He's got a tumbler of something in his hand, probably gin which is his go to if he drinks liquor.

I walk into the kitchen to get a bottle of water and he comes up behind me, almost scaring me to death.

"I think it's better if I sleep in the guest room tonight," I say.

"No, Lexi. I need you in my bed," he whispers as he strokes my hair.

"You should've thought of that before you accused me of cheating on you. How could you Noah? I would never do that especially when I know how it feels."

"I'm sorry. I lost my head. I don't know what I was thinking."

"JC is my ex and we work together. If you don't want me to talk to him outside of work, just say so."

"I want you to do what you think is right."

"Think of it this way. I'm not asking you to stop talking to Vivian, am I?"

"That's different, she's the mother of my child."

"But she's still your ex."

"Okay, I get it. Please sleep in our bed tonight."

"I will."

He buries his head in my shoulder and he inhales against my skin.

"You smell delicious. I could eat you."

"I'll take it under advisement."

Noah gives me a look of longing as he heads to the bathroom. I take off my robe and slip on my nightgown, forgoing a pair of panties. I'm dozing when Noah presses his body next to mine. He smells from minty toothpaste and something I can't put my finger on, a floral scent. I drift into a restless sleep unsure if we have a future.

CHAPTER 17

After our argument, things improve between us. Noah is a lot more attentive and sex is back to an every night occurrence. I do notice he fields daily phone calls from either Vivian or Rory. I can't stop that, and I don't want to be a wedge between him and his daughter, but something bothers me about the constant interaction.

By the next Friday, we're anticipating a visit from Lucian. I haven't seen him for months and I can't wait. He's four years younger than Noah and at thirty-two; he could pass for twenty-two with his boyish looks. I prepare the guest room for him, hoping he doesn't mind the boxes Noah's stored there.

"Everything all set in here?" Noah asks as he pokes his head in the guest room door.

"Yes, bed sheets are changed, and I dusted. I hope he doesn't mind using the hall bath."

"Why would he mind?"

"I don't know. I'm just saying."

"He's not a snob, it won't matter to him."

Noah's phone rings and as he walks away, I can hear him say Vivian's name. It's the third time tonight he's talked to her. I can hear him laughing in his office. I'm happy he's re-established a relationship with Rory's mother, but I feel envious he's so easy-going with her.

Maybe if I get a free chance with Lucian, I can question him about their relationship. It's not that I want to snoop, but I'm curious about how they were together.

After I finish in the guest room, I head to the kitchen to make sure the refrigerator is fully stocked. Beer is low and I know Lucian loves Killian's. I specifically bought a couple of six packs. I open the pantry door and add several bottles to chill.

It was a long day at work. JC was not in the office, he had to go see his divorce attorney. Amazingly enough, Brianna agreed to the divorce without much of a fight. His father is putting up more of an argument than she. Jonathan the third was plenty angry when he found out the marriage was over.

I sit down to read a bridal magazine I picked up a few days ago. We're getting close and I'm nervous. In a few short months I'm going to be Mrs. Noah Wilton. I must have dozed off because I feel lips on my cheek, and I wake to see Lucian's smiling face hovering over me.

"Luc, how are you?"

"I'm great. You look beautiful. I always tell Noah how lucky he is."

A hot blush coming to my face. "Thank you."

I stand up to hug him and he wraps his arms around me, lifting me up, then plants a kiss right on my lips. I see Noah over his shoulder scowling.

"Alright you two with the love fest."

Lucian puts me down and turns to his brother. "Jealous she might like me better than you?"

"I highly doubt that, Luc. You don't have as big a dick as I do."

"Would you like to compare?"

Noah's hands rest on his zipper and I stop the banter.

"Enough with the pissing contest boys."

"We're ordering in. What would you like, Luc?"

"I'm craving some good old New York pizza."

My mouth starts to water because it's been a long time since I've had it. Antonio's around the corner makes the best Neapolitan pizza. I beg Noah to get a couple of pies. He grumbles because they don't deliver but then smiles and grabs his wallet while I make the call.

"Luc, do you want to come?"

"I'd rather freshen up a little if you don't mind."

"Okay, be back in a little while. Keep your hands off my fiancée."

I stick my tongue out at Noah as he walks out the door with a smirk on his face. I'm sure he has his usual phrase in his mind "don't stick your tongue out unless you plan to use it."

Now is the time I can question Luc about Vivian. I'm bursting with curiosity. We head into the kitchen and Luc sits down at the island.

"Would you like a beer? I got your favorite, Killian's"

"You're awesome. If Noah wasn't marrying you, I would. Speaking of married, how's Megan. Is she married to that Jeremy guy yet?"

"Actually, no. They broke up and she's moving to Manhattan."

"Really?" I see his face brighten.

"What's up?"

"I like Megan, she's a great kisser."

I'm going to kill my sister if I find out she fucked Lucian. What is with her and messing around with my fiancé's brothers?

"How do you know that?"

"We messed around a few times."

"By messing around do you mean…"

"No. I wanted to but she said no."

"Speaking of kissing, can you tell me about Vivian and Noah? He doesn't really tell me much and I'm afraid he'll think I'm prying."

"What do you want to know?"

I realize I haven't given Lucian his beer and take one from the refrigerator, handing him a bottle opener from the drawer.

"What was their relationship like?"

"They were inseparable from the time they began dating. He would talk to her for hours if they couldn't spend time together. They had sex almost immediately, their chemistry was that strong."

"How do you know that?"

"My room was next to Noah's. Our parents had the downstairs master, so they didn't know what was going on. He used to sneak Vivian into his room, and they would fuck for hours."

"You listened?"

"How could I not. The moaning was so loud. He would sneak her out of the house just before the sun came up. Her house was even larger than ours, so I doubt her parents knew she was gone."

"Wow," I say as I begin chewing on the inside of my cheek.

"I remember we double dated; I was only fourteen at the time. They would spend the whole time kissing. It was so annoying and embarrassing. I knew what was coming that night. I eventually got a pair of ear plugs so I could sleep."

"Did you ever confront Noah about the noise?"

"He told me to mind my own business and if I told on him, he would beat me within an inch of my life. I knew he was kidding."

"He would never hurt you."

Luc nodded. "So, for months they would fuck almost every night, even if it was bad weather. She only lived one road over."

"They never got caught?"

"Almost. I was sick and my mother came up to check on me and heard them. I guess they heard us talking and stopped. She went to check on Noah, and he was fast asleep in bed. The minute she went back downstairs, they started up again."

Lucian takes a long pull of his beer before he continues.

"His grades started to slip toward the end of the year and my father got pissed. You know Noah had been accepted to Stanford. Vivian was going to USC and then it all stopped when she found out she was pregnant."

My mouth dropped open even though I knew the story.

"Noah was willing to marry her and go to USC, but my father forbade it and said he wasn't paying for his tuition. Noah said fuck it and enlisted in the Marines. I think the worst thing in his life was to leave Vivian and then have her hate him when he came home. He gave up being a parent because he wanted Vivian to be happy."

"I feel horrible he had to do that."

"Well you know old Richard. Have to keep up appearances. Noah was an embarrassment to him since he knocked up Vivian."

"I met her and Rory last week. She's beautiful."

"Which one?"

"Both."

I look down at my feet.

"Lexi don't read into it. Noah loves you more than anything. Vivian is his past. She's the mother of his child but he's moved on."

I'm not so sure with all the contact he's been having with Vivian since we all had dinner together. I want to ask more but Noah comes through the door with the pizza and the aroma reminds me I'm starving. I set out plates and we eat at the breakfast bar. Lucian inhales a slice as if he hasn't eaten in weeks and it makes me laugh.

"This is so good. We don't have pizza like this in Boston."

"You're here for the weekend, pace yourself," Noah says.

Right after we finish, Noah's cell rings again and he excuses himself to answer it. Again, I hear him in his office laughing and my face clouds. Lucian stares at me.

"What's wrong?"

"It's Vivian. This is the fourth time she's called since I've been home. I wonder how many times she called today."

Lucian frowns. "Let's sit on the terrace, it's nice out."

I know he's trying to distract me, but I can see he has a worried look on his face. I hand him another beer and pour a glass of white wine for myself. It's balmy out in the mid-June evening. I sit looking out at the city not saying anything. Down below, you can hear the traffic and I look out across the street at the trees of Central Park blowing in the gentle breeze.

"Lexi, I told you not to read into it."

"Luc, how can I not. Don't you think it's strange that he talks to her so much?"

"Rory's coming to school here. I'm sure that's what it's about."

"I'm trying to be rational about this but it's hard. Did Noah tell you that I work for my ex, JC?"

"No shit? Seriously?"

"Yes. I'm the director of marketing and he's the VP. I guess I should've paid attention when they mentioned who my boss would be. I was so excited to get the job."

"Has Noah said anything about it?"

"He was initially secure but then we had a spat and it got ugly."

"And you think this is why he's talking to Vivian? Maybe to get you back?"

"The thought has crossed my mind. I've never seen him jealous until now."

"I think you have nothing to worry about."

After twenty minutes, Noah finally joins us with a beer in hand. I let him and Lucian talk and go inside to take a bath. The water feels good and I doze off leaning against the rim. I don't know what time it is but when I wake, the water is cool and I'm chilled.

I get out and drain the tub then hop in the shower to warm myself. By the time I finish, Noah and Lucian are watching a ball game on television and sharing a bowl of popcorn. I leave them alone because I hate baseball and sit on the bed with my laptop to play solitaire.

It's close to eleven when they both turn in for the night. Lucian peeks in the door to say goodnight as Noah brushes his teeth. I'm under the sheet when he comes to bed and he takes his familiar spot behind me, with his arm securely around me. I fade off to sleep only to be awakened a few hours later by his cell.

I hear him in hushed tones on the other side of the bed and I wonder what the emergency is this time. I click on the bedside light and turn to me just as he's getting out of bed. His face is ashen.

"Noah, what is it?"

"Rory had a car accident. She was coming home from a party and someone hit her."

I feel panic because I don't want to ask the questions, but he instead offers.

"She's pretty banged up and asked for me. I'm going."

"Now?"

"Alexa, she's my daughter. I'm going."

We hear a knock on the door and Noah opens it. Lucian is at the door rubbing sleep from his eyes.

"Everything alright in here?"

"No, Rory had a car accident."

Now Lucian is wide awake. "Is she okay? I just saw her yesterday."

"She's okay but pretty banged up. She's asking for me."

"So, you're going now?"

"Yes. You can stay here with Lexi."

He says it like it's an order rather than a request.

"I plan on it, but I wanted to spend some time with you."

"I hope to be back by Sunday."

"Just in time for me to leave."

"Lucian, don't start. You can come to Boston with me if you want."

"I just got here today. As long as Rory's okay."

"She's fine. I'll be back on Sunday. Maybe Richard will give you a few extra days off and we can hang out."

It's strange to me how both he and Lucian call their father by his first name.

"I highly doubt that. He's leaving in about a week and a half for Japan, so he wants to make sure I'm briefed on all our ongoing projects. I'll try though."

Lucian disappears back into his room and I watch Noah pack a few things in a black duffel bag he took from the closet. It's more clothes than he'll need for a couple of days but I'm not going to comment. The last thing he does is kiss me goodbye. It's more like a peck rather than an "I'll see you in a few days kiss" and then he's gone. He garages an SUV a few blocks away for work. I assume that's where he's heading.

I snuggle back into bed and check my phone since I'm up. I have a few texts messages from JC. I wonder what time he sent me these. I check and it was after midnight and I think he's buzzed based on the nature of them. There are three in all and I read through them.

Hey gorgeous, want to join me at McCorvey's for a beer?

Come on, you can't be asleep you sexy thing. Put on something tight and join me.

I was so in the mood to see that hot ass of yours. I'll talk to you tomorrow.

I don't know why I don't delete them right away, but I don't. I know I better before Noah gets back or he'll have a fit. He already accused me of being with JC. This would just give him license to assume the worst.

I put my phone on the nightstand and go back to sleep. When I wake, the sun is shining through the window shades. I forgot to pull the string to shut them tight. Wondering what time it is, I pick up my phone. Holy fuck, it's almost ten. I received several texts from Noah about two hour ago.

I'm here at the hospital. Rory is fine and I'm going to stay at my parent's house. Text me when you get this message.

Hey babe, I'm glad that Rory is okay.

I wait a few minutes but get no reply, so I decide to get myself a cup of coffee. Lucian is sitting on the terrace when I enter the kitchen. There's a fresh pot of coffee already made. I pour some in a mug and join him. The fog in the park is lifting as the sun begins to blaze bright.

"Hey sleepyhead. I thought you'd never get up."

"I was tired. I had a busy week and with the 2:00 AM phone call, that just made it worse. Have you talked to Noah?"

"Yeah, he called me a couple of hours ago. Rory's fine. Sleeping comfortably and they should release her from the hospital later today."

"He texted me and I was asleep. I texted him back but got no answer."

"He might be sleeping."

"Noah said he was going to stay at your parent's house."

"Good luck with that. They said they were going to the house in Chatham this weekend. I'm not sure if he has a key."

"So where would he go if he couldn't stay there?"

"Maybe a hotel."

My mind starts racing. Would he stay with Vivian? I don't want that.

"What's the matter?"

"Nothing."

"Come on Lexi, I know you better than that."

"Would he stay with Vivian?"

"I doubt it."

Would he even tell me if he did?

"Are you sure?"

"As far as I know, no. What's got you so insecure? I've never seen you this way before."

"I'm just on edge with everything. In less than four months we're getting married and we still have so much to take care of.

"So, get on Noah's ass. I know he gets too involved in his work."

"What would you like to do today?"

"I'm game for anything but I'd love to go to Central Park."

I brighten because I love to walk around the park in the warm weather. I'm surprised he didn't say something like visit the South Street Seaport.

"I can handle that. I need to shower."

"Go, I'll clean up the coffee cups while you're in there."

I take a quick shower and put on a pair of khaki shorts and a white tank top. I'm in no mood to blow dry my hair so I put it in a ponytail. When I come out of the bedroom, Lucian is sitting on the couch reading one of my bridal magazines.

"Hey, are you serious?"

"What? These women look beautiful. I can't wait to see you in one of these dresses."

I almost wish that Noah felt that way. Lucian always says things to me that he would never. It's not that he's not complimentary, because he is but he would never get all sappy like Lucian. I can feel my face getting hot from embarrassment.

"Let's go."

Lucian gets up and offers his arm to me. I wrap my hand around his forearm, and we head to the elevator. The park entrance is just a short walk from the apartment. It's teeming with activity because the weather is hot and sunny. We walk around the moms with strollers, joggers and park entertainers. I'm beginning to sweat and release Lucian's arm, wiping my hand on my shorts.

As we forge a path through the park, I hear my name called. Turning, I look for anyone familiar but can't see who it came from. We continue to walk, and I hear my name again. I turn around and see JC behind me with Hunter in tow.

As usual, he's beautiful. His chest is bare, and every ridge and muscle is glistening with sweat. His light blue t-shirt is tucked into the waistband of his basketball shorts and hanging down his thigh. Hunter is dressed much the same but holds a soccer ball in one hand and a bottle of water in the other.

I know I shouldn't be having thoughts about JC's half naked body, but I can't help it. He looks so sexy. His sandy hair is soaked with sweat and hangs on his forehead in a mass of strings.

"Hey, what are you doing here?"

"Same as you, just hanging out."

He offers his hand to Lucian, "Camden. This is my brother Hunter and you are?"

"I'm sorry, where are my manners. This is Lucian, Noah's brother."

They shake hands and Lucian strikes up a conversation with Hunter about the New York Red Bulls Soccer team since he's wearing their shirt. I pull JC over to the side and he asks why I didn't text him back last night.

"I was with Noah and Lucian."

He raises his eyebrows and I know he's thinking about a threesome.

"You're a pervert," I whisper.

"How could you possibly know what I'm thinking?"

"Because I know you."

"Where's Noah?"

"He had to go to Boston early this morning for an emergency."

I'm not ready to tell him about Rory yet. I didn't even discuss it with Megan.

"Oh. So, you're out with your brother-in-law?"

"He had a scheduled visit and came last night."

Again, the raised eyebrows and I realize it's the word "came."

"Would you stop it!"

"I just love to get you riled up. You're so sexy when you get like that."

I gesture over to Lucian. "Stop it. That's Noah's brother for heaven sake. What were you doing at McCorvey's last night?"

"Drinking with Hunter and Megan."

This is news to me. I had no idea she got in touch with Hunter or JC.

"Really? Is that why you texted me?"

"No. I texted because I wanted to hang out. I miss you, Lexi."

"Shh."

"They aren't paying attention to us."

He removes his shirt from his waistband and wipes at the sweat on his chest and stomach. It's making me heated more than I am from the weather. Why is he having this effect on me?

"And what happened with Megan?"

"They didn't go home together if that's what you want to know. She did ask Hunter to help her move some stuff to her new apartment next week. I told her I would help if she could get you there, too."

"Next weekend I'm not sure what we're doing. I'll let you know."

"We should hang out tonight. Is Noah coming back?"

"Not until tomorrow. Do you really think it's a good idea to hang out?"

"Though I would love to, I'm not going to eat you."

"Fuck JC, stop. You can't say things like that."

I'm beginning to feel faint in the heat and I begin to walk over to the benches. Hunter and Lucian are kicking the ball around and JC sits next to me.

"Are you okay? You don't look good."

"I feel a little dizzy."

"You need water. I'll be right back."

He jogs over to a cart in the corner where a man is selling drinks and ice cream. When he comes back, he has four bottles of water and hands me one, Lucian and Hunter the others while keeping one for himself.

"Drink. You'll feel better."

I sip at the water and gradually the dizziness fades. He puts his water bottle which is almost full on the back of my neck. It feels good. We spend the next several minutes talking and decide to go to lunch. There are a couple of nice small restaurants a few blocks away. JC slips his t-shirt on thereby ending my peep show.

CHAPTER 18

We walk to a small bistro that has tables outside on the street. I want to sit inside but they all insist we remain, so I agree. The tables are small and made of green wrought iron and the patio is crowded. JC sits next to me and I'm sure that when his knee keeps hitting mine, it's done on purpose since Lucian's never touches me. I'm quite positive it's no accident when his hand grips my lower thigh and begins to knead me. I dig my nails in his hand and he yanks it away, giving me a wounded look.

Lucian and Hunter are deep in conversation about sports and I lean over and tell JC that was inappropriate.

"Remember, sexual harassment?" I whisper.

"I can't help it," JC whispers back.

I want to question him further but it's not easy in such close proximity to my fiancé's brother. I sip at my water while trying to avoid JC's gaze.

Fortunately, our lunch comes out though I've lost my appetite. My stomach is in knots. It's nearing almost 2:00 PM and I haven't heard from Noah. This is becoming a habit. I know his daughter was in an accident, but it seems like since she came on the scene, his communication is lacking.

I pick at my Cobb salad and JC gives me a hard stare. I know he's worried because I've been skipping meals since I started working. It's no big deal because usually I'll make up for my lack of one meal for another. I want to tell him I had almost three slices of pizza last night. When the check comes, I dig into my pocket for some cash, but Lucian pushes the money away and ends up buying lunch for everyone.

"What's going on tonight?" Lucian asks.

"JC and I are going out to a dance club in midtown. If you guys aren't doing anything you can join us. Megan said she might come." Hunter says.

Hmm, my sister is really getting chummy with JC and Hunter now that she is planning on moving to the city in a week.

"How come you know more about Megan than I do?" I said.

"You should've come out with us last night. Megan misses you."

"I miss her, too."

"I haven't seen Megan for such a long time," Lucian says.

"If you want to go out tonight, we can. Noah won't mind if you come with me."

"Oh, my big brother doesn't like you to go out?"

"No, it's not that. He just prefers that he's with me when I do."

We get up and say our goodbyes, promising to meet them at Vapor, one of the hottest clubs in midtown. I haven't been to one for a long time and I'm not even sure what I should wear.

After we separate and head back to my apartment, I tell Lucian that I'm not sure this was such a good idea.

"Why not Lexi? You're still young and if my brother gets pissed, too bad. You're getting married, not dying."

"I just don't want him to be upset."

"He won't be."

We spend the rest of the afternoon relaxing in the air conditioning. Around seven, Noah finally calls me.

"How's Rory?"

"Fine. She's home resting. I just got back."

"Where are you?"

"I'm at my parent's house."

"Lucian told me that they went to Chatham for the weekend."

I hear silence on the other side of the line as if he's thinking of what to say.

"I have a key."

"Oh, he said he wasn't sure if you did or not."

"Lexi, is there something you want to ask?"

"Not at all. I just was wondering is all. I'm going to a club tonight."

"With who?"

"Lucian, JC, Megan and Hunter."

"How did that come about?"

I explain to him how Lucian and I went to the park and met JC and Hunter.

"It should be fun. I haven't been to a club for a long time."

"Just make sure you wear your engagement ring."

"What's that supposed to mean?"

"It means that I don't want guys pawing my fiancée."

"I doubt you have to worry. Besides, I'll be with Lucian."

"He's not the one I'm worried about. I have another call coming in. I'll talk to you later."

Before I can say, I love you, Noah hangs up. So, he's jealous. I'm sure when he said to wear my engagement ring, it's not because of other guys at the club, it's because of JC. I know I'm on dangerous ground with him. Once Noah finds out he's getting a divorce, it will get worse.

After my call with Noah, I decide to take a bath. We aren't leaving the apartment until 10:00 PM so I have time to luxuriate in the tub. I fill it with vanilla scented beads and let the water get good and hot. I slip into the water and put my head back on the rim of the tub. The heat feels good and I love the smell of vanilla. A half hour later, Lucian knocks on the door.

"Lexi, are you okay?"

"I'm taking a bath. I was in the mood."

"Sorry, I didn't mean to disturb you. I'm having leftover pizza. Do you want me to heat a slice for you?"

"Yes, please. I'll be out in a few minutes."

I quickly got out of the tub and dried herself, then put on Noah's robe. If Lucian wasn't here, I would've put on my own, but the short pink satin barely covered my ass and was not appropriate. When I got out to the kitchen, Lucian had set a couple of places with paper plates.

"Do you want a glass of wine?" I asked.

"I'll have a beer. Any Killian's left?"

"Of course. I stocked the refrigerator yesterday."

I handed Lucian a bottle after I popped the top and poured myself a glass of white wine. The buzzer went off on the oven and I pulled the pan out while telling Lucian what Noah said.

"Do you think he's jealous?"

"Lexi, what's going on with you and JC?"

"Nothing. I work for him."

"It's so obvious he's in love with you. I saw the way he looks at you."

"Lucian, I don't think so," but I did. I know he has feelings for me and it's not good. I'm not sure I can continue to work for him. The sexual tension between us is very palpable. I try to ignore it but sometimes…

"I'll be watching him tonight."

"He's harmless. He knows I love Noah. JC had his chance and he blew it."

"Can you help me with my hair?"

"Really?"

"It needs to be calmed down. I can't wear this mop in the club."

I run my fingers through his thick sandy colored hair. It's the same color that Noah has though he wears is cut shorter and neatly combed.

"I think a bit of gel will help tame this. Come to my bathroom."

It took me fifteen minutes, but I managed to get his hair to wear perfectly. He's adorable and I'm sure he'll be getting female attention all night. It's close to nine and I want to get dressed. I push Lucian out of my bedroom and close the door so I can find a something to wear.

I don't have a ton to choose from. Most of my clothing is for business but I do have several dresses for going out. I find two short dresses, one black that's open to my lower back and one strapless burgundy dress. I keep comparing them and finally decide on the black one. I'm feeling sexy tonight and select a black lace thong. Because of the open back, I opt for no bra. I can get away with it.

I dress and when I come out to the living room, Lucian is waiting for me. He's wearing a pair of black jeans and a button-down gray dress shirt. He looks handsome and whistles when he sees me.

"You look great."

"So, do you."

I put on a pair of four-inch heels I brought out from my closet and a small purse I can wear on my wrist. I'm ready to go. My phone rings and I don't recognize the number, but I answer just in case it's Noah. It's not, it's Megan. I forgot to add her to my contacts. She's meeting us at the club and I'm glad to have another woman along.

The club has a long line when we arrive. I'm not looking forward to waiting for what seems like at least two hours. I text Hunter and a reply text tells me to come to the door. The bouncer lets us right in which draws protest from the people behind the rope.

Hunter is waiting just inside the door to take us to the table that he reserved. I wonder how he got us in and reserved a table with such short notice. I don't really care, I'm just happy to be out for the night. I was beginning to feel housebound night after night.

At the table, JC stands when he sees me and Lucian is right, I see the look on his face, it's love. How stupid of me not to notice before. Had he been looking at me that way since I started work three weeks ago?

Megan arrives shortly after and Hunter kisses her on the cheek, then pulls her out on the dance floor. I watch them swaying together, their bodies molded against each other. I glance at Lucian and notice a scowl on his face as his eyes are glued to them.

I'm sitting next to JC and he plants a soft kiss on my cheek and practically screams how beautiful I look. The music is quite loud and not really a great place to have a talk. I have so many questions I want to ask him. The first being if he's in love with me. I don't expect a truthful answer, but I want to see his body language.

Instead, I ignore him and sip the martini with extra olives that the waitress put in front of me. Leave it to JC to remember my favorite drink. Lucian decides to interrupt the love fest between Megan and Hunter by cutting in. They end up dancing together.

JC leans in and begins talking to me in my ear. I can feel his hot breath as it caresses my skin. His lips are practically pressed against the tender flesh. I'm half expecting him to take my diamond studded earlobe in his mouth, but he doesn't.

"Are you having fun?"

I nod so I don't have to lean in to talk. I don't want to be that close to his face.

"Lexi, what's wrong?"

"We need to talk," I yell.

He gives me a puzzled look and as Lucian, Hunter and Megan come back from the dance floor, I pull JC's arm for him to follow me. I look for somewhere quieter so we can have a discussion. I notice the club has a lounge area with a door that leads into the bathrooms.

I pull him by the hand through the door. There's a long hallway with several leather benches and I pull him past the line of women to the one furthest away. I don't want anyone to hear our conversation.

JC smirks. "If you wanted to get me alone, all you had to do was ask."

"Be serious. I need to ask you something."

"Anything."

"Are you in love with me?"

"I'm not going to lie to you."

"That's not an answer."

"I've wanted you ever since I saw your name come up on the candidates list for the marketing director position."

I frown. "Are you saying you told them to hire me? I didn't get the job legitimately?"

I know I'm avoiding the elephant in the room, but this is important to me that I get a job based on my merits not that the boss wants to fuck me.

"You did. You were the most qualified of all the applicants. The fact that I wanted you is just icing on the cake."

"It's far more complicated than that. I'm not available for you to love or fuck."

"That won't change how I feel. I love you. There I said it."

"You can't."

"That's self-righteous of you. Don't tell me I can't," JC growled.

"For how long?"

"I think forever. I've loved you for a long time. I gave you up and it was the biggest mistake I ever made but I couldn't undo it."

"You could've. I would've come back."

"You were hurt. What kind of dick would I have looked like if I came to you a day, a week, a month later and said I fucked up?"

"Someone who could admit they made an error. It's too late,

JC. You can't have me. That part of my life is closed. You had your chance."

"So, I'm just supposed to watch Noah take you off into the sunset?"

"Yes. He's marrying me in less than four months."

JC says nothing, then grabs my face between his hands and kisses me, hard. His tongue spears into my mouth, probing the recesses. I'm not sure what to do but my belly clenches and I begin to respond, then realize what's happening. I wrench my face out of his hands and pull away, slapping his cheek for good measure.

"Lexi, please, I'm sorry. Can't you see he's wrong for you?"

"He's not wrong for me. Noah has been nothing but decent. You hurt me all through our relationship and I kept letting you get away with it. Why wasn't I good enough for you, just tell me that?"

"You were more than good. I don't know why I couldn't stop. I knew I fucked up each time I did it."

"It's too late for you. You had your chance."

As I walk away from him, salty tears sting my eyes.

Back at the table, Lucian is sitting drinking a whiskey and twirling the cocktail napkin that came with it under his finger.

"What's the matter?" I ask.

He gestures with his head to the dance floor where Megan is pressed up against Hunter again. They should just get it over with and have sex already. I know it's going to lead there. The look on Lucian's face tells me he has a thing for Megan too.

"Do you like Megan?"

"Is it that obvious?"

"Yes, it is. Go ask her to dance. I'll run some interference with Hunter."

We both get up and I cut in-between Megan and Hunter and begin dancing with him. Lucian sidles up and takes my sister in his arms. In a couple of minutes, they're hardly moving, and their mouths are pressed against the other. I look at Hunter and he shrugs, continuing to dance with me.

For most of the rest of the night, I manage to stay away from JC. I know he's hurt because he stays seated at the table and nurses the Jack and Coke he ordered a couple of hours ago. I feel bad, but he had his chance long ago.

I go back to the table with Lucian and Megan, Hunter is off dancing with two women. He got over Megan pretty quickly. JC keeps glancing at me, and I give him a weak smile. I can't give him what he wants.

CHAPTER 19

It's nearly, 2:00 AM when we leave. We get out to the sidewalk and Megan announces Lucian is coming back to her friend Cindy's apartment. Her friend is away and gave her a key. I have a feeling a love connection is about to take place. So great, I get to sleep in the apartment alone. I'm not at all happy.

They're not even sharing a cab with us since Cindy lives a few blocks from the club. They'll walk and JC and I get to share an awkward cab ride home. I don't want to say no because it's late, so I let him hail a cab and slide in while he holds the door for me. Several silent minutes later, he starts talking.

"I'm sorry I did what I did. Please don't hate me."

"JC, I don't hate you. You're confused."

"I'm not confused. I've never been surer of something in my life."

"Why couldn't you tell me this years ago? Why now?"

"I was afraid you'd turn me down."

"I have to turn you down. I belong with Noah."

"I don't believe you do. I believe we were made for each other. If you just give me a chance to show you, I've changed."

"Do you know what you're asking? You're asking me to break

it off with Noah on the verge of my marriage to him. And suppose I did, and it didn't work out?"

"Are you saying you have feelings for me?"

"No, don't twist my words."

"I'm not but I want to know. You think I didn't see you looking at me yesterday in the park?"

"That was purely because you have a hot body, not that I'm attracted to you."

JC grinned. "Oh, so you think I'm hot?"

"We're getting off subject."

"It's a simple question. Do-you-think-I'm-hot?"

"No. Happy?"

"No, because you're lying."

"I'm not."

"Then do me one favor, kiss me and tell me you feel nothing."

"That's ridiculous."

"Why because you're afraid of what you'll feel?"

"No, because I'm faithful to my fiancé. What would it prove anyway?"

"That you love me too."

"No. I'm done having this conversation."

I cross my arms and look out the window. I can see from the corner of my eye that JC is staring at me but I'm not going to give him the satisfaction of meeting his gaze. A few more awkward minutes later and the cab pulls up to my building.

"JC, you need to get out so I can."

He doesn't move then finally slides out, once again holding the door for me. I say nothing to him as I head in. Then he grabs my arm just before I get there.

"Have coffee with me."

"I'm tired and I'm done spending time with you."

The fact is that I'm afraid of the emotions welling inside me. I do feel something for him but it's wrong and I need to be alone so

I can reconcile them. Maybe a good night's sleep and a rational head in the morning will prevail.

"Just one cup? Beansy is right around the corner."

It sounds tempting, a nice cup of coffee or a latte. But it's who I have to drink it with that worries me. I decline and leave JC standing on the street staring after me.

Finally, in my apartment, I realize I'm breathing erratically. I'm stuck when it comes to JC. I don't want to look for a new job and I love Noah. I'm going to have to figure out a course of action. I undress and slip under the sheets hoping that I fall asleep quickly, but I don't.

I toss and turn so much that by the time five rolls around, I still haven't gotten a decent fifteen minutes of sleep. So many things rattle around in my head. In a few short weeks many things have changed. I have a new job that's barely a month old, I'm a stepmother, my boss is in love with me, Noah has grown distant.

It's all a lot to take in right now. I lie on my side and look out the window. The sun is starting to rise and I'm exhausted. Maybe I can take a nap this afternoon. Noah is supposed to be home today, but I don't know when. Who knows when Lucian will come back? I wonder if he and Megan ended up sleeping together.

I get up and go back and forth between tea and coffee. In the end, I make a cup of ginger lemon tea. My head is feeling stuffy and I'm hoping that I'm not getting sick. The last thing I want to do is take a day off since I haven't worked at my new job for long. JC would probably think I was avoiding him.

I left my phone in the bedroom and can hear it going off. I hurry to see if it's Noah but it's not, it's JC.

Please tell me that you're not going to quit.

. . .

I'm not quitting. I deserve that job and you'll have to behave yourself when we're together.

Thank you.

I get no other text from JC, but I realize I need to delete the previous texts before Noah sees them. Not that he would snoop on my phone but just to be safe. I delete them and climb back into bed. It's where Noah finds me when he gets home at noon.

"Sweetie, wake up? Are you sick?"

"No," I mumble.

"What time did you get home last night?"

I'm seriously not in the mood to talk, but I answer him.

"Two. How's Rory?"

"She's banged up, but okay. Where's Lucian? Did he leave yet?"

"No. He's with Megan."

"Megan?"

I roll over on my back. "Noah, he likes her."

Noah raises his eyebrows. "Are you telling me he went home with her?"

"Yep. I'm sure they had a very active night."

"I'm going to have to have a talk with that boy."

"You certainly will not. Just because you don't like her doesn't mean you need to badmouth her to Lucian."

"But she's your sister."

"So? Big deal. Leave them be, they make a good match."

"That's your opinion."

"You just got home. Is this the conversation you want to have?"

He looks down at me. "No. I missed you."

"Then kiss me."

Noah pushes his lips against mine and I twirl my fingers into his hair. As we kiss, I get the distinct scent of perfume on him and it's not mine. My stomach starts to tighten, and I push him away.

"What's the matter?"

"I'm not feeling well. I don't want to get you sick."

He wrinkles his nose. "Thanks for letting me know."

He backs away from the bed and starts to undress, leaving his clothes in a heap by the closet. After I hear the clank of the glass shower doors, I race out of bed and pick up his shirt to smell it. It's rich with perfume, even his pants have the faint odor. The most worrisome part is that his boxers have the same scent.

How much perfume would someone have to wear for it to permeate right down to underwear? This is a familiar scent to me since I smelled it on Vivian when she was here with Rory. Maybe I'm overreacting but it's very suspicious. My mind starts going in a bunch of directions and none of them good. Did he fuck Vivian? The shower turns off and I quickly slip back into bed. The last thing I want is to have an argument with Noah.

"Are you getting up?" he says as he exits the bathroom.

"In a minute. I couldn't fall asleep this morning."

"I'm sorry I was away." he kisses me on the cheek and pulls on a pair of shorts and a tank top. His phone starts to chime, and he fumbles around the clothing he dropped on the floor to find it.

"Yes, hello. I got home a little while ago. How's Rory?"

Geez, can't he be home for fifteen minutes without her calling? Noah goes toward his office, but I can hear him laughing. He never laughs this much with me. I decide to take a quick shower and when I get out, I can still hear him talking to Vivian.

I'm making a pot of coffee when Lucian knocks at the loft door. It's nearly 1:00 PM. The smile on his face and his just fucked hair is answer enough for what he did last night. I don't want to ask anyway because we're talking about my sister.

"How are you?"

"In love."

"Luc, be serious."

"I am. Your sister bewitched me."

"And what are you plans?" I hope Megan doesn't break his heart because before Jeremy, she could be flaky with guys.

"We're seeing each other for the time being."

"Is it exclusive?"

"I didn't discuss it with you."

"Do me a favor? Don't tell Noah."

"I hadn't planned on it until it gets more serious."

"Tell me what?"

We both turn to see Noah coming out of his office.

"That he's leaving in a little while. If you want to spend some time with him, you better do it now."

"When did you get home?" Lucian asks.

"About an hour or so ago. Rory was fine and I wanted to get back. Vivian was really upset about the accident. The car is totaled so I'm going to get Rory a new car."

"Noah, does that make sense? She'll be living in New York soon." I said.

"She needs a car for the rest of the summer and when she goes back and forth from here to Boston. I'm not going to say no to her. I promised I would get her a new one."

"Okay, it's your decision."

"Yes, it is."

He turns and heads back to his office. Lucian looks at me and mouths "what the fuck is his problem?" I shrug because I'm not really sure and head back to the kitchen to make a cup of coffee. I'm put off by Noah's behavior and tone.

Lucian comes to say goodbye twenty minutes later. I wish he was going to stay because we spent so little time together. Plus, I need a buffer between Noah and me. I have a feeling that tonight will not go well after the exchange we just had.

"I'm coming down next weekend. Megan and I have a dinner. She also asked me to help her move."

I almost spit my coffee across the counter because she also

asked Hunter and I'm sure that little get together is going to be interesting. I don't think that Hunter was very happy that Lucian got Megan over him. I think I definitely want to be there to see the dynamic.

"Are you staying with us?"

"More than likely if you don't mind unless I stay with Megan."

I'm sure he'll be staying with my sister rather than us. He goes to Noah's office to tell him goodbye and I hear them arguing. They both stalk into the living room.

"What's going on?"

"Lucian told me that he's coming to the city next weekend to help Megan move."

"So, what's the problem?"

"The problem is that his niece's birthday is Saturday and I thought we could celebrate as a family."

This is news to me because he didn't even ask if I was free.

"We're going to Boston next weekend?"

"No. I'm going for her birthday."

I put my cup down and brush past Noah without saying a word. So, this is how it's going to be? I'm not family yet so I'm not welcome? Or will I ever be welcome? I hear Lucian telling Noah what an asshole he is and the front door slams.

"Lexi?" Noah calls.

"I don't want to discuss it right now."

He comes into the bedroom. "I'm sorry. It was last minute, and I didn't think you would be comfortable around Rory's family."

"The point is that you didn't even ask, you just assumed."

"You're right. I should've asked."

"Noah, what's happening to us?"

"What do you mean?"

"Things are so different between us in the last month."

"I don't think that."

"Then you haven't been paying attention."

"I think you're letting these changes get to you."

"It's a lot to take in. I've had very little time to absorb it. But that's not what I mean. I mean you don't seem the same towards me. Like I can't do anything right."

He sits on the bed and takes me into his arms, pressing my cheek against his chest.

"I'm sorry. This all came on so fast, but I want to be the best father I can. I missed so much of Rory's life that I want to make it up to her any way I can."

"You can't do it all at once."

"I know but I want to."

Noah rocks me and I inhale his scent. I feel safe in his arms, but something is gnawing at me and it's the fact that I now have to share him. I don't want to be selfish, but I don't get to spend a lot of time with him as it is.

Noah kisses the top of my head. "Are we good, Lexi?"

"Yes. I'm fine. I just want you to bear with me. This is a lot for me too."

He kisses the top of my head and lets me go, then heads back to his office.

I spend the rest of Sunday relaxing on the living room couch and reading. I'm tired from broken sleep and everything that's taken place in the last forty-eight hours. Tomorrow I have JC to deal with and I'm not sure how that's going to go.

Even though Noah and I haven't had sex since Saturday morning, he makes no attempt when we slip into bed. I find this unusual because normally when we're apart for any length of time, we have sex when we get back together. I shrug it off that he's tired and fall asleep with his arms around me.

I wake up a little after three and Noah is no longer next to me. I turn over and spread my arm out and feel around. He isn't in bed at all and the bathroom door is open, so I know he isn't in there. I listen closely and hear hushed tones coming from somewhere in the apartment.

Noah is on the phone with someone and I'm curious to know who. I'm wide awake now and I quietly pad to his office. The door is closed most of the way and I lean against the wall near it and listen. What I hear, I do not like. A one-sided conversation but the words spoken are like Noah talking to a lover.

I turn and bump my knee against the wall. In the quiet of the loft, it echoes, and I turn to run back to bed before Noah catches me. I hear the door to the office creak just as I slip into bed and pull the sheet over me. In the dark, his face is illuminated by his phone as he peers in at me. When he sees I'm asleep, he heads back to his office.

What the fuck was that? I have that sinking feeling again in the pit of my stomach. I wonder if Rory had an accident at all or Noah was using it as an excuse to see Vivian for the weekend. I don't know what the truth is, but I must trust Noah is telling it to me.

CHAPTER 20

The next morning, I want to ask about the call last night, but I hold my tongue. Instead, I give Noah the silent treatment, taking my shower and drinking coffee while reading the paper.

"Lexi, are you still upset with me for yesterday?"

"Not at all. I'm fine. I have a lot to do today so excuse me if I seem...disconnected."

He gives me a puzzled look but goes back to reading something on his phone. I need to get out of here before I explode. I'm angry and ready to boil over.

"I have to go," I say.

"It's only seven."

"I told you I have a lot going on."

As I'm slipping my heels on, he makes a snide comment with a nasty tone.

"Say hello to JC for me."

"Fuck you," I growl as I head out the door.

Noah has the nerve to talk about JC and it's very possible that he's doing something behind my back. We need to discuss this and soon. I'm hoping he's not preoccupied with work tonight.

The office is quiet when I get in, after all it's only 7:30. I go into the kitchen and fire up the coffee maker. I'm still tired and I feel groggy. My head feels stuffier than yesterday and I'm hoping it's just allergies. The hot coffee helps, and I feel a little better.

I don't want to talk to JC or anyone else, so I lock myself in my office. I hear his keys jingle as he walks by my door and I hold my breath. He stops and I see the shadow of his feet under the door, then he continues on. I'm glad because I really don't know what to say. At noon, I get a knock on my door and it's JC. He closes the door behind him and sits in one of the chairs in front of my desk. He's nonchalant, crossing his legs and leaning back.

"I think we need to talk."

"I don't want to discuss anything about Saturday."

"Lexi, why not?"

"Because. It's a moot point."

"Okay, then how about this. We have a rewrite on the Camilla campaign. They want to see it tomorrow."

"Fuck, are you serious? I'm swamped here."

"You might have to work late then. They're coming in at 10:00 AM."

The last thing I want to do is work late. My head is pounding, and I don't feel well. I might even have a fever. I have no alternative, so I nod at him.

"Let me call Noah and tell him I'll be late tonight."

JC exits my office to give me some privacy. I chew on my cheek waiting for Noah to answer.

"What's up?" Noah says when he answers. His tone is flat.

"I have to work late. We have a rewrite on a campaign."

Noah sighs into the phone. "What time will you be home?"

"It's hard to say."

He pauses. "Call me when you're on your way."

The phone clicks before I can say another work and we're disconnected, as disconnected as our relationship is right now. It makes my head pound harder. I need something hot to help the stuffiness in my head and I ask Nikki to order some soup for me.

It's not helping, and I feel quite warm. An hour later, the chills start.

I can't deal with this with all I have to do but I press on and by the time 4:30 rolls around, I'm miserable. JC comes in to see how I'm doing and immediately knows something is wrong. He touches his hand to my cheek.

"Geez, you're burning up. Why didn't you go home?"

"I have so much to do and you said that the Camilla campaign needs a rewrite."

"Lexi, you're sick. Go home. We can reschedule."

"Are you sure?"

"I'm sure. I'll explain to Vincent and Marco."

"Thank you so much."

I grab my purse and pack up my briefcase. I'm definitely not taking the subway the way I feel. I'm not sure I can handle the rush hour and standing on the train. I hail a cab and lay my head back as it moves through the city. I'm glad to see my building because the more the minutes tick by, the worse I feel.

The apartment is quiet when I get upstairs and then I hear it, soft moaning. I slip off my shoes and quietly walk toward where the sound is coming from, Noah's office. Then I see it and I want to scream. Vivian is naked, bent over the couch arm and Noah is fucking her from behind.

My head feels like it's going to blow. JC cheated on me, but I always found out after the fact. I never walked in on him fucking someone else. I can feel the soup I ingested hours before working its way up my throat and I force it down. Silent tears are rolling down my cheeks. What do I do? Do I burst in the door and tell him what a bastard he is and what a whore she is?

I can't deal with this right now, but I do have to deal with it. Where do I go? Megan doesn't have her apartment yet and Olivia hasn't returned from California. Those options are out. I could stay at a hotel or go to my parent's house in New Jersey. That's out because they'll ask why I'm there and not with Noah. The only other option is JC. He's close and he'll understand. I need his comfort.

I grab my shoes and silently slip out the apartment door, out of the life that I thought was going to be mine. My whole life will change, it's over with Noah. I can't go back to him. My intuition told me something was wrong, and I thought I was just being paranoid.

I can barely see the buttons in the elevator because my eyes are filled with tears. I jam on the one marked M and rush out of car when the doors open. On the street I lean against the wall of the building and call JC.

"Lexi? Are you home yet?"

"JC," I blurt out.

His voice is full of concern. "What's wrong? Where are you?"

I'm sobbing so hard I can barely get words out of my mouth. Passersby are looking at me.

"Calm down. Is it Noah?"

That makes me cry harder and I start to cough.

"He cheated," are the only words I can get out of my mouth before a new fit of sobs take hold.

"Are you home?"

"In front of my building," I choke out.

"I'm in a cab. I'm coming to get you. Calm down."

Twelve long minutes I lean against the building, wiping my nose and eyes with a crumpled-up tissue I found in my purse before JC reaches me. He jumps out of the cab and puts his arm around me while he escorts me to the waiting car.

"Do you want to tell me what happened?"

I shake my head and he pulls me against him. I try to back away, not because I don't want his comfort but because my mascara is going to stain his crisp white shirt. He holds me to him, and I stop struggling. A few blocks later, JC is helping me out of the cab and into his building.

My crying has subsided but I'm hiccupping now, and he rubs

my back. I feel horrible and my head is killing me. I don't know what hurts worse, the betrayal or the pain. JC takes me by the hand and leads me to his apartment. The décor is masculine, lots of blues, beiges and grays. He sits me on an overstuffed leather couch in his living room and gets me a glass of water.

"Lexi, what the fuck happened?" he says as he sits next to me.

I gulp the cold water and it soothes my tortured throat. "Why do my fiancés keep cheating on me? Is it me?"

"No, it's not you. It's us. We're stupid fucking idiots. At least I can speak for myself. He cheated on you? With who?"

I realize I'm going to have to tell JC the entire story and I do. I can tell he's having a hard time believing it because he just sits there with his mouth gaping open.

"Let me get this straight. Noah has a daughter he hasn't seen for years. He gets in touch with her and meets back up with his old flame and cheats on you with her?"

"That's about the size of it. I wonder if I came home late tonight would I find them in our bed together. I knew something was going on."

"What are you going to do?"

"It's over. I can't go through this again. I was done being a doormat when we broke up."

I see JC wince and I know I struck a nerve.

"I'm…I can't apologize to you enough. I was stupid. He's even more stupid because you're an even better catch than when we were together."

"I can't go home. I feel terrible and I'm nauseous. The last thing I need is a confrontation with Noah tonight."

"You can stay here. I'll sleep on the couch."

I was hoping JC would say that because it's either here or I beg Hunter to let me stay at his place. I don't have a lot of friends in the city since most of mine are still in Jersey.

"I appreciate it."

"It's the least I can do. Let's get you into bed. You need to rest. You're going to have to tell Noah you're not coming home."

I'm dreading it but I'll text him in a couple of hours when Vivian decides he's fucked her enough. JC takes me to his bedroom. A king-sized bed is centered in the middle of the far wall. The room is painted in a royal blue and several reproductions of Picasso adorn the walls. I didn't know JC was an art lover.

"I need something to wear to bed."

He opens his dresser and finds a pair of shorts that look too small for him and probably are since they have a stamp on the left leg from our high school. He also hands me one of his t-shirts. I thank him and go to the bathroom to change. It's half the size of the one in my apartment but it's decorated nicely with a large tub, walk in shower and double sink vanity.

The shorts are big but I'm able to pull the drawstring tight to keep them securely around my waist. The t-shirt is huge but it's soft and smells like JC's cologne. When I come out, he has the covers turned down and is waiting with a glass of water and some aspirin which I take before slipping into bed.

"I'm sorry this happened. I can't make up for what I did but maybe you should talk to Noah before you end it."

"It's over. There is nothing to talk about."

I turn on my side and he pulls the sheet and light blue cotton blanket over me. He doesn't leave but instead sits on the bed next to me and strokes my hair. It soothes me and I fall asleep in a matter of minutes.

I wake up with a start, disoriented and not sure where I am. My head feels a little better but not much. The bedside clock reads 9:43, so I've slept almost four hours. I sit up in bed and cough loudly.

"Are you okay?"

I look up to see JC standing at the door. He's no longer in his dark suit but instead dressed in a pair of worn blue jeans with holes in the knees and a black muscle shirt.

"I'm fine. Where's my purse?"

"Living room, I'll get it for you."

He comes back and hands me my purse. I take out my phone and my fingers pause on the keyboard as I think of what I should tell Noah.

I'm not coming home tonight.

Why not? Are you that busy?

No, I'm not coming home, EVER.

What the fuck do you mean you're not coming home, ever?

I'm done with you. I know what you did, and I can't forgive you.

My phone rings and I let it go to voicemail. It rings several more times and each time, a voicemail is left. Then I get a text.

It just happened. I'm sorry. I don't love her. Please call me.

I can't call him because I begin to sob again. I don't want to give him the satisfaction of knowing he destroyed me. JC comes to me and takes me in his arms, holding me against his chest. I know I shouldn't let him, but I need the comfort. He doesn't let go until I'm all but sniffling.

"I have some tissues in the drawer of the nightstand."

I pull it open and besides the tissues there's a bunch of condoms and some lubricant. Just what I need to see. JC looks at me sheepishly.

"I'm sorry."

Why is he apologizing? We're not together and he's separated. I don't expect him to wait around for his divorce to be finalized before he sleeps with someone else.

"I didn't just buy them. I've had them for a while. Brianna has a thing about messing up the sheets when they've just been changed. I haven't slept with anyone since her and that was a while ago."

"You don't need to explain. I don't expect you to wait."

He takes the tissue out of the drawer and wipes at my cheeks. I close my eyes as he cleans my skin. I realize my phone is still in my hand. Noah hasn't texted me again and I'm curious to hear the voicemails. I dial to listen. Four messages and he sounds like he's been crying. It would break my heart if it wasn't already broken.

"Lexi, as much as I want to tell you to tell him to go fuck off, I'm not going to. I know you're hurt but you should let him explain," JC says.

"I can't. Your cheating on me was hard enough but now Noah. I feel like I've been punched. I love him but he betrayed me."

"I wish I could make it better, but you have to give him a chance."

"Why JC? Why should I?"

"Because he's good for you. He made a mistake."

"I bet if I fucked you, he wouldn't be saying the same thing."

"You want to do it and then tell him?" he says as he smirks at me.

"Stop it. You're trying to make me laugh."

"I want you to just hear him out."

217

"Can you explain to me why you're not jumping for joy? I would think that you would be happy I'm going to leave him."

"I don't want you by default. I want you to be with me for your own reasons, not because you left him because he cheated."

I can understand what he's saying, and I appreciate that he wants me to be sure about Noah before I end it. I think I should hear Noah out but not tonight. I need rest and I'm not going to run back to him like a dog that's been beat. He's going to have to suffer the way I am right now.

"Should I tell him that I'm willing to talk?"

"Do you think he deserves to stew in his own juices for a night?"

"Yes. I can't get it out of my head, seeing him with her."

"He fucked up bad. Tell him tomorrow."

I take JC's hand and kiss the palm. I can see that the small gesture has caused his face to flush. I don't want to lead him on, and I drop his hand, slipping back under the covers.

"Lexi, are you going to work tomorrow?"

"I feel horrible. Do you mind if I stay home? Maybe I can do some work while I sit in bed."

"Are you going home tomorrow morning?"

"I probably should. I want to get my discussion with Noah over with. I want to know what the fuck was going on in his head when he decided to cheat on me."

"He was thinking with his dick. It's not a complicated process."

"Vivian is beautiful and hot so I'm sure you're right."

He raises his voice slightly. "Why do you discount yourself all the time? You're beautiful and hot. If you were mine again, I would treat you right."

"I'm not like her."

"You don't need to be. You're you and it's more than appealing."

He gets up and heads to the door.

"JC, I'm sorry I can't give you what you want."

He smiles at me, but I know it must be killing him to send me back to Noah. Nothing is set in stone. It might not work out anyway. Noah better have a convincing story because at this point, I'm ready to walk.

I pull the covers over me and go back to sleep. During the night I feel a cool hand on my head. JC has come to check on me and I smile a little. He walks out of the room and closes the door. *Why couldn't he be this sweet when we were together?*

The next morning, I wake up and call out to JC. I get no answer and a glance at the clock tells me that he probably left already. I feel a little better and get up to use the bathroom. A note is taped to the mirror.

Lexi,

You were sleeping so peacefully I didn't want to wake you. You're welcome to stay as long as you like. If you go out just be aware the door closes and locks behind you automatically. I left a key on the counter.

If you speak with Noah, let me know how it turns out. Know that I only want the best for you. As much as I want you, I would never stand in the way of your happiness.

Hugs,

JC

. . .

He really is trying to score some points. I'm grateful that he didn't pressure me to just end it with Noah. I want to see what he has to say though I saw it with my own two eyes. What excuse could he have to do what he did? I text Noah because I want him to know I'm willing to talk.

I'm coming home to talk. I should be there soon.

I'm sorry. I fucked up. Where are you?

The last thing I want to tell him is that I stayed at JC's apartment last night. I can just imagine how that would go over. If he asks me when we meet, I'm going to tell him I stayed with Hunter. He likes him.

It doesn't matter where I stayed. I'll be home in a little while.

Ok.

That's it, ok? I prepare myself to go home. JC neatly laid my clothes on a chair by the bathroom. I change back into them and fold the t-shirt and shorts I slept in, leaving them on the dresser. I start to feel crappy again and I'm not at all ready to have this conversation.

I walk the few blocks to Noah's apartment. Funny how I'm not even considering it my home anymore. I'm not sure I can forgive him for what he did. I hope he has the decency to tell me the truth. I want to know how many times he fucked Vivian and if he even went to Boston this weekend. It's curious how she just happened to find her way to his apartment. When I get upstairs, I knock on the door and Noah answers.

"You didn't have to knock. This is your home too," he quietly says.

He reaches out to take my briefcase, but I pull it away. I don't want him helping or touching me.

"Alexa, please. I made a mistake. I don't want to lose you."

I wheel around to look him square in the eye.

"How many times, Noah?"

"Huh?"

"How many times did you fuck her? Did you fuck her in our bed?"

"Of course not. I would never."

"But you would fuck her in the apartment we shared. That you had no problem with."

"Please sit down. I need to explain."

"How could you possibly explain your way out of this? I saw you."

"I know and I'm not trying to make excuses. Just let me tell you how it happened."

As if I want a play by play of how his dick ended up inside Vivian. I'm weary and all I want to do is go to bed. I can feel my fever starting to ramp up again. Bile is rising in my throat and I turn to run to the bathroom but don't quite make it. The next thing I know, I feel Noah's arms cradling me as he carries me to the bedroom.

"What, what happened?"

"You passed out. You're sick. You need to rest."

"I want to talk."

He presses his hand to my forehead. "We can talk later. You're burning up."

He sits me on the bed and begins to undress me. I let him because I'm too exhausted to fight. When I'm down to my panties, I slide under the covers and promptly fall asleep. I don't know how long I slept, but when I wake up, the sun is sinking in the sky. I've been sleeping all day. As I stir, I see Noah sitting at the foot of the bed, cross legged with his laptop.

"What time is it?" I croak.

"Nearly six. I was worried, you were moaning in your sleep. I've been here most of the day. Would you like something to drink?"

My throat is dry as a bone and it feels scratchy, but my head feels a little better.

"Can I have some juice? Do we have any?"

He gets up and puts his laptop on the bed, then goes in the kitchen. I hear a glass clink and drawers opening. He's back in a minute with a glass of orange juice and a straw.

"Sit up so you don't choke."

He reaches over to help me, and I shrink from his touch. The look on his face is painful and I know he's hurting to see me react this way. Instead he pops the straw in the glass and holds it until I'm in sitting position.

"We can talk when you feel better."

"Let's talk now. I want to get this over with. I need to decide my next move."

"There is no next move. I'm not going to let you go."

"You can't make that decision for me. You cheated on me. I swore I would never be with a man that did that to me again. Do you understand?"

"I do and I can never take back what I did. All I can ask is your forgiveness."

"Did you fuck her this weekend when you were in Boston? Did you really stay at your parent's house?"

"No, we didn't have sex. I stayed at my parent's house. The maid was cleaning when I got there and let me in. I found a key in my father's desk drawer. I was lucky because I would have had to stay at a hotel."

"Why did she come to New York?"

"Rory wanted to do some shopping."

"Where was Rory while you two were fucking?"

"She was with the young woman that she'll be sharing the apartment with. They wanted to explore. She needs to get to know Manhattan without me, so we let her go."

"Who made the first move?"

"Vivian did. It brought back memories from years ago. Before I knew it, we were undressed."

"You could've said no and sent her home. Why didn't you?"

"I don't know. I just thought…I wasn't thinking. You and I haven't been getting along and…"

"And you thought fucking someone else would make it all better? Did it?"

"Obviously, no. I wasn't thinking it would make it all better. I should've said no."

"You should have. How many other women have you fucked behind my back?"

Noah gasps. "None. I would never."

"Don't say never because clearly, never doesn't exist," I caution.

"No one but her."

"Say her name, Noah."

"Vivian."

"If you wanted her why didn't you just end it with me? It would've been far less painful for you to just dump me than to have me catch you fucking her in my home, our home."

"I don't want her. I want you. I want to marry you."

"I'm not sure if that's going to happen."

Noah's face twists in pain. "Don't say that. Please don't."

"I can't trust you. The problem still exists. She's the mother of your child and that will never end. I don't want to take you from Rory but I'm not sure how you can be her father and not see

Vivian. How will I know when you two are together you're not having sex behind my back?"

"Because it won't happen again. I told her it can't happen."

"How many times did you tell her that before you two fucked?"

"Lexi, please, can you stop saying that."

"What, fucked? You don't like it. What should I say then?"

"Anything but that."

"You want me to pretty up the act. Call it a beautiful symphony."

"No. I just don't like to hear that word from you so much."

"Well to fucking bad, you fuck. You shouldn't have fucked her and I fucking wouldn't be saying fuck so much."

I watch as he scrubs his face with both hands. My expletives have the desired effect. I want to make him as uncomfortable as I was when I saw them yesterday. Of course, nothing could compare to the shock that I can't erase from my mind. I have to make it more visual for him.

"How would you like it if you walked in on me screwing JC? Would you forgive me the way you want me to forgive you so easily?"

"Probably not."

"Then give me time to think. You owe me that."

"So, you're staying?"

"I am but I can't share a bed with you. You're going to have to sleep on that heinous fuck couch in your office or in the guest room."

"I wouldn't touch you if I slept here."

"You're damn right you won't. I need more sleep. Please go away."

I watch Noah slide off the bed, take his laptop and walk with hunched shoulders out the door. Good, let him think about what I said. How do you try to explain fucking someone else and then expect me to forgive so easily? I decide text JC to let him know I'm okay.

. . .

We talked.

And?

I'm staying for the time being.

When will I see you?

More than likely I'll be at work tomorrow.

I drift off to sleep and that night, I hear the bedroom door open. Noah is standing in the doorway looking at me. I see his face illuminated by the small blue nightlight we keep on by the bathroom door. He looks older than his thirty-six years. He created his misery and now he's going to have to wallow in it.

CHAPTER 21

I trudge into work just before nine. I slept okay the night before and when I woke up, Noah was locked in his office. The minute he heard me moving around, he came out and offered to make me breakfast. I'm still not feeling well and told him I could make my own tea. I know my tone and actions are hurting him but the punch in the gut I took on Monday is like an open wound.

I didn't say goodbye when I left. I just walked by his open office door and said nothing. I hope he had a shitty night of sleeping because he deserves it. He called me before I walked out the door, but I ignored him.

Now I'm sitting at my desk deciding what I should start on. The copy for the Camilla campaign is in the electronic file and I pull it up to take a look. It's different, it's good and I see that the sign off for completion has the initials JCL, which means that JC finished it. I'm grateful and again think that if he had been this way when we were together, I wouldn't be dealing with any of this shit.

We would be several years married and maybe have children by now. I know he wants them. We talked about it all the time. He used to kid me and say he wanted fourteen children. I told him if he didn't mind screwing a wind tunnel, it was fine with me. After all of those births I would be stretched to high heaven.

He pokes his head in, disturbing my thoughts.

"How are you this morning?"

"Better but still not one hundred percent."

"Is everything alright?"

"It's okay but I need time and Noah knows that. I'm not going to forgive him so easily. I'm not even sure if we're going to make it. I have a few months to decide if I want to marry him."

"I'm glad that you are trying to be levelheaded about this."

"Levelheaded has nothing to do with it. I'm just not sure I want to start over once again. Maybe I'm being stupid about this but even with what Noah's done, I still love him."

"Is he walking around with tail between his legs?"

"For the most part. I made him sleep elsewhere last night. I couldn't deal with him being in the same bed with me."

Nikki shows up and asks JC to move aside so she can enter my office. She's holding a large white box which can only be flowers.

"This came for you a few minutes ago. Either you did something very good or very bad."

I didn't do anything of the sort.

The box is heavy and inside are two dozen long stemmed red roses. I don't have to look at the card because I know they're from Noah. He's trying to make it up to me but it's going to take more than roses to do that. I hand the box to Nikki and ask her to find a vase for them.

I look up and notice that JC is still standing in the doorway. His face has clouded, and his eyes have darkened. I know what he's thinking because this was the exact pattern he followed. Cheating, begging for forgiveness and the showering of gifts. I wonder if men have a cheater's handbook on how to make it up to their significant others.

Maybe there's a section labeled, "How to fix your fuck up." I smile because the image is funny even though this situation is not. JC now has a puzzled look on his face.

"Lexi, what's funny?"

"Nothing."

"You're smiling."

Should I tell him? Might as well and I do to his shocked look.

"You did the same thing. Is there some sort of handbook cheater's follow?"

"That's a shitty thing to say."

"It's true. You would cheat, beg my forgiveness, send me roses and little gifts. I bet Noah will buy me some bauble or piece of jewelry to try to patch things up."

"Did it ever make it better?"

"No. My self-esteem was in the toilet. It's why I took it so long. You're breaking up with me was the best thing for my self-confidence."

"Excuse me if I don't see it that way. It was the worst thing I've ever done in my life. I set you up for this which is why you're so forgiving. Why didn't you dump me the first time?"

"Because I loved you JC, can't you understand that? You wrapped me around your little finger, and I was done."

"I'm sorry our relationship was so terrible for you. I always wish I can take it all back."

"You can't but it made me stronger. I'm still not sure that Noah deserves me. I might end it after all. I just need time."

JC nods and runs his fingers through his thick hair, then turns to leave. I'm sure I've given him something to think about. Maybe the next woman he gets involved with will be treated better even though I know she will. He was much better with Brianna than he ever was with me.

I go back to work and by lunchtime, I feel even better. At least my body does. This upcoming weekend, Noah is supposed to go to Boston for Rory's birthday. This is not going to happen. I can't trust him to be alone with Vivian and frankly, I don't fully believe that she was the one who initiated the sex.

Based on what Lucian told me about their relationship when they were younger, I think they just can't keep their hands off each other. I still want to question Noah as to why his clothing smelled like Vivian's perfume. I have an idea and if he wants to make it up to me, he needs to follow through. I dial his cell and he answers immediately.

"Lexi, did you like the roses?"

"Yes, thank you. I need you to do something for me this weekend."

"I...this weekend is Rory's birthday. I was going to Boston."

"Hold on a sec."

I close my door because I'm ready to lay into him. Is he really that stupid?

"Do you actually think I'm letting you go to Boston after what just happened?"

"Not alone. I expected you'll come with me."

"Well you expect wrong. Do you think I want to see Vivian? I have the urge to tear her eyes out that I might not be able to control."

"But I promised."

"Noah, the last thing I want is to get in the way of your relationship with your daughter, but you created this by fucking Vivian. I can't trust you, not yet anyway."

"But you are getting in the way."

"Then this conversation is over and so is our engagement."

"No! What do you want me to do?"

"You're going to help Megan move into her new apartment and you're going to be nice."

"When?"

"Saturday morning. JC, Hunter and Lucian are also helping. Those are my terms. You will just have to figure out another time to meet Rory here in Manhattan without Vivian."

"I need to explain it to Vivian."

"Why? Does she deserve an explanation after what she did?"

"She doesn't know you saw us."

My mouth must have dropped open without me realizing it because I can feel my tongue getting dry. Did I hear what I thought I just heard?

"You didn't tell her? When were you planning on revealing this little tidbit?"

"I was going to call her today. I don't want to be a dick about it."

"Excuse me?" I say raising my voice.

"I know she's expecting more. She wants us to be together."

"You're really making a good argument for why I should dump you. You seem to give a shit more about her feelings than mine."

"I don't but I left her once before. I owe her."

"I'm hanging up now. Don't send me any more flowers and don't buy me anything. Trinkets are not going to fix this."

"Lexi, I'm sorry. Please come home tonight."

"I'll take it under advisement."

I hang up and can't believe the exchange I just had with Noah. Is he fucking kidding? I need to pinch myself to see if this was a dream. Unfortunately, it's not. I float through the rest of the day, not particularly concentrating on my work. At five I gather my things and get ready to leave. JC's door is closed, and I don't want to bother him, so I text him goodbye instead. He must be busy because I receive no reply.

Arriving home, the apartment smells wonderful. Noah's made homemade chicken soup which I figure is because I'm sick. He's also baked fresh sourdough bread which is surprising since it's summertime. He rarely bakes in the warmer weather. I find him in the kitchen wearing his "Kiss the Cook" apron which I won't do.

"Hungry?"

"Starving."

I barely consumed anything today except three cups of tea and a small container of tomato soup for lunch. My stomach growls at the aroma of the bread he just took out of the oven. The loaf smells heavenly and he slices a piece off with a crunch as the knife goes through the crust.

He places a bowl of soup he just ladled in front of me and it too smells delicious. I begin to eat, not looking at him but concentrating on the small cubed carrots and diced celery floating in the broth. At least he can cook, but the way back to my heart is not through my stomach.

"Lexi, what time do you need me on Saturday?"

"Eight. Megan is having the moving truck come from Jersey by nine, so we need to move whatever is in her car upstairs before then."

I know he's upset that he can't spend Rory's seventeenth birthday with her but it's his fault and I'm not giving in.

"Did you talk to Rory?"

"Yes. She's not happy she won't see me, but I told her to come down this week. She can stay with us and I'll make it up to her."

"And what about Vivian."

"She's aware why I can't come."

Good, the bitch. She knew what she was doing, and I hope her heart is in shreds.

"Fine."

I silently finish my dinner and for good measure, leave it on the table for him to clean up. My days of being nice are over. If Noah wants me back, he's going to have to earn it.

The next few days go well, at work and home. Noah is overly attentive though I'm still not allowing him back in our bed or to touch me. I did grant him permission to kiss my cheek before he retired to the guest room on Friday night.

Now here it is Saturday at 6:00 AM and I can hear him taking a shower in the master bath. I feel much better physically. Emotionally, I'm healing but I still can feel the sting of the slap in the face I received on Monday. I need a girlfriend to talk to and I know that Megan will freak out if I say anything. Olivia is coming back to live in Manhattan in two weeks. I wish she was here now.

Olivia has been my best friend since we were seven. She has always been there for me. I lived with her after the breakup with JC. We had a great time until she got transferred to California. I'm thrilled that she's coming back. She's a computer programmer and is giving up a great job with Google to come back here.

The last time I saw her was five months ago which is much too long. If she wasn't on vacation in Australia for almost the last month, I'd spend an hour pouring my heart out to her. Oh well, two more weeks and she'll be here. I need her anyway because she's my maid of honor.

Noah comes out of the shower with a towel wrapped around his waist, hair dripping a little in the back. He smiles at me as he passes through the bedroom to get dressed in the guest room. I'm glad he's giving me my space. I'm still not sure we're going to make it.

I take a quick shower and pull on a pair of cut-off jean shorts and a blue polo shirt. The shirt buttons open down to the middle of my chest and I make sure to wear a bra which creates cleavage. Noah hates this shirt and I'm sure I'm going to get a dirty look but too bad. I know I'm being immature, but I want to make him jealous.

Sure enough when I come into the kitchen, I see the look he's giving me but it's not one of anger, it's one of lust. We haven't had sex in more than a week. Of course, he last had sex on Monday. I ignore him and pour some coffee in my travel mug. I can see his reflection in the frosted glass of the cabinets and his eyes are centered on my ass.

I miss him sleeping in our bed but I'm angry and confused. I want things the way they were a month ago when all the distractions we have now didn't exist. I want my old Noah back. I can't look at him because I'm afraid I'll give in and want him to make love to me. Instead, I walk to the bedroom to get my purse.

"Ready to go?"

"Yes. Can I make a request? You can say no."

"Sure, what is it?"

"Can I kiss you?"

"Talk to me tonight."

I see his face fall and my heart clenches. I feel bad but I know I need to be strong. Noah needs to realize that he has a lot of making up to do.

By the time we get to Megan's apartment, everyone is there. Hunter and Noah greet each other as if they're old friends. He nods at JC and when he's not looking, JC strokes my arm. I can see him from the corner of my eye looking at my cleavage. If Noah saw, he would blow a gasket, but I want to have some fun.

Megan's place is fairly large one bedroom with a big picture window that faces the street. It's an open floor plan which means that except for the bedroom and bathroom that have doors, it's one big space. The kitchen is along the wall as you enter but has a nice sized black granite island. The floors gleam with fresh varnish and the walls have just been painted a bright linen white.

Between all of us, her car is unpacked within twenty minutes and two minutes after that, Lucian walks in. He got his hair cut since we saw him a week ago. When he kisses me hello, he tells me he wants to have a talk. I can only imagine why.

We sit around on the floor and granite island eating donuts

that Hunter brought and drinking coffee. The moving company is a half hour late. The apartment Megan shared with Jeremy was filled with half her furniture including the king-sized bed. I guess he's sleeping on the floor now.

The truck comes and Lucian, JC, Hunter and Megan head downstairs while I fill my travel mug. When I turn, Noah is there and his hand sweeps down the bare skin of my chest right in between my breasts. His fingers linger there and I'm becoming heated.

"No," I whisper and push his hand away.

"Lexi, are we ever going to be the same?"

"Give me time."

We break apart as Megan comes through the door leading the way for the moving men. She directs them where to put each piece of furniture with the organized nature that she's had since we were kids. I back against the counter to avoid getting in the way and watch as they place each piece of furniture where she points.

Lucian brushes against my hand and startles me. I glance over at Noah who is helping one of the moving men center the large square coffee table just right.

"I want to talk to you," Lucian whispers as he gestures to the hall.

I follow him before Noah sees us and we go through the heavy steel door marked "stairs."

"I know what happened. Vivian told me. My brother is an asshole."

"She told you, not Noah?"

"I confronted him on the phone yesterday."

"Lucian, I'm not sure what to do. I'm conflicted."

"Do you love him?"

"You know I do, but he betrayed me."

"Vivian can be very manipulative and seductive."

"You can't blame her for everything. He had free will and chose to give in."

"I know. I'm just so pissed at him. I can't believe what he did. Does Megan know?"

"She'd string him up by his balls so please don't tell her. Are you staying with her tonight?"

"She asked me too. I really like her."

I lean in and kiss his cheek. He's so different from his brother. We peek into the hallway making sure that no one sees us. The apartment is empty when we get inside and I breathe a sigh of relief. At least I don't have to explain where we were. I'm sure Noah would figure it out and be angry at Lucian.

Forty-five minutes later and the moving men are tipped and have left us in a fully furnished apartment. Megan is directing us like minions to put dishes in cabinets, towels and sheets in closets and wiping a thin layer of dust from the tables. Many hands make light work and by the time noon rolls around, the apartment is done except for a few pictures needing hanging.

She calls for pizza and we sit around on the couches eating off paper plates and toasting with glasses of soda. Noah is sitting across from me and keeps glancing up hungrily at my cleavage. The problem is that so is JC. Maybe I should've buttoned my shirt. I look down and creamy halves of each breast are visible between the vee of my shirt. The push up bra I wore accentuates them.

Hunter is the first to leave. He needs to go meet some of his buddies in the park at two. Megan is practically sitting on Lucian's lap and I announce it's time to go and JC agrees. I'm sure the minute the door closes behind us; they'll be in bed together. I kiss my sister and Lucian with promises to come for dinner soon. Noah scowls at me.

The elevator ride is an awkward silence and so is the walk back to our apartment. Megan lives just twelve blocks from Noah and I and sixteen from JC. If we all got along, we could hang out but that's not going to happen. It's obvious to me that Noah is jealous and JC looking at my cleavage hasn't been lost on him.

In front of our building, JC hugs me goodbye and I can see the frown on Noah's face as he holds me longer than necessary. I tell him I'll see him at the office on Monday. Another awkward elevator ride and we arrive in our apartment. Noah is on me the minute we walk through the door.

"Why did you wear that shirt? He wants to fuck you," he barks.

"Are you serious? Suppose he does want to fuck me? I'm not going to act on it. How dare you. Just because you're guilty about what you did. Stop it. It doesn't make me any more forgiving when you act like this."

I want to forgive Noah, but I'm not sure I can, yet.

"How long will it take?"

"I don't know. I need time. I told you that and you think I'm like a light switch, turning off and on. It doesn't work that way. I need to trust you again."

We go our separate ways. I head out to the terrace and Noah goes to his office. Our distance is apparent, and I don't mean geographically. I'm not sure we can get back to where we were.

CHAPTER 22

Two weeks later, things still aren't great. Noah begs me to forgive him and I tell him I need time. My feelings for him haven't changed, I still love him but in a different way. That way is some good and some bad. We haven't slept in the same bed in all that time.

Work has leveled off now that summer is in full swing. JC still looks at me with sadness, but he's trying to forget by dating. On July Fourth, we met by accident in Central Park, the woman that was with him looked very much like me, except she was taller and thinner. She definitely wasn't his type and I think it was a last-minute thing since she kept calling him Cameron.

It's Friday and I'm excited because Olivia is finally moving back to New York. I need some girl time with my best friend. Her brother, Matty, who's a real estate agent, set her up in an apartment in my sister Megan's building. How convenient for her to be so close to me. Matty even took care of getting it furnished as a homecoming present, but Olivia doesn't know this.

I went with him to select a couple of couches, end tables, lamps, a dresser, a bed and few other items. Once again Noah's jealousy got the best of him and he snapped at me when I got

MJ MASUCCI

home two hours later than expected. These days he doesn't trust me alone with any man which is funny since he's the one who cheated.

I'm not sure how long I can deal with this or if I even want to. We've done little about the wedding. Virtually all our preparations have stopped. We're getting married in three months and nothing has moved forward. I know Noah wants to still marry me, but even he hasn't mentioned anything. I have a fitting for my wedding dress tomorrow. Just in time to take Olivia with me.

When I get home from work, Noah isn't there. He didn't tell me he would be out which he usually does even with our current circumstances. I text him but receive nothing in reply. I'm not going to worry because sometimes he likes to take a run in the park with his headphones on.

I decide to change my clothes and have a sandwich for dinner. When it's warm out, I prefer not to cook. I could live on convenience food the whole summer if I needed to. Three hours go by and I still haven't heard back from Noah. I'm just about to call Brice to see if he's had contact and the door to our apartment opens.

Noah's with Rory and they're laughing, their hands full of packages from stores on Fifth Avenue, Saks, Victoria's Secret, Anthropologie, Versace and Hollister.

"Wow, you two really went on a shopping spree."

Rory scowls at me but isn't rude. "I needed clothes for school."

"I was wondering where you were, Noah."

He doesn't look at me. "Sorry, lost track of time."

Maybe I should throw a tantrum since he did the same thing when I was with Matty longer than expected. But I don't want to make a scene in front of Rory, so I keep my mouth shut. Noah ignores me and goes to the guest room to leave the bags. When he comes back, he lets me know Rory will be staying with us until Tuesday. I'm not thrilled.

"I have to go for a dress fitting tomorrow. Olivia just arrived

238

back from California and she's going with me. I'd like to spend some time with her."

Noah's face is passive. "It's not a problem. I can spend the day with Rory. She wanted to do some more shopping, this time for some items for her new apartment."

Really? You haven't bought her enough?

"We can meet back up for dinner. I might bring Olivia with me."

"I'll discuss it with you later," he says and goes to answer his ringing office phone, leaving me with Rory.

"So how was your day?"

Rory frowns at me. "I'm not sure I want to talk to you."

I'm shocked and I return her frown. "Excuse me?"

"My father told me you forbid him to see me on my birthday."

"That's not true. I said no such thing."

And maybe if he didn't stick his cock in your mother, I wouldn't have had to say no. I'm pissed off that Noah would even tell Rory something like that.

"He said he couldn't come because you told him no. Ask him."

"I will, later on."

She kicks off her shoes and leaves them in the middle of the living room.

"Rory, I'd appreciate if you put those in the closet."

She lowers her voice. "You're not my mother and I don't have to listen to what you say."

I grind my teeth. "But this is my home and I want it kept in order."

"This is my father's home, not yours. You just live here."

I can't believe she's acting this way since she's seventeen. I feel like I'm dealing with a spoiled little girl. My anger is beginning to boil over and before I can reply, Noah returns from his office. He can see I'm upset.

"Would you please tell your daughter to put her shoes in the closet?"

"Rory, put your shoes away."

"Yes, Daddy."

When Noah's back is turned, Rory sticks her tongue out at me. I've had enough. I went to the kitchen to pour a glass of wine and sit out on the terrace. The last thing I needed after a full week of work was to deal with this little brat. A few minutes later, Noah joins me.

"Lexi, what's wrong?"

"Everything. You, your daughter, this situation."

"What me? I've been trying to make it up to you."

"You could've texted me and let me know where you were. I was getting ready to call Brice. You had me worried."

Noah puts his hands on his hips. "You did the same thing last week."

"You knew where I was. I lost track of time."

"But you didn't let me know you'd be late."

"I think you were more worried about me being with Matty. You cheated on me, not the other way around. Yet I feel you have no trust in me. Also, you told Rory that I forbid you to see her on her birthday?"

Noah shook his head. "I didn't actually say that."

"She said you did. You make me look like a shrew. Maybe I should tell her why I forbade you to go. How would that look?"

"You're all worked up. Calm down."

"Noah, if you tell me to calm down once more, I'm walking out of here."

A look of fear crosses his face but then he smirks.

"Come on Lexi, I love you. Don't make threats you have no intention of keeping."

I'm fuming. I want to punch his beautiful face. Make his perfectly straight nose crooked. I take a big gulp of wine, emptying the glass and brush past him. Noah follows me as if he can't sense how pissed I am.

"I need to sleep in the bedroom tonight, preferably in bed with you."

"You're really pushing it. We'll see. I understand you want to make it look like everything is perfect in front of your daughter, but it's not. In fact, I think I'm going to Megan's. I need a break from all this shit."

"I think that you're…"

I put my hand up to stop him. "Don't you dare say that I'm overreacting."

Noah's quiet and I grab my purse, cell phone and slip on my shoes before I'm out the door. I just can't deal with him and now his obnoxious daughter. This wrinkle puts a whole new perspective on how life will be with Rory in the city. Yes, she will be living in her own place near New York University but I'm sure she'll come by.

It's early evening and still warm. Instead of heading to Megan's, I turn and go toward JC's apartment. I need an ego boost and he's just the person to give it to me. I hope he's home and not out on some date. I decide to call him before I get too far in case I need to walk the other way to my sister's. He answers and he sounds groggy.

"JC, it's me."

"Me who?"

"Stop playing. You know who this is."

"If it's that incredibly hot, sexy and gorgeous woman named Lexi, then yes, I do."

"Very funny. I needed a break. Can I come by?"

His once groggy voice is now clear. "Absolutely. I'll see you in a little while."

It takes me ten minutes to walk to his place. The sidewalks along Central Park are busy with people out enjoying the warm summer evening. When I get to JC's, he answer's the door in a pair of basketball shorts and a tank top that frames his muscular torso. I look away before he catches me ogling him.

"Hey, come on in. What's up?"

I tell JC what happened a short while ago and why I needed a break.

"I'm sorry. I know you haven't been happy lately. I can see it in your face and the way you act. Is it his daughter and what he did or something else?"

"It's everything. I'm not even sure I want to marry Noah. Nothing has improved over the last month. He tries but I'm miserable and I've been hiding it from him."

JC takes me by the hand and leads me to the couch. I don't know why, but I start crying. He's so tender and sweet to me. I press my face to his chest and cry. He holds me until I stop. JC swipes his thumbs across my cheeks and uses his shirt tail as a tissue to wipe the mascara that's blackened underneath my eyes. Then he does something I didn't expect. He kisses me.

I'm caught up in the softness of his lips and I respond. He presses harder and his tongue spears into my mouth, moist and hot. Before I know it, I'm stretched out under him and we're making out as if we're at a drive-on movie. My belly clenches and I can feel his growing erection pressing against my thigh.

I want him and I'm not sure if it's because I haven't had sex in a month, want to get Noah even for what he did or just because I really want JC to fuck me. We have to stop, and I try with all my might to push him away. He finally realizes what I'm doing, sliding off me and sitting up.

"I can't. If I do this, it's no better than what Noah did. I can't use you for revenge."

"Lexi, I would love for you to use me for revenge. I've wanted you for a long time, but I know what you're saying. I'm sorry I kissed you."

My heart is pounding and I'm breathing heavy and so is JC. There's a throb between my legs that I will away. I start to feel like garbage, not because of what I just did to Noah, but to JC. He's been a much better man than Noah has in the past few weeks.

Kind and sincere, only caring about my feelings. I wish he was this way years ago.

We both sit back against the couch, not speaking. Gradually the ache down below subsides but I'm horny as hell. It would be so easy to give into temptation and JC is oh so tempting.

"I think I better go. This was a really bad idea."

"It wasn't. You needed some comfort. It just got a little out of hand."

"But I never should have let it happen. I know how you feel about me."

"I love you and if you marry Noah, that's for you to decide. I don't want to get in the way of your happiness."

But was I happy? Am I happy? I don't know. I don't want to look like I'm needy, but the fact is that right now, I am. I quickly change the subject.

"Olivia is back."

JC groans. "Fuck, just what I need since she hates me."

"She doesn't hate you. She just thinks you're an asshole."

"Have you told her about what happened with Noah?"

"Not yet. She's been on vacation in Australia for the past month. I think it's a conversation best had in person. Why do you care if I told her or not?"

"Because it's going to make me look like less of an asshole. The story is so weird. Noah doesn't see his daughter for years and then all of a sudden, bam. Then he fucks his ex."

I think about what she's going to say when she finds out that yet another of my fiancés cheated on me. Olivia tells it like it is. I guess she has that sharp wit because she's had to protect herself all her life. She was always overweight as long as I've known her. Not by a lot but enough to always be overlooked by the guys she was in love with. It pissed me off because she's gorgeous. It goes to show what a shallow society we live in.

"I don't know about weird, but I wonder if we were married if Vivian would've tried to seduce Noah."

"I have no question she would've. If a woman wants someone enough, they're going to do what they need to so they can sleep with them."

"Is that how it was with you?"

"No. I was stupid. I didn't appreciate what I had at home. Can I ask you a question?"

"Sure."

"Have you slept with Noah since you found out?"

"No. I make him sleep in the guest bedroom. Tonight will be the first time he's sleeping in bed with me since that time."

"Why?"

"Rory has the guest bedroom and Noah said he doesn't want to make it seem like anything is wrong between us. Isn't that a joke? I have to play a part, so his daughter doesn't run back to mommy and tell her how fucked up daddy's relationship is."

JC laughs and then immediately stops when he sees the sadness on my face.

"Lexi, when are you going to make a decision?"

"I don't know. Soon. Tomorrow I have a fitting for my wedding dress."

"I want you to make it based on what's right for you. Yes, I love you and I want to make love to you, but don't let me sway how you feel about Noah. I gave up my chance and if he makes you happy, then you marry him."

JC picks up the remote and puts on the television. I lie down with my head on his leg and he strokes my hair. He used to do this when we were living together. JC would soothe me when I had a bad day at work or didn't feel good. He has a lot of great qualities and will make a great husband for somebody, just not me.

I stay with him for another couple of hours and by that time, I'm calm. I should get back to Noah. I know even though we aren't getting along, he still worries. JC walks me to the door and hugs me, hard.

"Thank you for being a friend. I needed that," I say.

"I'll always be your friend."

I kiss his cheek and he rides down in the elevator with me, giving me another hug in the lobby. The street is still busy with pedestrians and jazz music is playing across the street in the park. I love summer in Manhattan.

When I get back, Noah is sitting in the living room watching a baseball game. He smiles at me and I come over to join him on the couch. He takes me in his arms and kisses me. I let him even though I have reservations.

"Lexi, you're very important to me. I want our relationship to be as strong as it was before I fucked up."

I shush him because I don't want Rory to hear us.

"Rory's not here. She went to visit her friend, Ella. Her father lives here and she's visiting him for the summer. She's sleeping over."

My ears perk up when I hear she won't be here for the night. I need sex and I'm ready to forgive Noah so I can get it. I begin kissing him and then fear hits me. I'm worried that I smell like JC's cologne. I noticed the faint scent of it when I left his apartment.

Noah pulls me onto his lap and kisses me hard, his hands tangled in my thick hair, gently tugging it so he can have access to my throat. He plants soft kisses until he reaches the hollow at the base, then he sucks. I moan and my core begins to floor. I can feel him harden under me.

He expertly unbuttons and unzips my shorts so he can slide his fingers down to my clit. My breath hitches when he touches me and I whimper.

"So wet for me," he whispers.

I'm digging my nails into his arms as he caresses my swollen nub, then he stops, removing his hand from my pants. I protest because I'm so close to climax.

"Let's go to bed."

He leads the way into the bedroom and makes me stand in

front of him while he undresses me. First, Noah pulls of my tank top, kissing my shoulders and upper chest. I feel his fingers working on the clasp of my bra while he sucks on my earlobe. When he has it open, he gives a gentle tug and it falls to the floor at our feet.

Next, he kneels down in front of me and pulls my shorts and panties off in one move, helping me step out of them. Noah places his face in front of the apex between my thighs and uses the tip of his tongue to massage my clit. I feel shockwaves go through me as his fingers plunge into my opening. I'm so close to coming, my hands gripping his hair, then he pulls away.

"No, Noah."

"Get on the bed," he growls.

He doesn't wait for me to obey, but rather scoops me up and lays me down. He quickly strips, leaving his clothing next to the bed then gets between my legs. His thick cock is kissing his belly and I can see the head glistening from pre-cum. Oh, how I want that in me.

As if Noah hears my thoughts, he positions himself at my opening and swiftly thrusts into me, hard enough for me to gasp. Then he's hovering over me, his head dips to suck my aching nipples, nibbling, biting, and licking. I cradle his ass, pushing him deeper with each thrust.

"Yes, fuck me."

My request spurs him to move faster. My heart is ready to burst out of my chest and I close my eyes tight as I draw nearer to orgasm. I'm panting when I fall into a million pieces as my climax hits. It's been almost a full month since I've had sex and I come so hard that my insides burn like white hot fire. Noah follows with several loud grunts as he spills everything he has, then collapse on top of me.

I stroke his sweaty hair as he plants kisses along my upper chest, whispering how much he loves me. Then I feel wetness on my breast and grow alarmed.

"Noah, sweetie?"

He looks up at me and his cheeks have tears on them.

"I thought you were going to leave me."

"I love you. I don't want to leave. Don't push me away."

"Can we start fresh?"

"I want that so much."

I know it's probably stupid of me to forgive him so soon, but I can't help it. I love him. I have two choices, forgive him or forget him. I'm glad Rory stayed at her friend's house. It gave us time to make up.

The only problem is, I feel I let my body make the decision for me. Maybe I'm stupid for giving in so easily. I don't know if what I did makes sense or I'm following the same pattern I did with JC several years before. I'm supposed to be older, wiser and more experienced, but I still have some doubts.

CHAPTER 23

Doubt is still eating at me for what we did the night before. I don't have time to analyze my more than likely bad decision. I have an appointment with the bridal shop to have my wedding dress fitted. Olivia is meeting me and then we're going to lunch. I can't wait to see her.

I slowly untangle myself from Noah's embrace and head for the shower. I'm sore and the soap stings a bit when I wash. It doesn't surprise me since we went at it pretty hard. After I dry myself, I wrap the towel around me and start for the closet. Noah's awake and watching me with lust in his eyes.

"Bring your pretty ass over here. I have something for you."

"Noah, can we pick this up when I get home?"

"You don't want to?"

"I want to but I'm a little raw."

He frowns and his sapphire eyes darken.

"I was rough last night. I'm sorry. It's because you're so damn hot."

"I need a rest. When is Rory coming back?"

"Not sure but I think we can work something out even if she's here tonight."

I finish dressing and sit on the bed and run my fingers through his sex mused hair. His hand slips up my shirt and I playfully slap at it, squirming out of his reach.

"You really are sexy. My sexy Lexi."

"Ugghh. That sounds so childish."

"It's true."

"I have to go. I want to arrive before Olivia does."

I hurry out the door. Doubt is deep inside me that I made a big mistake having sex with Noah.

In the elevator, I think I should wait in the Olivia's lobby and surprise her. I text her to see when she's leaving, and she tells me she's already on her way. Dammit, she's going to get there before me. I better hop to it. I hail a cab and hope Olivia isn't too far ahead of me.

The cab I'm in pulls up just as I see Olivia go into the bridal shop. At least I think it's her. I hurriedly pay the driver and run to the door. She's at the desk and I stop short when she turns to me. She's slim, slimmer than I've ever seen her before. In the months since she visited me in New York, she's lost the excess weight she has carried for years.

"I can't get over how beautiful you look. Why didn't you tell me you lost weight?"

"I wanted to surprise you."

It's a huge surprise. Olivia was beautiful before with gorgeous thick wavy black hair that shines like glass, almond shaped green eyes the color of soft moss, long eyelashes, high cheekbones and perfectly straight teeth framed by thick full red lips. Her body is now curvaceous with lush firm breasts, full hips and a flat stomach.

Two men are sitting in the corner more than likely waiting for family members and I see them looking at us. I'm sure they're looking at her more than me. I'm a bit envious but she's my best friend and I'm thrilled for her.

After we chat a bit, I give the clerk my name and she

retrieves my dress. I grow impatient while the seamstress pins spots that need altering. She tells me I must have lost weight because my measurements have changed. Fact is that she's probably right because I haven't been eating much, especially in the last month. I can't wait until this is finished so I can have lunch with Olivia.

As we walk to a restaurant not far from the shop, I reach out to hug Olivia. It startles her a little, but I love knowing she's home for good.

"What was that for?"

"I need you. The past few weeks have not been good."

She stops short and looks at me, but I don't want to start my conversation about everything on the street. I pull her arm into the restaurant and the hostess leads us to a table in the back. The place isn't full yet, so we have some privacy. We're sitting in the corner near the window and I stare out at the sidewalk.

A couple walks by holding hands. They look happy and I remember when I was happy without doubts eating at me. I'm interrupted from my thoughts when our pink haired waitress with too many facial piercings takes our drink order and we're finally left alone.

Olivia leans forward, her arms folded in front of her. "Tell me, what's been going on?"

"Everything has been fucked up. I told you I got a new job. Guess who my boss is?"

"You know I hate playing this game. Who?"

"JC."

I let that sink in, watching as Olivia's mouth becomes a thin line and she wrings her hands. Olivia always does that when she's upset or annoyed.

"Are you serious? How's that going?"

"It's stressful at times but we're getting along. He kissed me."

"He kissed you!"

"It was yesterday at his apartment."

"Whoa, did I miss something? What were you doing at his apartment?"

I gloss over the argument I had with Noah and make no mention of Rory. I'm debating whether I should tell her about his cheating. I decide that she needs to know even if it creates tension between us. I trust her more than any other person in my life.

"You should've stayed and worked it out rather than run to JC."

"There's more to the story with Noah. Maybe we better have a cocktail."

Olivia starts to wring her hands again. The waitress is on her way back with our soft drinks and we order cocktails.

"Why don't you start?"

"I'm waiting for the alcohol. You're going to need it."

"Geez, just tell me already."

I blurt out the entire story of Noah reconnecting with Rory and sleeping with Vivian. Olivia's eyes grow wider by the minute. By the time our cocktails arrive, she's agitated and gulps half her raspberry cosmo.

"That bastard. Why didn't you call me?" she growls.

"It's not something that you reveal on the phone when your friend is thousands of miles away. There was nothing you could do."

"I would've cut my vacation short."

"That's why I didn't do it. You need a break without having to deal with my fucked-up life."

"I'm sorry I wasn't here for you."

"Tell me about Australia. Did you meet anyone?"

Olivia eyes me for a moment, realizing I don't want to discuss my shitstorm of a life. I need a distraction. She goes on to tell me about the hot Aussie she met on her first day in Sydney. He owns a computer software company and his name is Jake. She showed me pictures and boy, was he handsome, with blond hair, a square jaw and gorgeous sea blue eyes.

At the conclusion to lunch, I feel better though I'm afraid if she sees Noah, she'll cut his balls off. I didn't tell her I finally gave in and slept with him the night before. She would probably chastise me for that, saying I let him off the hook too soon. Olivia is right. I've been beating myself over the decision.

We share a cab to Olivia's place, and I get out with her. I want to see the apartment since Matty had the furniture delivered two days ago. Upstairs, the place is much like Megan's. It's open, airy and sunny. The furnishings look wonderful in the space and I inwardly pat myself on the back for having a good sense of style.

"Were you surprised?" I asked.

"I was. I can't believe you and Matty went through all this trouble."

"You said you sold all your furnishings, so we wanted you to be cozy when you got here. What would you have done without furniture?"

"I was going to rough it with a sleeping bag and some crates until I could pick out some."

"I think that would have worn thin and you would've slept at Matty's. You could have gone downstairs to sleep at Megan's."

We talk about girl stuff and things we missed about each other over the past several months. I've been with her for hours and I don't want to leave, but I'm sure that Noah will want to have dinner with me, and I text him to let him know I'm on my way. I hug her tight as I get ready to leave with promises to get together in the next few days.

On the walk home, I see a dark car pass with a woman that looks very much like Vivian in the passenger seat. I must be seeing things because Rory told me she was in Cape Cod for the weekend.

The apartment is quiet when I get home and as I traverse the large space, I hear the water in the shower. Why is Noah taking a shower so late?

"Hey, I'm home," I say as I peek in the bathroom.

"Hi, baby."

"Why are you showering now?"

"I decided to workout. You didn't want me all sweaty, do you?"

"I appreciate a clean Noah. I'll be in the kitchen. I'm thirsty."

I find his explanation strange because he either works out in the morning or after dinner. I'm suspicious and I look for his sweaty workout clothes in the dirty clothes hamper in the closet. I don't find any, only his boxers that he had on this morning. Maybe it's my imagination but I smell perfume and it's not mine. I try not to jump to conclusions.

Noah finds me out on the terrace drinking a bottle of water. His hair is damp from his shower and he's only wearing a pair of shorts.

"How was your day with Olivia? You were gone a long time."

"I haven't seen her for months. I missed her."

"What did you do while I was gone?"

"Oh, a little of this and a little of that."

"Was it a productive day?" I try not to sound accusatory.

"What are you getting at?"

"Nothing. I'm just asking what you did."

"I was busy. Is there something you want to say?"

"Noah, stop reading into it. I don't want to argue."

"How was your dress fitting?"

"It was fine though they said my measurements are smaller. They had to take the dress in."

"Why? Did you lose weight?"

"Yes. A few pounds I guess."

"Lexi, are you eating?"

"I'm stressed. Sometimes I forget to have lunch."

"You can't do that. You're going to get sick."

Well maybe if you didn't cheat on me, I wouldn't be so stressed.

"I know. I'll keep it in mind when I'm at work."

"Please do." Noah gets up to go inside and I watch him walk away.

Really? You're going to start telling me what to do?

I'm tired from lack of sleep the night before and even though it's later in the afternoon, I decide to take a nap. The minute my head hits the pillow, I fall asleep. It's not until a while later that I'm awakened by laughing. It sounds like Rory is back. Thanks for the consideration.

I might as well get up since it's well past seven. I'm not sure I'm even going to sleep tonight because I slept so late. I come out to the kitchen where Noah and Rory are sitting at the breakfast bar eating chicken parmesan wedges from Antonio's.

"Did you get me anything?"

"Of course. I wouldn't order without getting you something."

He slides the bag with *Antonio's Pizzeria* emblazoned across the front in bright red letters, toward me. Inside is a twelve-inch wedge. I can eat the whole thing I'm so hungry. I tear at the tinfoil and take a large bite. It's wonderful and I relish the savory sauce as it hits my tongue. Noah reaches over to wipe a spot of it from my cheek and Rory gives me a scowl. Fuck you, little girl, he's mine, I want to scream. I don't care if she doesn't like me.

After dinner, Noah cleans up and Rory goes to her bedroom to play on her tablet. The wedge was filling, and Noah opens the freezer and takes out a large white plastic container, popping the top. Inside is lemon ice which is my favorite. I reach for the container, but he pulls it away, spooning some up and holding it out.

I take it into my mouth and seductively slide my lips over it as I pull the ice off the spoon. I can see the look on his face, it's smoldering. Another few spoonfuls and it's necessary for him to adjust the shorts he's wearing. My little show has aroused him, and I run my tongue over my lemon-flavored lips.

"I wish I could take you on this counter right now," he whispers.

I curtly smile and pull up my shirt so he can see the lacy pink bra I'm wearing. He bites his lower lip and I smile. I wonder if we're going to have sex tonight with little miss primrose next door to our bedroom. I leave him to relax on the couch. I channel surf but don't find much that interests me. I'd rather read and I still have several chapters of Pride and Prejudice to finish.

I'm settled on the bed with my book and I hear Rory talking in the room next door, probably on her cell. She's making some very disparaging remarks about me, comparing me to her mother who apparently, I can't hold a candle to. I know I shouldn't, but I got to the wall that we share, and I listen until I hear her end the call.

I'm fuming but more so because she said something else that tells me Noah lied about staying at his parent's house when he was in Boston after her accident. She said that he had stayed with them and she heard them talking about getting back together. I'm dismayed and feel like an asshole. He duped me.

What do I do? Do I confront him? Now I'm wondering if that was in fact Vivian I saw when I was walking home. How do I know he wasn't fucking around with her all day while I was gone? I decide to go to Noah's office and let him know at least that his daughter is speaking ill of me. The conversation about him lying and his duplicity can wait until the little bitch leaves tomorrow.

The door is slightly open, and I push it more to poke my head in. He's sitting at his desk with what looks like a second phone, looking back and forth between it and his primary. He's typing and I can only assume that he's programming something into it. His behavior is getting more and more shady which makes me wish I hadn't given in to my sexual desire last night.

He doesn't see me, and I pull the door almost closed and back away, then call his name and push the door open. I see him scramble and slide the second phone into his desk drawer. What the fuck?

"Your daughter was talking to a friend about me and it wasn't very nice. I appreciate if you have a talk with her because I'm not going to allow that in my home."

"Are you sure?"

"Noah, I'm not deaf."

"Let's get her in here and we'll straighten this out."

"No. I prefer not to be around when you do it. I can leave. I can go see Olivia or Megan."

He glances at his watch. "it's almost ten. A little late for visiting isn't it?"

"No, not really. Either that or talk to her tomorrow. I can go to the park or something."

"We should all sit down and get this out now."

I sigh deeply. "No. I don't want to deal with it at this time. She's your daughter, you deal with her tomorrow. If this is how it's going to be then when she comes for the two weeks next month, I'll stay with Megan or Olivia."

"Don't be ridiculous. You can't just run every time something doesn't go your way."

Is he joking? The last time I left was because he was fucking Vivian in OUR home. I wouldn't say that's running because it didn't go my way. I was perfectly in my rights to leave. All of a sudden, I feel totally drained. I want to relax, watch television and not think about the conflict in our lives. I head to our bedroom and snuggle into the chaise in the corner while I flick through the channels. I don't know what the future holds, but I don't want to continue like this.

CHAPTER 24

On Sunday, I'm working on my laptop. The animal rescue needs help with a marketing plan for more adoptions. I hear yelling from the kitchen and realize I'm too late. Noah's having the talk and Rory's denying she said those horrible things to me.

Her door to her bedroom slams and she's talking to someone on the phone. After she hangs up, closet doors and drawers are banging. Noah tells Rory she can't leave but she insists on going to her friend Ella's house until tomorrow when she's leaving. He tells her that he'll take her and I lean back on my pillows and pretend I'm dozing when he comes into the bedroom to get his sneakers on.

"Are you awake?" he says softly.

I pretend I'm not. I don't want to talk to him right now. As soon as he shuts the bedroom door, I'm up, waiting for the apartment door close. I want to see the phone he was fiddling with yesterday. I run to his office and pull the middle drawer, it's locked. It makes no sense to lock it when I know where Noah has the key.

From inside the desk, the phone goes off several times. Who can that be? I fumble for the key in the little box on Noah's desk and jam it into the lock, quickly turning it and retrieving the phone. It has a security code and I punch several in before I figure it out, my birthday, the month and the day.

The phone has several texts from an obvious code name "My True Love." As I read through them, I'm ready to puke up the contents of my stomach which is nothing.

I haven't heard from you.

Thank you for yesterday, I needed to feel your touch.

When are you telling her? It's time for you to end it.

I'm tempted to carry on a conversation with this person who I'm pretty sure is Vivian. That son of a bitch lied to me and has been lying to me for so long. I wonder how many times he fucked her? It wasn't just once; it was more than once. He has no respect for me and has been carrying on this charade.

I have no idea what Noah's end game was. He seemed so happy when we made love on Friday night. Was he planning on marrying me and carrying on this secret love affair? What was he waiting for? Me to get pregnant? Then he would spring it on me that our marriage was a horrible lie?

I jump into action which is hard since tears are clouding my eyes. But they're more anger than sadness. I yank my suitcase out of the foyer closet and begin shoving clothing inside. When it's full, I sit on it to zip it up then slip it off the bed. It weighs a ton, thank god it's on wheels. Next, I fill up a smaller bag with shoes and sneakers. I'll come back for the rest.

I left out a pair of jeans and a polo shirt to dress in, pushing my feet into a pair of sneakers. The last thing I do is take all my toiletries from the bathroom. I'm not sure where I'm going and if it's a hotel, I want to have all my own things. I roll the case by his office door where I left the phone on the desk along with the key to the drawer.

My phone buzzes and it scares the shit out of me so much that I almost drop it. I glance at the screen and see that it's Noah. He's letting me know he'll be home in an hour or two because he had to take Rory to her friend's house. Yeah, I bet, you take her and then go see Vivian wherever that cunt bitch is holing up.

I text Olivia and hope she's awake. She has two bedrooms and even if I have to sleep on the floor, I'll do it until I secure my own place. The last thing I do is remove my engagement ring and leave it in the middle of the granite countertop in the kitchen. It's over. Noah deceived me and I know that saying about fooling me twice. Thank god, Olivia texts me back.

It's early, what's up?

That whole thing I told you about with Noah and his ex? He never stopped seeing her. He's been cheating on me this whole time.

I'm dressing and I'm going to cut his balls off. Fucking bastard!

No, I'm packed and need a place to stay. Can I bunk with you until I find my own place?

Are you kidding? You don't have to ask. I'd love to be roommates again. Are you okay?

. . .

I have to get out of here. I'll be there in a little while.

I roll the case out of the apartment and realize that except for when I pick up the last of my things, this will be the last time I'm here. This isn't my home or my life anymore.

I forgot to take a coat and I roll the heavy case down the sidewalk as it pours on me. I don't care, in fact, I feel free as my clothing becomes soaked. It's like the rain is washing away all the worry and insecurities I had about my relationship. In a way, I feel untangled from a web.

By the time I get to Olivia's building, my sneakers squish as I walk into the lobby. My purse and bag with the shoes are like rocks in my right hand. But I'm here and this will be my new home. I ask the front desk to buzz Olivia's place and she comes down to help me.

"You look like a drowned rat. Why didn't you take a cab?"

"I needed something to wake me up. I feel alive."

"Let's get you upstairs and out of those wet clothes."

We take the elevator and I see her staring at me. I know she's trying to assess my level of agitation.

"I'm fine, Olivia. Stop looking at me that way."

"I was there for the breakup with JC, remember."

"I was a lot younger and not as stable. Noah and I haven't been right for weeks. I think even before he cheated on me, there was something wrong."

I begin to shiver as the air conditioning hits my wet clothes. I need to get changed. Once we get into her apartment, I open my suitcase, praying that the clothing is not damp. Fortunately, the inside of the case is dry, and I grab a pair of sweats and a t-shirt.

"You can take the smaller bedroom. We're going to have to get you some furniture, but you can sleep with me until then."

"Oh, Liv, I don't want to inconvenience you by sharing your bed."

"Are you serious? It's a king-sized bed. I have plenty of room."

I roll my suitcase into the bedroom and leave everything sitting in the corner, then plop down on Olivia's couch. My phone starts going off like crazy with calls and texts. I keep letting them go to voicemail because I know they're from Noah. Fuck him. When I finally check, I have five voicemails and tons of texts. He must have gotten home and found my ring on the counter and the privacy of his office invaded.

What does he care? Now he's free to be with Vivian. I hope they have a good life because I need to get mine back together. He built my trust in men up after JC and now it's torn down again. I'm not sure I'll ever be able to be with a man without checking to see if he's doing something behind my back.

To have it happen once was bad enough, but twice? I feel like the world's biggest jackass. Who even knows if Noah did this before? He went on so many trips early on in our relationship, he could have been screwing women and I would never have known.

I delete all the voicemail messages but before I delete the texts, Olivia yanks the phone out of my hand. I watch her mouth gape open as she reads each one. I can only imagine what they say because I really don't want to know.

"Do you want me to tell you or you don't care?"

"I'm curious, but should I give a shit?"

"I can give you the general story."

I ponder whether I should just have her keep it to herself and tell me at another time but it's like a wound. It's open and bleeding now, do I want to rip it apart when it's healing. I ask her to tell me.

"Noah said you should've waited and given him a chance to explain. He wanted to sit down with you and have a discussion."

"Is he fucking kidding? Noah's acting like this is something up for discussion. Did he want me to say, hey, fuck Vivian on the side and we can still get married. I'm totally open for it."

"He said he never meant to hurt you, but it was hard for him to break away from her after they met again. He tried to make it work with you."

I grab the phone back from her and type a text to him.

Why the fuck did you bother after I caught you fucking her? You had an entire month to break it off with me, yet all you did was make it seem like you were in for the long haul. And what was Friday night, a mercy fuck before you let me down hard?

You're right. I should've been straight with you. Sex with you was never about mercy, it was about love. I love you, but I love her just a little bit more. I'm sorry.

Fuck you, Noah. I want to pick up the rest of my things tomorrow and I don't want you there. Say about noon. I'll leave the keys to the apartment on the counter where you found my engagement ring. And I'm not paying any cancellation fees on our wedding venue. You caused this; you pay.

You should split it with me.

Is he fucking kidding? I didn't break off the wedding. I didn't cheat on him and I certainly am not paying anything. He can fight me in court for all I care. We used his credit card so the venue will charge him.

. . .

If this was mutual, yes, but it wasn't. I had no say in the matter when you slipped your dick into Vivian. Have a nice life.

I shut my phone off and bury my head in Olivia's lap. All the anger I felt has now drained from me. The tremendous weight of sadness presses as it overtakes me, and I start sobbing.

"You cry it out," Olivia says as she strokes my hair.

I'm more than glad she's back because I need her. She's always been there for me; a lot more than I have for her. I don't know how long I cried but when I finished, my head hurt, and my jaws ached. I had nothing left in me.

"I need to lie down."

I sit up and rise from the couch, heading to my small unfurnished bedroom.

"Lexi, no. You sleep in my bed."

"I don't deserve to be comfortable. I feel so foolish."

"You have nothing to feel foolish about. You tried to make it work."

She stands and pushes me towards her bedroom. When I'm settled in her bed, she sits next to me and strokes my hair until I fall asleep.

Later on, I hear her hushed tones. It sounds like my sister has come by. It's definitely her because she bursts into the bedroom and plops down hard next to me.

"That fucking piece of shit. I can't believe he did this. I wonder if Lucian knows?"

"He knows." I mumble into my pillow.

"He knows and didn't say anything?"

"I told him not to. I'm not sure how much he knows."

I sit up and turn to my sister. Her face is pained, and she hugs me. "Why does this keep happening to you?"

"I guess I'm a good doormat. I keep picking men that like to cheat on me."

"Lexi, you're not a doormat."

"Then how come I feel like I've been stamped on and had shit rubbed in my face.

"Noah's an asshole. It's his fucking loss."

Funny but she said the same thing about JC years ago and now look? Their like best friends, hanging out all the time. Fuck, I forgot about JC.

"You cannot tell JC. I don't want him to know."

"Why the fuck not?"

"Because. I just don't. It's too embarrassing. If you see him, don't say anything, to Hunter either."

"I won't. I'm sorry for this. I should cut it off with Lucian."

"No, he likes you. He's not Noah. He's much more decent."

"Won't it be painful to see him when you're not with Noah anymore?"

"I love Lucian. He shouldn't be held responsible for Noah's shit."

"Fine. I won't dump him."

"Megan, do you like Lucian at all?"

"Yes, he's wonderful but I'm not sure he's my type."

"You have a type?"

"Well certainly not Jeremy. I don't know why I wasted my time with him for the past few years. He just wanted me as eye-candy."

I sit there staring at her wondering how our conversation gravitated toward her issues.

"I need your help tomorrow. I have to get the rest of my stuff from Noah's. I told him not to be there."

"What time?"

"Noon. Olivia is helping too. Maybe I can get Matty to come."

"Matty. He's dreamy."

"He's not your type."

"He's beautiful. I'd like to hang out with him."

"If you're not serious about Lucian, please let him know now."

"I don't know what I want. I've spent the past few years being tied to one guy. Now I want some freedom especially living in the city."

I can see that she's going to break Lucian's heart if she isn't careful. Wonderful. I have my own shit to deal with. Thinking about entering my former apartment causes my stomach to knot and that feeling of nausea begins to take hold. I shove it down because I don't want to throw up.

I spend the night wallowing in a pint of pistachio gelato and a glass of white wine courtesy of Megan. We all sit around chatting about things other than men and it's then that I realize how much I've missed my sister and best friend. I've spent so much time with Noah that I lost myself.

I announce we should plan a girl's weekend somewhere. We can invite Emma since I haven't seen her in months. She's probably itching to get away from my parents for at least a weekend. Megan and Olivia agree and say we should just plan something here in the apartment. It probably makes sense since both of them are starting new jobs next week.

That night I can't sleep, tossing and turning. I get up to lie on the couch since I'm in Olivia's bed and I don't want to disturb her. How did I get so lucky to have such a good friend?

The next morning Olivia shakes me awake. I'm bleary eyed since I got maybe three hours of worthy shut eye.

"When did you come out here?"

"I don't know. Maybe two or three this morning. I didn't want to wake you."

"I doubt that. I sleep so much better now that I lost weight."

"Good to know next time I can't sleep."

I trudge to the bathroom and look in the mirror. I have dark circles under my eyes and my face is pale. My light brown eyes look dull. I'm not in the mood to do what's before me. To pack up my life and start anew but I have to.

At eleven-thirty, Matty shows up and Megan is right behind him. She bats her eyes at him, and I nudge her to knock it off. Matty is very handsome. He shares the same shade of black hair with Olivia except it's short and spiky. Matty has heterochromia, two different colored eyes.

His left one is the same shade of green moss that Olivia has, the other is a soft sea blue. Couple this with his strong square jaw and dark permanent stubble and it makes for a gorgeous picture.

I take a deep breath and lead the way to my former life. During the walk, Megan won't shut up. She keeps chattering away to Matty about this and that. I'm nervous and Olivia grabs my hand and holds it which elicits some whistles from a couple of male passersby. Jerks, they must think we're lovers. The next thing they'll yell is for us to kiss.

As we enter the building, I nod at the man at the front desk. The wait for the elevator is excruciating because I just want to get my things and be done. The apartment is quiet when I enter and I'm thankful that Noah at least had the decency to allow me to get my things without intervening. But as I dig through my side of the closet for shoes and other items, I hear the apartment door open and my heart sinks.

I hear him arguing with Megan and Olivia, then he barrels into the bedroom and slams the door, locking it, trapping me inside with him.

"How dare you go through my desk. I have confidential papers in there."

I scramble to my feet and point at him while narrowing my eyes.

"Go fuck yourself. Maybe if you were straight with me, I wouldn't have to snoop around to find out what you were up to. You're disgusting. Now get out of my way and let me finish what I have to."

He grabs my wrist as I try to pass by and squeezes hard enough to make me yelp. I try to wrench free, but he holds fast.

"Get off me," I scream.

"No. We have to talk about this."

"The time for talking is over."

I swing my other hand hard and connect with his face. It startles him enough to unhand me and I run to the door, unlocking it and running right into Matty's arms.

"Is he your new boy toy?"

"Go to hell."

He approaches and Matty pushes me behind him telling him to back off. Noah might be a formidable opponent, but Matty boxes with a world class trainer and I'm sure wouldn't have any problem with him. I watch as Noah stops short.

Matty takes me by the hand and stands guard while I finish cleaning out my stuff in the closet. Meanwhile, Olivia and Megan have packed up my clothing and shoes from the foyer storage. I hear nothing more from Noah, but he does stand in the bedroom glowering as I complete what I came to do.

I turn to him before I slip through the door of my former home. "Goodbye, Noah. Maybe in the future you'll have regrets about what you did and how you handled the end of our relationship."

His face is grim. "I think it was for the best."

I shake my head as I pull the door closed. This is not the Noah I fell in love with. He's changed over the past few weeks. It doesn't matter, he's not my problem anymore. I have nothing but wide-open future ahead of me. Single future.

CHAPTER 25

To keep my mind occupied, I spend my off hours at the animal rescue. Caring for creatures abandoned and thrown away by uncaring owners makes me feel better. I took to a particular dog we called Bonnie, a shepherd golden retriever mix. She was picked up wandering the streets and we discovered she was pregnant and ready to give birth.

I watched her give birth to her four pups, three boys and one girl who we named for the characters from the television show Seinfeld, Jerry, Elaine, Kramer and George. They were sweet and I couldn't wait to get to the shelter each evening to pet them and see how they were doing.

A month later, they were walking around and exploring the kennel where they were kept. Kramer and Elaine were my favorites, climbing on my lap and rubbing their soft heads against me. I was dozing in the corner of the cage with them on my lap when a fellow volunteer, Jessica, woke me up.

"Lexi, it's nearly eleven."

My eyes fluttered open to see her standing over me. She smiled as I rubbed my eyes.

"Shit, I'm tired."

"You should go home. You have work tomorrow."

She lifted the sleeping pups from my lap and placed them next to their mama and brothers. I yawned as I rose from the floor.

"Why don't you take the day off tomorrow evening? You've been here every night since these little ones were born."

"It's okay, I like spending time with them."

Jessica gave me a sympathetic smile. "Go out and enjoy yourself. You're a young woman."

"Thanks."

I stepped out into the late-night humidity of early August. I couldn't believe it had been one month since I left Noah. How things change.

The next day, I'm sitting in my office nursing an extra-large cup of coffee and working on a new campaign for barbeque sauce. The client had sent over a case of it and I hate to say it, but it's god awful unless you like the overpowering flavor of pepper which I do not. But my job is not to like the product; it's to make others buy it.

JC has been suspicious of me. I've been coming in early and working later than usual until I head to the shelter, making no mention of Noah. He questioned my missing engagement ring. I told him the stone was loose and was being repaired. He didn't seem to buy the explanation but didn't push the issue. I know Megan hasn't told him anything, though she did tell Hunter and swore him to secrecy.

This morning JC comes into my office asking if we can have lunch at French's. We haven't spent any time together since the night we made out at his apartment. I feel bad but I'm afraid if I spend time with him, it will turn into something it shouldn't. I need to be alone right now.

"I can't. I have so much to do today. I'll just have Nikki get me lunch."

JC closes my door and comes to sit down in one of the chairs in front of my desk.

"Lexi, what's the matter. You seem sad the past few weeks."

"I'm just overwhelmed with a bunch of stuff."

The truth is that I am sad. Lucian has provided Megan with information about Noah. Apparently, Vivian is taking my place as the bride and he's removed my name and inserted hers. They're getting married in October, my wedding date that I painstakingly picked.

"I don't believe you. Work has gotten lighter the past few weeks. Are you going to tell me what's wrong or do I have to guess?"

I keep my focus on the work in front of me, not looking at JC. "I don't feel like discussing it and if you don't mind, I'm busy."

"Go to a movie with me tonight."

I put down my pen. "Excuse me?"

"A movie. You know friends do go to movies together. We haven't been out for a while. I'm sure Noah can spare you for a few hours."

It's Friday and I don't want to be alone. Olivia and Megan are going out to a club, but I declined their invitation. The last thing I want to do is be pawed over by some sweaty guy with his shirt half unbuttoned.

"I'll ask him and let you know. What do you want to see?"

"Pride and Prejudice is being shown at the Cineplex. My treat."

The Cineplex often played older movies for a five-dollar ticket price. Pride and Prejudice was one of my favorites and I'm surprised JC remembered. When it came out, I dragged him to it several times until he begged me to stop.

"You remembered."

"Sure, I did. When I saw they were showing it, I wanted to take you. It's only for this weekend. Please say you'll go."

Since I don't want to stay home by myself indulging in butter pecan ice cream and watching television, I should go.

"Let me text Noah."

I put on a good show for JC by texting Megan and asking her to play the part. She texts me back so he can hear the ping and I let JC know I can go.

"Great. I'll pick you up at seven."

This is a wrinkle I forgot about. He can't come get me because I no longer live with Noah.

"How about I meet you at the Cineplex?"

"What's the problem? Noah might get jealous."

"JC, the Cineplex or nothing."

"Fine, I'll meet you in front of the Cineplex at seven. Movie starts at 7:30."

He leaves my office and I begin to feel nervous. Why? I've been out with JC before. Of course, that was when I was engaged. Now I'm single again and the sexual tension I always feel when he's around is lingering in the air.

The Cineplex is busy, and I search around for JC. I finally find him standing near the front door. He's casually dressed in worn jeans with a few frayed areas. His t-shirt is form fitting and shows the carved muscles of his torso below. I'm also dressed casually in a pair of dark blue capris and a pink t-shirt.

"I thought you stood me up," he says as I approach.

"It's only 7:05."

"I already bought tickets. Let's go inside."

He offers his arm for me to take but I shake my head. A look of disappointment crosses his handsome face and instead he opens the door for me.

"We should get some snacks. Do you want something?"

"I should buy them since you got the tickets."

"Nope. I said my treat. What do you want?"

"Some snowcaps and a bottle of water."

We wait in line and I can't help leaning close to him to smell his cologne. He always smells so good. I want contact with him but I'm afraid where it will take us. After we get our snacks, we head for the theater. It's not very crowded, even for a Friday night. We decide to sit almost in the back row. No one is behind us and the next closest people are four rows ahead of us.

The movie starts and I concentrate on my snowcaps and the screen in front of me. The theater is chilly, and I look up to see we're under the vent. I hug myself to see if I can warm up.

"Are you cold?"

"A little."

Without asking, JC places his arm around me and pulls me toward him. I automatically feel flushed and suddenly, I'm not cold. My cheek is leaning against his delicious smelling shirt and I can feel the curves which make up his muscles underneath. I'm overwhelmed by emotion. I want to kiss him. My lips meet the side of his pec and I press them against it.

In the dim light of the theater, I see his face as he looks down at me. He shifts and his fingers find my chin, tipping my face up. The next thing I know, JC's lips are against mine and his tongue is pushing into my mouth. I run my hand along his stomach feeling the tautness below his shirt.

He softly moans into my mouth as my hand slips to the growing bulge in his pants. I desire him and I know he wants me. JC pulls away, pushing my hand off him.

"Lexi, what are you doing?"

"I...I'm sorry. I should go."

I stand up to head down the aisle and he pulls me back down.

"Tell me what's going on with you?"

The patrons a few rows downturn and tell us to be quiet. I can feel tears welling in my eyes and I'm afraid to speak so I point to the exit and get up again. As I'm walking towards the aisle, I realize he isn't behind me. JC is looking at the floor and I call his name to break the trance, gesturing for him to follow. I breathe a sigh of relief as he does.

Outside in the warm evening air of August, he gently pushes me against the wall of the theater, caging his arms around me so I can't slip away.

"I want to know why you did that. Why are you teasing me when you know you're all I want?"

"I don't know."

"That's not an answer. Do you know how hard it is for me to see you day after day knowing you'll never be mine?"

"I want you too," I say quietly.

"But even if we sleep together you belong to someone else. I can't deal with that. I don't just want to sleep with you. I don't want to share you with someone else. It's not fair to me or Noah."

"I'm not with Noah," I whisper.

His arms drop to his sides and he straightens up, staring into my eyes.

"When?"

"A month ago. I didn't want you to pick me up tonight because I don't live with Noah anymore. I live with Olivia."

JC shakes his head back and forth as if he doesn't believe what I just told him. He's silent, just holding my gaze and I turn away because the look on his face tells me he's hurt. I begin to walk away, and he grabs my arm.

"Where are you going?"

"Home. I'm sorry if I upset you."

In one swift move he pulls me into his arms and slams his lips onto mine. His tongue forcing its way into my mouth to explore. It leaves me breathless and I feel like I'm going to pass out.

"Lexi," he moans.

"JC," I choke out.

"I'm taking you home with me. I want you so badly it hurts."

I know how he feels because there's an ache in my belly that pushes its way down between my legs. I want his touch. I want to feel him inside me. He breaks the kiss and practically drags me to a cab exiting passengers. He barks out his address to the driver and pulls me onto his lap.

"If I could get away with it, I would fuck you right here," he whispers.

I shudder because I want him so much. Instead we kiss and his hands roam my body. It's still light out and he doesn't want to give the pedestrians a show, so he keeps his hands on top of my clothing. I can feel his growing bulge beneath me, and he shifts his legs.

A short cab ride later and we're in front of his building. He shoves a twenty at the driver and lifts me off his lap toward the door. In the elevator, he pushes my arms above my head, holding them in one hand while he kisses me and his other hand cups my breasts. We can't get into his apartment soon enough.

When we do, it's a frenzy to remove clothing. I need no foreplay because I'm soaked. Amid a mass of clothes, he tears at my panties, lifts me and pushes me against the wall next to the foyer closet door. His cock is poised at my opening and I'm ready for him. When he slips inside me, it's heaven as his hot steely length fills and stretches me.

I feel a bit uncomfortable since it's been a month since I last had sex but, in a few seconds, the feeling turns to ecstasy as he moves inside me. I wrap my arms around his neck, sucking on his shoulder as his fingers lace under my ass, lifting me against his thrusts as I wrap my legs tightly around his waist.

"JC, yes, yes. I've wanted this for so long."

"Look at me."

I lift my head and my eyes flutter open to look at his. He stops moving and I can feel him pulsing inside me.

"How long?"

"Please," I plead.

"How long, Lexi."

"Since forever."

The answer satisfies him, and he continues thrusting into me, lifting me by my ass. I'm so close and I start to moan louder letting JC know that I'm going to come, he moves harder, his breathing and mine, ragged. In seconds, I start to break apart and shatter as I climax. He keeps up his rhythm and I watch his face as he bites his lip hard, grunts and releases, filling me.

When he finally stills, he presses my back hard against the wall and moves his hands from my ass to under my arms. Pulling up, he pops out of me and he puts me down. My legs are like jelly and walking doesn't agree with me. Seeing this, JC scoops me up in his arms and wades through our clothing to take me to his bedroom. Laying me down on the unmade bed and slipping in behind, he embraces me.

"You said forever. How can that be if you had Noah?"

I'm not sure I should tell him that I occasionally fantasized that Noah was him when we made love.

"I sometimes fantasized about you."

"When you got yourself off or when you fucked other guys?"

"Both. I don't think I ever stopped loving you. This is so screwed up. I'm not even a month out of my engagement and I'm sleeping with my ex. I made a mistake, I should go."

"You're not going. I'm not letting you go."

"This can't work. I shouldn't have given in."

"Why can't it work? You already know I love you. I'm in love with you. I don't think I ever stopped either. I was too stubborn to admit it but I'm admitting it now. I want you forever."

"What are you saying?"

"I'm saying I want you to marry me. I fucked up once before and I thought I would never get another chance. This is my second chance. Say yes."

All the emotional turmoil that I've felt for the past few months come spilling out of me and I begin to cry. I can't stop and JC looks bewildered at my response to his proposal.

"Lexi, sweetheart. I didn't mean to pressure you."

I continue to cry, and he uses the top sheet to wipe my tears. It's tender and sweet. Something I wished he had done when we were together years ago. Not that he wasn't kind to me back then, it's just different now.

"It's not that. So much has gone on in the past few weeks. It's not you."

But really it is. I felt feelings leak out of me the minute I saw JC the first time at Barker and Perez. Maybe Noah was not the full cause of the breakdown of our relationship. I had a hand in it too, if even indirectly. Our hearts belonged to other people we just didn't know it.

I know now that my heart always belonged to JC. It's probably the reason why I forgave him time and time again. If he didn't end our engagement, I would've married him. Now I have another chance.

"Do you want to marry me, JC?"

"I do, more than you know."

"I want to marry you, too. But wait, aren't you still married?"

"No. Brianna wanted it over quickly. She went to live in Vegas after we broke up. I received the filing a week ago. I'm officially divorced."

"So, you're free to marry?"

"Yes, but we're not going to get married that soon."

"What? Why not?"

"Because I took away your chance to have the big wedding that you wanted. We need to plan."

"Why can't we get married in my parent's backyard?"

"In Jersey?"

"Of course. It's a nice backyard."

"Lexi, your parents hate me. How did they take it when you broke up with Noah?"

I look down at the pillow and begin pulling at a stray thread.

"You did tell your parents you broke up with Noah, didn't you?"

"No."

"When the hell were you planning on telling them?"

"I was waiting for the right time. My sisters know."

"You have to tell them. I'm not sure what's going to be a bigger shock. The fact that you're not marrying Noah or the fact that you're marrying me."

"I think the fact that I'm marrying you will be more of a shock."

He chuckles and then kisses me. We start to make love again. A while later when I call Olivia to let her know I won't be home; she can't understand me. The music behind her is blaring since she's at a club. I hang up and send her a text letting her know I'm with JC. The response is immediate.

Are you fucking kidding me? You're really with him.

Yes, I have so much to tell you. I have news. I'll let you get back to dancing.

Hell no, you tell me right now Alexa Stanford!

JC's hand is between my legs and I drop my phone on the bed only to be interrupted by the phone ringing.

"Let me get it or she'll nag me all night until I do."

"Olivia."

"You tell me what's going on. I can't wait until tomorrow or whenever you get back to the apartment."

I get out of bed naked and pad to the hallway watching JC hungrily survey my body.

"We're getting married."

"When? Tomorrow?"

"No, but soon."

"Explain to me how this came about."

I tell her everything and want to tell her more, but JC comes out and moves my hair away from my neck, kissing and nibbling. His fingers start rubbing my clit and I gasp and point to the phone.

"I don't care. Hang up or I'll make you come while you're still talking," he whispers.

"Liv, I have to go. I'll call you tomorrow or Sunday."

"Alexa, don't you hang up on me."

I do and JC pulls the phone from my hand, pressing the power button, then leads me back to his bed.

"She's not going to be very happy."

"You told her enough. Now hush so I can make you come."

We spend the entire weekend in bed, only taking breaks for food and showers. I'm happier than I've been in a long time even when I was with Noah.

On Sunday afternoon, I prepare to leave. I've done nothing but make love with JC and I have a bunch of stuff to do at my apartment. He lazes in bed watching me pull on my clothes. I have no panties since he destroyed them on Friday night.

"Going commando?"

"It's not like I have any extra clothing here and my panties are in shreds thanks to you."

"We'll have to remedy that. You should move in with me."

My stomach clenches and I swallow the now forming lump in my throat.

"Can we just live apart for a little while?"

He sits up in bed and stares at me, feeling the change in my demeanor.

"Lexi, what's wrong."

"When we lived together, that's where it all went wrong."

"You think I'm going to cheat on you again? Those days are long over. I won't. I've changed. I know that you deserve better and I want to give that to you."

"Can you just bear with me for a little while? I can sleep over here a few nights a week. I need to ease into it."

"I'll let you have your time but we're going engagement ring shopping next weekend. I want everyone to know you're mine."

"Oh, do you?" I can't contain my straight face and start laughing.

"Be serious. We have a lot of planning to do and a lot of people to tell. When you leave, I'm going to call Hunter. I'm sure that my father with be skeptical but I don't have to answer to him."

"I'm glad to hear that."

"I need to go. I should be back later."

"You're staying with me tonight?"

"Of course. Why did you think different?"

"You said you needed your space. Would you mind if I came with you?"

"Sure. Any particular reason why?"

"I want to see Olivia's face when I walk through the door with you."

"We should probably stop by Megan's and tell her too."

"You just want to knock everyone off today, don't you?"

"Is that a bad thing?"

"No but remember, we need to tell my parents and it's got to be in person."

JC sighs loudly because my parents aren't his biggest fans. I don't care because I love him, and I need to make my own decisions.

"Well, if you're coming you should probably get dressed."

∾

Twenty minutes later we enter my apartment. Olivia is sitting on the couch painting her toenails with a black polish. She jumps up when she sees us and waddles to pass out hugs.

"I can't believe it," she says as she clings to JC.

"Hey girl, look at you! You're gorgeous."

I forgot to tell JC Olivia lost weight and he hasn't seen her since she got back to New York. I let them have their moment and go to my bedroom to find a pair of panties to wear. I hear her tell him if he breaks my heart, she'll have his balls. JC nervously laughs but he knows she means it.

After I put on a fresh pair of panties, we go downstairs to Megan's apartment. It's 2:00 PM but when she answers the door, she's bleary-eyed and her blonde mane is a mess.

"What are you two doing here, together?"

"Let us in and we'll tell you."

She does and we spend the next half-hour explaining how we're newly engaged. Her mouth gapes open as the story unfolds. I wasn't quite sure what her reaction was going to be but it's positive.

"I didn't want to say anything but I'm glad you're not with asshole anymore."

"Megan! I thought you liked Noah."

"I really didn't. I tolerated him for you. He was always a dick to me when you weren't around. It's why I left your apartment when you weren't home."

"How come you never said anything?"

"Because you loved him. I didn't have to be the one to marry him."

"Yes, but you're my family and you should have said something."

"It doesn't matter. I definitely love this new fiancé."

"I'm glad because you're coming with me to tell mom, dad and Emma."

"You mean you need a buffer."

"Megan, I need you. We need you."

"Fine. When is this going to take place?"

We decide to visit my parents next weekend. I need to break the news about Noah during the week and spring the news about JC when we see them.

~

The work week goes quietly since it's August and business is slow. I find it hard to concentrate with JC nearby since I want him all the time. At night, we usually spend it at his apartment and most of that time is spent making love.

On Friday night, he's secretive and tells me he wants to take me somewhere. I'm not sure if he means out to dinner or another place but I go along without questioning. We take a cab right from the office and it pulls up to a small jewelry store. The window is dark, but JC places a call and a small man with thick glasses comes to the door to let us in.

JC introduces him to me as Mr. Juri Polsky. He shakes my hand and ushers us into the back of the store which is his workspace.

"Mr. Polsky has been my father's jeweler for years. I asked him to do a special favor for me."

I'm misty eyed as the man picks up a small black velvet box, popping it open. The ring inside is a square cut two carat diamond mounted on a simple platinum band. He hands it to JC, who plucks it out of the box and holds it for me to slip on. It fits perfectly.

"It's beautiful. When did you do this?"

"Remember last week when I said I had a client meeting? I came here. Mr. Polsky was kind enough to rush the order."

I can't stop looking at it even though it's not the first time I've had an engagement ring on my finger. We thank the jeweler and he lets us out of the store. I'm giddy with excitement because now it's official. We're engaged. Now I have something to show my parents when we go to their house tomorrow.

"Would you be upset if we went to show Olivia and Megan?"

"No, I expected it."

On the drive to my apartment, I can't stop touching JC. His handsome face has a permanent smile. He's going to be my husband. Our marriage is almost eight years in the making. In another week on September first, I'll be thirty. I thought it would be at least another few years until I found someone to marry after my breakup with Noah. But here I am.

The next day, Megan, me and JC set out in a rented sedan for the drive to Glen Rock, NJ where my parents live and JC used to live. I go over in my head what I'll say to them. I think it's best that I ask JC to stay in the car until I break the news to them. While I'm thinking I absentmindedly twist my engagement ring around my finger. JC sees me and reaches out to hold my hand.

I glance behind me, Megan is sleeping, and I take his hand to my mouth and suck on his fingers, nibbling on the tips.

He mouths, "Don't." and withdraws his hand.

I've riled him up. We made love most of the night before and it's still not enough for him, or me. I'm not sure I'm going to be able to make it through the day. I smile because it's funny how for the past few months we worked together and denied our passion for each other. Now, all I want is to spend all my waking moments with him. I know he feels the same.

We pull up to my parent's large colonial. It's the same as it was when I came here with Noah about six months ago. All except for the fresh summer blooms of flowers. I kiss JC and wake Megan. My stomach is in knots because I know my parents are going to be flabbergasted by the news. Might as well get this over with.

It takes over an hour to get out the entire story of how my

relationship with Noah ended and why. My mother is sympathetic but my father, more reserved. Megan tries to lighten the mood with some jokes, but it doesn't go over well. I'm ready to tell my parents about JC when my sister Emma comes in and blows the whole plan out of the water.

"Hey, why is JC Lawson sitting in a car in our driveway?"

I clap my hand over my mouth and roll my eyes at Megan.

"Might as well go get him," I say to her.

I stand leaving my parents and Emma to wonder what is taking place. On the way back from the car, I pull my engagement ring from my pocket and slip it on my finger. My parents are cordial to JC but there is a frosty overtone. I hope they accept him because I love him.

"JC and I are engaged," I blurt out.

Now it's my mother's turn to cover her mouth with her hand. My father just sits there shaking his head. Emma begins questioning how this happened.

"If you just give us a chance to explain."

In twenty minutes, the story is out. We proclaim our love for each other and the plans that we want to make for our wedding. My father takes JC aside and when they return, it's like their best buddies again as they were years ago before we broke up. It's then I realize that everything is going to be alright.

EPILOGUE

I'm nervous as hell. My sisters, mother and Olivia fawn all over me while I wait to walk down the aisle. I spent the night here at my parent's home while JC stayed with a friend from high school. His parents drove from Manhattan where they now reside as did Hunter and many of our other friends.

I check and recheck my hair and makeup. It's perfect but I still look for anything out of place.

"Lexi stop it. You look beautiful and JC is going to lose his mind when he sees you in this dress," Megan says.

I was lucky to find this dress on a rack at the same bridal shop I bought the dress for my impending wedding with Noah. I was prepared to wear a simple white dress rather than get all decked out. I had gone to the shop to let them know they could donate the other dress to someone. It was already paid for and the recipient would just have to pay for the alterations.

Olivia was with me and pulled out the dress off a rack. It was a size four which was just right. I needed a small alternation to the waist, and it fit like a glove. She took it home for me so that JC wouldn't see it since I've been sleeping over at his place almost every night since we've been back together.

My sisters and Olivia look beautiful in the light blue dresses they bought off the rack at Macy's.

Emma has matured so much in the six months it's been since I saw her. She's become more focused and has been working for the local newspaper. Her figure is just darling with soft curves and an ass to die for. Her long wavy blonde hair looks wonderful, pinned up with soft tendrils around her face.

We pose for pictures in my bedroom, then on the stairs and finally on the front lawn. I don't need to worry about JC seeing me since he's not here yet. Once I get a call from Hunter that they're on their way, I duck into the house to hide. I see him from my window exit the car and he's gorgeous in his black tuxedo with white shirt and tie. He wipes at his forehead with a handkerchief in the heat of mid September.

Once the music cues up, everyone including my mother leaves me to be seated. I'm alone in my bedroom thinking about how far we've come, the secrets we've kept and revealed, the discussions we've had and how we promised to be honest with each other. However, I have one more secret I'm keeping from JC.

The ceremony is short and sweet. I'm now Mrs. Jonathan Camden Lawson IV. I'm excited to start my life with my new husband. A life we should have started years ago. The night is spent in my parent's backyard that's been decorated by Glen Rock's finest wedding planner. The food is wonderful as catered by our friend, the owner of French's, Paul Borrego. Not that I feel much like eating.

At the end of the night, we're whisked away in a limo to a luxurious suite at The Park Hyatt in Manhattan, courtesy of my father in law, Jonathan Camden Lawson III. He has made peace with JC telling him that marrying me was the best decision he ever made. Before we arrive at our destination, I let JC know that

I haven't been honest with him like we promised. I have a secret and I need to get it out now.

"You should have discussed whatever you had to tell me as soon as you found out. Didn't we promise?" he says sternly.

"Don't be upset with me. We've been so busy that I didn't have time."

"This is a hell of a way to start off our marriage. I demand that you tell me now."

"I will."

I start to giggle, and he looks at me puzzled. Soon he'll know. I lean in to whisper in his ear.

"I'm pregnant."

"When did you find out?" he says with a giant smile.

"This morning. My period was late, so I took a test. I didn't have time to tell you."

"This is the best wedding present you could ever give me."

"I think I'm about three weeks along. Next summer we could be welcoming Jonathan Camden Lawson the fifth into the world."

"No way. That name stops with me. Besides, it could be a girl. I would love to have a daughter."

He leans down to kiss my stomach through my dress.

"Daddy loves you. I can't wait to meet you."

Then he looks up at me and tenderly presses his lips to mine.

"You're my love and my soul mate. Thank you for becoming my wife."

I love this man. A man who I initially thought was the worst mistake of my life...now I know better.

The End

ADDICTED BY LOVE

If you like this book, get ready for Hunter's story in Addicted by Love, Book 2 of The Full Circle Series, to be released in February 2020.

I thought I could forget her, but she's my addiction.
She made me change my mind about love...
and now I'm addicted.

Printed in Great Britain
by Amazon

19730794R00171